Take Me Home

SLOAN PARKER

DEDICATION

For all who have fallen in love with their best friend.

ACKNOWLEDGEMENTS

Many thanks to the following:

To Connie, Patrice, and the rest of the MV-BIC/coffee groups for your invaluable support and insights on this book and its title. To Johnny Miles for helping me land on a title and for the wonderful encouragement and friendship when you didn't even know I needed it most. To S.J. Frost and Jambrea Jo Jones for teaming up with me to tackle part of the mysterious aspect of this business we call author promotion. To all my writer friends and the many writers in this genre and others who have taken the time to share their knowledge and expertise about writing, publishing, and promotion. Your willingness to give up your own writing time to share with others is greatly appreciated. To all the readers, authors, and editors on Twitter, Facebook, and my blog who gave me much-needed support and encouragement.

To my mom, dad, sister, brother, and the rest of my family for helping brainstorm ideas one night at a holiday get-together.

To Rosie, who continues to silently suffer behind the scenes through my crazy writing life and offers her unending support in everything, every day.

And lastly a special thank-you to my dad, the former locomotive engineer, who answered every annoying train question with patience and care as though this story was as important to him as it was to me. Thank you!

Chapter One

"Have you guys done it yet?"

"No!" Kyle Bennett rolled his eyes at the camera on his laptop and sank back against the couch cushion, wondering how long his sister would go on about it this time. "Jeez, Lorrie. I'm sorry I ever talked to you about it."

"It was Mom's spiked eggnog talking, not you." She laughed, and her image in the video chat window shook. She was two thousand miles away in the bathroom of her mobile home, sitting fully clothed inside the empty bathtub with the laptop Kyle had given her last Christmas perched on her lap. He wasn't sure if she was hiding out from her husband or her kids. Maybe both. A bright red shower curtain, covered in images of footballs and the Ohio State University emblem, was pulled around the bathtub, creating a pink glow across her face. It didn't camouflage her dark hair and eyes, though, a perfect match to his own, or the excited look on her face.

Kyle loved seeing the smile that wasn't always there, loved her laugh, but he wanted to kill her for bringing up the same topic she always did. He'd been doing good all day, not thinking about Evan, not thinking about everything he'd been dreaming of doing to his best friend's body—or vice versa, to be more precise.

Lorrie raised her eyebrows repeatedly in a playful look. "So?"

She was a nut. She never could stop herself from asking. Probably because her life hadn't quite turned out as she'd dreamed when they were kids and she'd danced around the house with her pillowcase draped down the back of her head, calling it her wedding veil. He doubted she'd been picturing the shotgun wedding at the local courthouse she'd ended up with. A ceremony that had lasted less than five minutes. No veil. No declarations of eternal love in the wedding vows. No bouquet of flowers or music. Just the sound of her soon-to-be father-in-law spitting chaw into an empty Mountain Dew bottle.

Kyle stared at the ceiling of his West Hollywood apartment, not sure what she wanted to hear. No need to keep staring at the ceiling, though. He'd long ago memorized the perfect swirls of textured paint. The side effect of working—or, in his case, not working—from home.

Still, he stared at it every day. Something to pass the time.

Hell, he might as well turn in his Mystery Writers of America's Best Novel award for that level of creative thinking. He focused in on the laptop screen again. Lorrie's dark eyes had gone from wide-eyed excitement to a squinted judgmental stare that reminded him too much of the one their mom gave their dad.

"Don't look at me like that," he said. "I told you I wasn't going to do anything."

"And why not?" she asked.

"Evan's not the kind of guy who fucks and forgets it."

"So you're saying you're usually forgettable in bed?" She laughed again.

"Shut up," he said, also laughing. It was hard to resist her good mood. He loved his big sis, and if he was honest with himself, it was nice to finally have someone to talk to about his attraction to Evan Walker.

For the past ten years, his best friend had been off limits, but then six months ago, Evan's partner had dumped him. Now that Evan was sleeping in his spare room, it was driving Kyle crazy, being so close to the man and not making a move.

Which explained his recent fascination with ceiling paint rather than his latest manuscript. Too bad he didn't write romances. Or erotic-as-hell romances, for that matter. Most days his imagination had been focused on one thing: sex. Pretty specific sex too. And not his usual brand of fucking at all.

He never took it up the ass. Not anymore. He'd only done it three times in his life. The most recent had been seven years ago. He'd been drunk on more Jack and Coke than he'd ever had since, and he'd agreed to bottom because the other guy wouldn't do anything otherwise. It was over before Kyle had a chance to react to the sound of his own voice saying, *"What the hell. All right."*

The time before had been with a D-list actor who worked out at the same gym and who Kyle had pursued for weeks. A guy who'd told himself he was straight and would only do another guy up the ass. No getting fucked for Mr. D-list. No intimate touches. No kisses. And no sucking, probably because he didn't want anyone asking him to return the favor.

The first time for Kyle had been when he was sixteen. His first time in a lot of ways. Before then, he'd messed around with other boys, even college guys, but the first man who'd given Kyle the chance to do more than a quick BJ or a handjob had been a forty-three-year-old, twice-divorced dentist who also didn't want anything but the fucking. And he'd been the one doing the fucking, no question about that. Kyle'd been the one on his hands and knees in the back of the guy's minivan.

Kyle had done it, his forehead scraping along the carpeted floor of that minivan with each shove of the guy's dick into him. The carpet had smelled of urine, old fast food, and hay. Sort of like walking into the barn on his grandpa's farm as a kid, minus the petrified, over-salted fries.

He hadn't hated the experience, but it had left him feeling used and powerless. He didn't go for that. Even at sixteen, that night with the dentist—who must have been paying a shitload in alimony what with state of the reeking van—had taught Kyle two things: he wanted to feel in control, and from then on, he'd be the one doing the fucking, with the occasional slip due to Jack and Coke and D-list actors.

Then what the hell was up with his dreams lately? Well, not just his dreams. His every fantasy. Awake. Asleep. Staring at the damn ceiling swirls. Thinking about him and Evan together. Evan sucking his cock, his balls. Evan licking his ass. Evan ramming into him from behind, thrusting Kyle face-first into the black sheets of his own bed.

He drew in a deep breath and spoke to Lorrie again. "Evan doesn't do the casual thing. Not even with a friend. I'm not going to lead him on."

There was a long pause, and then Lorrie said, "You're in love with him."

Kyle bolted upright and smacked his knee on the edge of the solid wood coffee table. The laptop skidded backward six inches, stopping just short of falling off the table. Which was good. He didn't need another excuse not to write.

"Ow." He rubbed his kneecap. "I am not in love with him." He sounded like the time he and Lorrie were fighting over whether he'd left the barn door open, which led to the escape of their grandpa's prized horse. Only love and sex were not something he and Lorrie had ever argued about during their teen years. Which was fine by him. Catching her making out with Carl Babcock, her tits hanging out of the top of her bra as Carl fondled her on the couch in their living room, had been enough.

He didn't want to think about tits, his sister's or any other woman's.

He'd rather give up on the ceiling swirls and spend the afternoon dreaming about cock—Evan's cock. He'd seen it a number of times over the years but had never had the pleasure of touching it, with hands or mouth or anything else.

There he went again.

He gave another rub to his knee and sighed. "I just want him."

God, how he wanted him. Since before the night over ten years ago when they'd been driving across the country to go to college and he and Evan had ended up fumbling around in their shared room at the Motel 6 off Interstate 80 in Des Moines, Iowa. It wasn't about love then. Still wasn't. "I want to fuck him. All right?"

"Don't give me that bullshit," Lorrie said. "You love him."

"No… Well, yeah. Like a brother."

"Ew." She scrunched her face and looked at the red shower curtain to her left as if she could see through it to know if her two kids and husband had heard what they were talking about.

"What?" Kyle asked.

She whispered, "You just said you wanted to fuck him."

"Jeez, Lorrie. I really am sorry I ever mentioned it to you."

She laughed again, the sound reminding him more of their childhood in Ohio.

"So what are you going to do?" she asked.

God, she was more excited than usual. Since Kyle had told her about Evan moving in six months before, she'd bugged him about it every week when he called. The iPhone and two-year plan with unlimited texting might not have been the best gift idea for her this Christmas. She'd never let up.

"You're nosy," he said. For years, he'd kept his desires for Evan a secret. Until he'd confessed to Lorrie in a drunken stupor last Christmas that he'd been wanting Evan since the first time he saw him in their high school English class.

"I'm not nosy," Lorrie said. "I just want to know all the details. I mean, if you do go for it, what happens if he turns you down? Can your ego take that?"

Kyle didn't want to think about Evan rejecting him. It was a real possibility, though. Like he'd done to Evan in that motel room.

Or worse yet…Evan might see something between them that wasn't there. It had been a long time since Evan had been alone. He didn't do casual sex.

No. Evan Walker fell in love. Hard.

Kyle didn't. Never had. He liked his life uncomplicated, easy. Just the way he liked his sex.

"So," Lorrie said, clasping her hands together in front of her chest as if she were praying for something to happen, "when are you going to, uh…make your move?"

A pair of black running shorts was draped over the arm of the couch where Evan had left them the day before. Kyle almost reached for them but stopped before he did something stupid like take them to his room for a sniff during a jerk-off session. "Told you, I'm not going to sleep with him."

"Why not? He's not a kid anymore. Neither are you."

"What does that mean?"

"Maybe it's time for you to have a real relationship. Take a chance. You know how Evan is. Someday he'll move on and meet someone new. You might never have another shot."

That left him speechless. Would Evan always be a fantasy for him? Always out of his reach?

"Don't you have anything better to do than bug me about this?"

"No," she said. "They cancelled my soap opera."

"You're *not* turning my life into a soap opera."

"It would be an improvement."

He laughed at that. He didn't want to admit to Lorrie he'd been trying to make a move, to talk to Evan about it for a week. The words lingered in the back of his throat. As if they were stuck in a motel room ten years earlier when he'd last gone for it with Evan, and Kyle had freaked over the intensity of his feelings. He'd practically been a kid and hadn't been ready for that kind of connection with anyone.

Hell, he was almost thirty and still wasn't.

Would it be like that again if they touched? If they kissed? Could he deal with that?

One night had been all they'd had. Kissing, shirts off, their bare chests pressed together, Evan's hand down Kyle's pants, rubbing his dick through the underwear, their tongues moving to a rhythm that was so new, so different, and all their own.

Then Kyle had pulled away, and Evan must have seen something in his face. Evan had jumped off the bed and said, "We can't. We can't fuck this up."

At the age of eighteen, he'd been screwed over too many times, trusted the wrong boys too often in his youth to believe sex wouldn't fuck up a friendship, let alone with someone like Kyle. Evan knew the truth.

So did Kyle. They'd fuck, and then he'd leave Evan. That was his MO then. Still was. No wonder Evan couldn't trust him.

But that was a different time. A different Evan.

He'd spent the last ten years in a relationship and was just starting to get over that loss, the heartbreak. Evan wasn't ready for something more with anyone. Not yet. This would be about doing what they'd always wanted. About giving in to desire. About a night together that would blow their minds. No matter what Lorrie thought, this would not be anything other than sex.

"Do guys talk about stuff like this?" Lorrie asked.

"How the hell would I know?" Kyle dropped his head to the back of the couch and focused on the ceiling swirls again. Yep, still there. Still that disturbing bright white that practically damaged the retinas. Still too perfect in their uniformity. Like everyone in Hollywood. He needed to get away from it all.

"What are you going to do, pounce on him?"

"Lorrie…"

"I wish I could be there."

"God." He sat up. She had a dreamy expression in the chat window. "I do *not* wish you could be here. If something does happen, I hope we'll be naked and…" He didn't say more. Didn't say he hoped he'd be buried inside Evan like he'd been dreaming of doing for years. Evan's body underneath him. Those blue eyes watching him. That blond hair resting on the dark sheets of his bed. Only, the recent fantasies had Kyle on the sheets, Evan staring down at him, buried in his ass. A knock came from the apartment door. "I gotta go," he said. "Someone's here."

"You're still coming home for Christmas, right?" she asked.

"No matter what." Kyle wasn't going to miss their usual trip home. Evan loved spending Christmas in Ohio. He loved the snow, the lights and decorations, the Christmas carols, the whole sappy affair. No matter how long they'd been living in California, Liberty Falls, Ohio—known as the Home of the Perfect Christmas Tree—would always be home.

"And what about moving?" she asked. "Are you still planning to move back here after the holidays?"

"I think so. I don't know. I gotta go. Tell the kids I've got surprises for them."

"You spoil them too much." Despite her words, she couldn't hide the grateful smile. Money had been tight since her husband, Brett, had been laid off in April.

"There's no such thing as too much spoiling from Uncle Kyle. See you soon." He gave her a wave, ended the call, and went to answer the door.

A guy in his early twenties stood in a uniform of a short-sleeved button-up shirt and shorts that were a little too tight around the hips and ass like they were stripper pants and he'd be ripping them off as soon as the music started. He held a package wrapped in plain brown paper. "Kyle Bennett?"

"Yeah."

"Package for you." He handed it over. Kyle took note of the visible bulge the tight shorts did nothing to hide, the muscular thighs, the eye contact that lingered between them. Yep, gay. Kyle almost laughed. Hadn't he seen a dozen pornos that started out like this? So he did what he always did. He licked his lips, ran his gaze over the guy's body, and met his stare again.

"I need you to sign for it." The guy didn't look away as he held out the electronic signature pad.

"Sure." Kyle reached for the pad and let his fingers brush the man's knuckles. "You must get pretty tired doing all these deliveries."

"You got that right. I sure could use a break."

Kyle smirked as he signed his name. Yeah, he still had it. "Well, I'd invite you in, but I'm supposed to be working." He passed back the signature pad and added, "Maybe another time."

The guy nodded. "Just order something else from"—he moved in close and read from the package in Kyle's hand—"Powers, Hunt, and Weinberg." He gave Kyle one last stare and turned away.

The man's ass almost had Kyle calling him back. He hesitated, doorknob in hand, but he knew how it would go. The same way it had the last time he'd been with a guy. Things would get started, then he'd think about Evan, about all the things they could do together, and when he looked down and saw the guy on his knees didn't have blond hair or those sharp blue eyes, the disappointment would hit hard. So he had avoided the scene.

Truth was, he'd rather be home with Ev. Sex or no sex.

There was no one he enjoyed spending time with more. Evan was funny and smart and, despite his small stature, was the toughest person Kyle had ever known. He admired the hell out of him and…

Kyle slowly closed the door and leaned his forehead against it.

"You're in love with him."

"Goddammit, Lorrie."

He tossed the delivery onto the coffee table and headed for the bathroom down the hall. The cool water he splashed on his face did nothing to ease his racing heart. He bent over, gripping the edge of the sink in both hands. A bead of water dripped from his chin and ran down the drain. This wasn't him. He didn't get panic attacks or worry about what he was or wasn't feeling for anyone. But this wasn't just anyone. He stood, not recognizing the wide-eyed, pale, wet-skinned man looking back at him from the mirror.

Yeah, this was what love reduced a man to. Nothing recognizable. He wasn't about to lose himself like that. Or lose Evan. Because, even if Kyle gave in to what he was feeling, it would never last. He braced his hands on either side of the mirror and spoke to his reflection.

"Don't you dare hurt him."

He grabbed a hand towel, scrubbed his face dry, and threw it at the towel rack. It hung there for a second, then hit the floor. He groaned as he picked up the towel and slammed it on the countertop before heading back to the living room and the plain brown package on the table.

Had he ordered something? Porn? No. He hadn't watched any in a long time. No need. One thought about Evan sleeping in his guest room, and Kyle was hard and reaching for his cock. It was embarrassing how fast he came. And how often he'd been jerking off lately. Sort of like high school all over again. Like the week he'd met Evan.

Damn. He had to get his mind on something else.

He plopped onto the couch and read the names on the package again. Sounded like a law firm. He'd heard those names before. Maybe his agent or editor had requested it be sent to him. Or not. It wasn't from New York. It was from Ohio. That was where he'd heard of the law firm. His dad had mentioned them once when dealing with the paperwork after the funeral. Kyle's chest grew tight with the grief he still carried.

He removed the brown wrapping and opened the box. Inside was another box, this one thin, with a letter taped to the top. It read:

Mr. Kyle Bennett,

> *This completes your portion of the estate for the late Victor Bennett. Please sign the enclosed record of receipt in the presence of a notary public and return to our office at your earliest convenience.*

Kyle dropped the letter to the couch, unsure if he could pick up the thin box. Two years since his grandpa's death. Why were they sending him this now, and what the hell could it be?

He couldn't deal with opening the box right then. He had to get going. Only an hour until he'd get the news he'd been waiting years to hear.

Chapter Two

"Shit." Evan Walker checked his watch for the fifth time as he waited for the highway crew to flag him on. He'd never been late before. Sucked to think the only time would be his last day. He'd had the job for ten years and didn't want Miguel to think he didn't care. Castillo's was more than a place of employment for him.

Which was a nice feeling, because after four years of college and six years submitting original and spec scripts all over Hollywood, waiting tables had seemed like the only career he'd have.

Not any longer. He'd just gotten the official word and would be signing the paperwork soon.

Traffic started moving again, and Evan eased the car past the roadwork crew laying asphalt. A shower of debris rained on the trunk of the car as he drove by. He winced.

Please don't let that ruin the paint job.

He needed to buy a car. He'd been borrowing Kyle's for months now. A part of him didn't want to admit buying a car would mean his relationship with Dennis was really over. That the man he thought he'd spend his life with was never going to take him back.

Not that the car had been Evan's. A gift. That was why he'd left it in the garage the day he'd packed his stuff—the last day he'd tried to get Dennis to change his mind. Evan had told himself to walk out of there like a man, his head held high.

It hadn't quite gone as he'd planned. Unless tears and groveling were synonyms for pride. The next morning at Kyle's, Evan had woken up on the couch with a hangover, another part of him relieved it was over. He wasn't sure he could face Dennis after that level of embarrassment.

Evan reached the back parking lot of the restaurant and pulled in. The lot was full, and he almost didn't find a space. Castillo's had to be swamped if the valets were using the employee lot. He'd never seen it this busy after they'd just opened for the night. He got out, grabbed his bag with his uniform, and jogged to the back entrance. He found Miguel standing by the door.

"Well?" Miguel asked, bouncing on the balls of his feet, despite his large stature. Miguel had played college football and liked to brag there hadn't been another player who could take him down.

"They offered me the job."

"To write for *The Agency*?" Miguel asked.

"Yeah."

"Damn. Congratulations." Miguel tugged him into a bear hug and squeezed tight, plastering Evan's head to his chest. Miguel had been like a father to Evan since the night he'd been a freshman in college, standing in the doorway of the restaurant, soaking wet, desperately in need of a job and ready to convince Miguel he could handle the busy crowd on Friday nights. Miguel had taken one look at Evan and handed him a uniform. Evan had figured it was the desperation in his voice Miguel had been unable to resist.

Or maybe it had been the fact he'd been dripping water all over the restaurant's entranceway. He'd walked from his USC dorm room to Castillo's through the pouring rain as soon as he'd seen the help wanted flyer at the campus job fair. The same day he'd found out about the fee for the special lecture series featuring fifteen of the top TV and film directors. He hadn't had enough money to cover the class and get through the year without a better job than scraping plates in the campus cafeteria.

Castillo's was supposed to be a temporary gig. Now, ten years later, here he was.

"This is great," Miguel said and gave Evan's back a series of heavy pats. He drew away, and for a moment, Evan thought he saw tears in the man's eyes. "You worked hard to get here."

Yeah. He had. It seemed like it had taken a damn long time too. Evan knew better. He was lucky to be landing the shot he'd gotten. A shot a hell of a lot of writers waiting tables in LA would kill for.

"Come on," Miguel said as he turned to the door. "Everyone is dying to hear how it went."

"Not yet. I want to wait until the paperwork's all signed."

Miguel stopped, a shocked look on his face. "But everyone already knows about the meeting. And you're leaving for your vacation. I told them if it went well today, this would be your last night."

"I know... I don't want to jinx anything until it's a done deal." Evan had to wait until the network finalized the terms of his contract with the show's executive producer. If all went well, he'd have a seat in the writers' room for one of the leading dramas on network TV in two weeks. If not, he'd be back waiting tables.

But the real reason he wanted to keep the news to himself for now? He wanted to tell Kyle before anyone else.

Kyle had not only given him a place to stay, he'd read every screenplay and teleplay Evan had written since their senior year of high school. Kyle had always believed Evan would get to this place.

"Well," Miguel said, "then you should take tonight off. Go on home and celebrate."

"Nah. You'll need me. Looks like a busy crowd already." Evan had promised Miguel even if the interview had gone well, he'd finish out any scheduled shifts until he left for his usual holiday trip to Ohio.

"All right," Miguel said. He opened the employee entrance to Castillo's. "I've got to take care of a little crisis up front." He paused and made eye contact with Evan. "I'm proud of you, kid." Then the big man was gone before Evan could say anything in response.

Evan ducked into the employee break room, changed into his uniform, and stashed his clothes in his locker. Well, not his locker for much longer. He couldn't believe he wasn't going to be working at Castillo's anymore. He dropped onto the wooden bench that ran the length of the room. He couldn't believe his life was about to change yet again. He barely recognized it as it was. He didn't have his car. Didn't have a home. Didn't sleep in his own bed. He was sleeping in Kyle's spare room.

Kyle.

For weeks now, things had been getting strange between them. He'd been trying to figure out how to describe Kyle's behavior. Flirtatious. Tense. Uneasy?

He should just ask Kyle what was up.

Evan bit his lip and tried not to fret, as his mom always called it. He leaned back until his head collided with the wall of metal lockers behind him. He needed to relax. Or he might do something stupid. Like the night before.

He'd almost gotten on his knees and blown Kyle right there on the couch while they were watching *American Treasures*. Evan still couldn't believe he'd almost done it. Kyle had just looked so damn good, laughing at the retired history professor on the show who thought he'd found a key to a long-lost Al Capone safety deposit box but wound up with a key that opened the local Dairy Queen instead. That laugh, the way Kyle had sunk back on the couch, his long, lean legs stretched out, his dark hair sticking up all over in that sexy-ass way that looked like he'd just run his hands through it.

"Shit." Evan stood and slammed his locker shut. He had to stop this. Had to give up on the teenage crush. Kyle didn't do boyfriends. He didn't even date. Evan was not going to be just another fuck on the long list.

The quiet left in the wake of his locker door rattling shut didn't sound right. No chatter from the employees or clank of dishes from the kitchen, no hum of conversation from the dining room. Something was wrong.

He headed into the hall and made his way to the kitchen. It was empty. The dining room at the end of the hall was dark.

"Miguel? Where is everyone? And what's wrong with the lights? Is the power out?" He crossed the dining room for the back wall where the main light switches were located. The dark figure of a man stood in his way. Evan jerked back. "What the—"

All the lights came on, and a crowd of people sprang out from behind tables and chairs and the dividing walls of the dining room. They clapped and shouted, "Congratulations!" The mariachi band made up of Miguel's four older cousins started playing in the far corner.

Everyone Evan worked with was there, including the entire Castillo family. Miguel's brothers, his wife and daughters, his nieces and nephews.

And Kyle. Standing across the room, hands tucked in his low-slung jeans. He was the only one not clapping, but the smile on his face was the widest in the room. Evan couldn't help but smile back. Kyle knew. He knew what this job meant to Evan. He knew how much Evan needed this to work out.

Miguel's youngest daughter rushed forward and squeezed Evan's legs at his thighs. The force of her small body smacking into him almost had him toppling over. He patted her head as the chefs rolled out a table with a decorated cake on top. It read *Today Staff Writer, Tomorrow Executive Producer*.

He might kill Miguel.

Maybe.

It was kinda cool to have the recognition, to know they wanted to celebrate his success. Especially after the loss he'd lived through six months earlier.

His heart was still pounding from the shock of the surprise. And the sight of the man in jeans still smiling at him from across the room.

Miguel made his way to Evan and gave a wink. "Sorry, but there was no changing their minds."

"That's okay."

Evan wouldn't miss the rude customers, the long hours on his feet, or the scent of chilies and fresh-baked tortillas that clung to him after his shift, but he was going to miss the people. He was going to miss being with Miguel's family and how they treated him like he belonged. He'd never been a part of a big family before.

Never would again, at this rate. All he had was his mom. And his best friend.

After the crowd of fellow employees took turns shaking his hands and clapping him on the back, Kyle approached. "You did it."

"I guess I did."

"They want you."

"I guess they do."

"Congratulations, Ev."

"Thanks." Evan bit his lower lip and stared at Kyle's. He forced himself to look away.

Kyle took a step closer. The scent of his cologne reminded Evan of the night before on the couch. So close to his first taste of Kyle's dick.

"Remember the first time we drove out here?" Kyle asked. "That summer after high school?"

"Yeah." They'd both wanted to go to school in LA, and when it came time to leave, they'd driven Kyle's beat-up pickup truck from Ohio to California. How could he forget? That was the trip when they'd almost—

"That's when you first told me the idea for that spec script you were going to write about the terrorism survivors. I knew then you'd make it."

"Let's cut into this cake," Miguel called out.

Kyle moved backward as Miguel rounded the cake table and gave Evan a knife.

"Here, kid," Miguel said. "You do the honors."

Evan had forgotten about the cake, about the room full of people. He took a deep breath and hoped Kyle didn't notice the shake of his hand as he slid the knife through the layer of icing. It was ridiculous how nervous he'd been around Kyle lately. Because no matter how Kyle had been acting, it wasn't like he would ever say what Evan had been dying to hear ten years earlier.

He cut the cake and handed out slices. Miguel had said they were opening the restaurant an hour late, which he'd never done before.

"Mr. Walker," said a man from behind him.

Evan handed off a piece of cake to Miguel's wife, who chatted with Kyle and was a little too fascinated with his biceps, if her hands were anything to go by. Not even married women could resist him.

"Yeah," Evan said. He cut another slice and didn't face the man speaking to him.

The guy cleared his throat.

Evan turned toward him and almost dropped the knife. He caught it before it slipped free. "Mr. Hastings. What are you doing here?" *Great. Nice way to talk to one of your new bosses.*

"I was told your meeting went well today, but that you were heading out of town for the holidays. I wanted to speak with you before you left. Someone mentioned you would be"—he glanced around the room—"here tonight."

"I was supposed to be working. My last night, but they threw me a party first." Evan stepped in front of the cake. He didn't want the vice president of the network's entertainment division to see *Executive Producer* forecasted across the cake in giant letters.

Hastings looked out of place in his tailored-to-perfection gray business suit, solid dark tie, and rigid stance. Castillo's was full of lively music and vibrant colors, the waitstaff in bright red shirts. Hastings didn't fit. He said, "The legal department has informed me there's a problem with your contract."

Evan set the knife on the table as he found his voice. "What kind of problem?"

"I don't think it's going to be a deal breaker. I should be able to talk you through what we need from you, and then we'll move ahead as planned, but..." He looked around again. The waitstaff and other employees were spread out around the dining room. No one sat at the prepped tables, but all were chatting and laughing over their pieces of cake. The mariachi band still played. "Can we talk somewhere private?"

"Sure." Evan caught Miguel watching them. He gestured with a head tilt toward the hall leading to the offices.

Miguel nodded.

Evan led Hastings through the dining room and stopped at the door labeled MIGUEL CASTILLO, OWNER. He held the door open and squeezed his eyes shut as Hastings passed by. *Please don't let me have fucked this up already.* "Have a seat."

Hastings stood for a moment more, glancing around the small, cluttered office with its stack of restaurant supply catalogs on every flat surface, an oversize decade-old computer monitor, and the various hats and sombreros Miguel forced the staff to wear for birthday parties hanging on nails all over the bright yellow walls. Funny how he hadn't made them wear those tonight. Or not so funny. Miguel took Evan's news more seriously than a customer's birthday.

Evan tried to relax as he sat in Miguel's chair, hoping the position of authority behind the desk would help him speak with a confidence he didn't feel right then.

Hastings sat opposite him and slowly folded his arms in front of his chest. He leaned back. "Mr. Walker, I need a guarantee you're the kind of writer we want working with our network before you sign the contract."

"Guarantee?"

"We have a little show in need of your help. Maybe you've heard of it. *American Treasures*."

Little? Only the top-rated show on network television for the past five years. A reality show that featured real-life treasures hidden in the United States and provided clues to contestants while viewers watched to see if anyone uncovered the treasure. If the contestants located it, they won a cash prize and fifty percent of any unclaimed money. "I'm familiar with the show, but if what I've read is true, none of it's scripted."

"Right," Hastings said. "We don't need you to write anything. We need you to help with our research. Every clue we give our contestants is a real lead. The treasure's existence is real. The fact that it is still missing today is real. We validate all this information. The one thing we don't guarantee is if the clues lead to the actual treasure. That's the show."

"And why it's so popular."

"Exactly. Which is why we don't take chances. We know going into each episode what the outcome could be. We know if the treasure is there for anyone to find. Right now, we're at ten percent of our contestants who locate what they're after. Which is good. If they don't occasionally win, we won't have viewers."

Evan nodded, feeling more uneasy with each word from Hastings.

"At any given time, we have about twenty treasures we are investigating as potentials for the show. One thing we look for is a story with strong human interest appeal. The more money involved, well, that's even better. There's a production team in charge of tracking down the clues." He paused, tapping his hands together at the fingertips, staring at Evan as if trying to figure something out. "They've received word a piece of information we need has fallen into the hands of someone you know. We want it. And we want you to get it for us."

"What is it?"

"A journal."

"What does it say?"

"That, I can't tell you. If you can secure this journal for us, then your position as staff writer with our network is a done deal."

So there was nothing wrong with his contract. They were blackmailing him. Holding his dream hostage. He wanted to ask what the fuck was going on but held it in check. Staff writers didn't have much leverage. Not-yet-officially-hired staff writers had less. Evan needed them a hell of a lot more than they needed him. Or maybe not. One of the network's top brass was sitting across the desk. There were not many people above Hastings in the chain of command.

"Who has this journal?" Evan asked.

"Kyle Bennett."

"Kyle?" His Kyle? How long had the network been sitting on this information? He held back the question. Instead he asked, "How do you know this?" *He* didn't even know Kyle kept a journal. Or was it someone else's?

"We make it a point to know everything about the treasures we're hunting."

"If the journal's worth money what makes you think I'll tell my friend to give it to you?" He hadn't meant for his tone to sound so harsh, but he wasn't about to sell out Kyle. Not even for his dream job.

"First off," Hastings said, "we don't want to keep it. We want to get a look at it. If it contains what I think it does, then Mr. Bennett can keep the journal, and we'll offer him a payment for allowing it to be a part of the show. Contestants will track him down to find out what he has that could help them. The journal itself is not worth anything. It's what the journal leads to."

"And that is?"

"Again, not something I'm willing to share."

"And again, I'm not going to screw over my friend." Evan clamped his mouth shut and stifled the anger. He didn't want to ruin his first shot at a writing job when he didn't know what the hell was going on.

Hastings leaned forward, a smirk on his lips. He pointed at Evan. "And here is where you prove yourself to us."

They stared at each other in silence for a moment more. Evan stood, rounded the desk, and opened the office door. "I'll let Kyle know you'd like to discuss it with him. I'm afraid that's all I can do."

Hastings laughed, the surge of it overwhelming as the sound bounced off the walls and the sombreros outlining the small room. He stood. "Mr. Walker, I'd like to see you do well. You are a talented writer, but *American Treasures* makes us more money than all our other shows combined. We will do what we have to in order to keep the ratings going."

Evan dropped his hand from the door and waited as long as he dared before speaking. "I get it."

"Good. You have until the New Year to convince Mr. Bennett. We look forward to working with you." He handed over a business card. "My direct line. Call me when you have an answer." He smiled like they'd been discussing Evan's salary and vacation benefits, then turned and left.

Evan held the card in his hand. Hasting's direct line. It was a rather big coincidence the person the network needed to talk to was the same person Evan currently lived with. The deal for him to join *The Agency* midseason had moved quickly. Too quickly? He'd been flying high on the excitement and had thought his writing had been so well received the network couldn't wait to get him on staff. Apparently there had been more to it than that.

A wave of exhaustion overcame him. He felt numb. And tired. Like he could sleep for three days. He wasn't sure he could take this disappointment on top of everything else. Could the worst year of his life get over with already?

He shoved the business card into his back pocket. He'd take this one step at a time. After work, he'd ask Kyle about it. Maybe he didn't have the journal.

"Hey." Kyle stood in the hall outside Miguel's office. "Things are winding down out here. Miguel says they're going to get ready to open soon."

Evan didn't say anything.

"You okay?" Kyle stepped into the doorway. "Was that about the new job?"

"Yeah. Something they need me to take care of."

"Anything I can help with?" Kyle leaned against the doorjamb, looking more at ease than he had in weeks. He had white frosting at the corner of his mouth. How did he make frosting look like a planned accessory, like a sample everyone would be dying to lick off him?

Evan reached up and ran the pad of his thumb over Kyle's lower lip, traveling the length from one corner to the other before swiping at the frosting.

Kyle's eyes widened.

What the hell was he doing? Evan dropped his hand. "Frosting. On your lip."

Kyle trailed his index finger along the same path, then followed it up with his tongue.

"Uh, sorry to interrupt." Miguel was standing in the hallway, shifting on his feet. "You should, uh, come on out and have some cake before everyone gets to work."

"Sure," Evan said. How was he supposed to go eat cake, let alone wait tables, with a raging hard-on? Two minutes with Kyle and he was out of control again. He had to find his own place soon. Or maybe he didn't. At some point, Kyle was going to go through with his plans to move back to Ohio. Maybe Evan could keep the apartment. Living alone for the first time in his life could be a good thing, couldn't it?

Guess he'd find out.

"I'm going to take off," Kyle said.

Evan wanted to ask if he was headed to the apartment to write, but he held back. Kyle didn't need the pressure. "Thanks for coming."

Kyle nodded and smiled, and Evan couldn't look away. Kyle said, "See you at home later." He left before Evan could respond.

"Thanks for inviting him," he said to Miguel.

"No problem." Miguel watched Evan for a moment more, then added, "You'll remember your promise? You won't become a stranger?"

"Not a chance."

"I'm going to hold you to that." He pointed toward the dining room. "Cake."

"Sure thing, boss." Evan didn't want cake, though. Now that Kyle had left, his stomach was in knots.

Tonight he'd talk to Kyle, and they'd figure out what was going on with the network and this journal. After he gave Kyle the surprise he'd picked up earlier, though. He didn't want anything to get in the way of that.

His priority for the next week was to help Kyle through his writer's block. It'd been going on for far too long.

That was what friends did for each other.

Actually, more like that was what boyfriends did for each other, but he had no illusions Kyle Bennett would ever be anything more than a friend.

Chapter Three

Kyle sat on the couch and held the flat box in his hands. The grief was like a shot to his heart again, like the day of his grandpa's funeral.

When he'd gotten home from the party at Castillo's, he'd been grateful to spot the package sitting on the coffee table. Something else to focus on other than Evan, than the way Evan had touched him in Miguel's office and the words Lorrie had said to him earlier. He'd needed the distraction, but it still had taken him an hour of goofing around on the Internet and two movie rentals before he'd been able to lift the box onto his lap.

He forced down a stiff swallow as he thought of the last time he'd seen his grandpa. Lying so still, looking pale and puffy, not like the smiling, crinkly-eyed old man Kyle had adored, and wearing a dark blue suit which hadn't been anything he'd worn in his life. He'd always been in his cowboy boots, jeans, and a long-sleeved flannel shirt. A farmer. A down-home family man.

Losing him had hit Kyle hard. Especially after living so far away for the last several years. Without words, Evan had seen the pain. He'd stayed with him after the funeral. They didn't talk. Instead, Evan had put in a DVD of *Captain Blood*, then *Mutiny on the Bounty* and *Captains Courageous*—all the movies his grandpa had shown them once he'd found out Evan liked the old black-and-white classics. They'd watched movies until the sun had come up the next morning.

Whatever was in this box couldn't be as bad as losing the old man.

Kyle removed the lid. A leather-bound journal lay inside. He couldn't bring himself to touch it. Why hadn't it been with the others?

His grandpa had kept journals all his life. He'd made them sound as if they were no big deal, describing them as daily logs about life on the farm in northern Ohio, about the weather and the crops, an emotional moment mixed in when his kids and grandkids were born.

When Kyle's grandpa had passed away four years after his wife, they'd found dozens of journals in boxes hidden under his bed. Kyle had sat on the edge of the bed, leafing through the pages of book after book, tears in his eyes at one point as his grandpa wrote about helping search for a missing seven-year-old girl after a tornado had ripped through the county one spring day in 1964. His grandpa had been the one to find her body in a field three miles north of her home.

While Kyle had read more, his dad had packed the closet full of clothes, shoes, and stacks of back issues of *The Old Farmer's Almanac* into boxes, ignoring Kyle and the journals. That night, his dad had taken the boxes of journals home with him, along with the clothes and the aging yellow hardcover almanacs. Kyle had never asked his dad what he'd done with the journals. He didn't want to know. They were probably boxed up in the attic or under his dad's bed, the dust mounting until you couldn't read the embossed year on each cover.

Except for this one.

Its cover was blank, and the overall size was smaller than the others. A sealed envelope was sticking out from between the cover and the first page. Kyle slid it out. On the front was his name, written in his grandpa's handwriting. The same handwriting he'd seen in the other journals and in the letter his grandpa had sent after reading Kyle's first as-of-then-unpublished mystery. That letter had praised Kyle for the excellent story he'd crafted, stating it was only a matter of time before Kyle found his success.

His grandpa had died a week after the release of his first book.

Kyle set the journal on the couch beside him and opened the letter.

> *Dear Kyle,*
>
> *I am asking my attorney to see you get this journal two years after I'm gone. I want you to have distance from my passing before you receive it. You are the only one to ever read what is written inside. I am ashamed of few things in my life, but what I did all those years ago to hide the truth is something I could never bring myself to tell anyone. Until now.*
>
> *I want you to know one thing before you read this. I loved my wife, my family, and the life I've had. All my children and grandchildren are special to me, but I know if anyone could read this journal and understand, it would be you. I thought about burning it before I go, but I can't bring myself to destroy the*

words—it would be like destroying the memories. I
am the only one left who knows the truth of my youth,
and a part of me can't stand that dying with me.
Please read these words and carry them with you
through your life. For me. And for yourself. I hope
you learn something from my mistakes.

I am proud of you for all you have accomplished,
and I was honored to have been the first person you
shared your story with. Don't ever lose faith in
yourself.

And always remember to follow your heart.

Love,
Your proud grandfather
Victor Bennett

Kyle refolded the letter and held it in his hands. The last person to hold that paper had been his grandpa. Oddly, he felt more distant from the old man than he had in the past two years.

He picked up the journal.

Could he open it? Read his grandpa's secrets?

Not yet.

He tucked the letter back inside, carried the journal to his bedroom, and stashed it in his top dresser drawer.

Later. He'd know when it was the right time.

All he knew now was he didn't want to tell Evan he'd gotten it. Talking about his grandpa would lead Evan to asking the question Kyle didn't want to answer.

When are you moving to Ohio?

He'd made the decision six months earlier. It had felt like the right call at the time. Now? Who knew. He sure as hell didn't. The quiet charm of Liberty Falls sounded good. He could write. Think. Breathe.

But…what about Evan?

When Kyle had first had the idea, he'd waited a week to tell Evan. He'd expected him to be pissed, but there was no response. Evan had been too busy with the new house and the screenwriting competition. All Kyle could wonder was, *Will he miss me?* When had he turned into such a damn sap?

Three days after that, Evan and his boyfriend had broken up, and Evan had moved in with Kyle. The breakup had come completely out of the blue and had left Evan reeling for months. Yet another reason not to take Lorrie's advice.

Kyle returned to the couch, set his computer on his lap, and stared at the screen. If only he could concentrate on his work, he might not be so obsessed with what he wasn't getting in his bedroom lately. As usual, nothing came to him. He slammed the laptop lid closed.

"Fuck it."

He stretched out on the couch and rubbed his temples with both hands. He'd tried everything he could think of. Every technique he'd ever read on how to overcome writer's block. Including the one that suggested standing on his head while clearing his mind and humming. All he'd gotten out of that was a headache.

Nothing had worked. The results were always the same. Documents full of crap he wouldn't be caught dead with on his laptop. Knowing his editor, Sue Ann, she'd want to publish every last word. Even if he were dead, he wouldn't want anyone to know about his failures. He'd deleted the files and started over.

Except…he hadn't really started yet. For the last two weeks, he'd done nothing but stare at a blank screen. And the stupid fucking ceiling swirls.

It had been a year since his previous release, and he'd spent that time shooting the shit on Facebook and Twitter and teaching workshops on writing. Two books on the *New York Times* Best Seller list, and he felt like a fraud instructing more talented writers on the secrets of his success. He'd finished the last workshop a month ago. Since then, he'd wondered how many had asked the financial office at UCLA Extension for their money back.

He should've invited that delivery guy in earlier, released a little tension. He had to write something. Anything. He sat up, opened the laptop, and placed his hands over the keyboard.

Start with the body.

In a car? In an alley? Along the road?

"How's it going?"

Kyle glanced up, and his breath caught. His writing, the journal, the delivery guy, everything else vanished from his thoughts. All he could see—all he wanted—stood across the room.

Evan. Holding a bag of takeout, his blue eyes focused on Kyle, a smile on his face. He had on the red dress shirt from Castillo's. It was untucked, the top three buttons undone, the black tie hanging loosely around his neck.

From the day they'd met, Evan had no idea how good looking he was. In high school, he'd been shy and quiet and hadn't had many friends. At almost thirty, a part of Evan was still that kid who never got the attention he deserved. He thought his geeky hobbies and intelligence made him undesirable. The little fucker had no idea what he did to most guys.

To Kyle.

"It's going the same as yesterday."

"Sorry." Evan held up the bag. "I brought dinner."

"Thanks."

Evan shrugged. "Thought you might be working and would want something easy." He carried the bag with him to the kitchen and kept talking as he went. The apartment was small enough you could hear another person from any room in the place. "Did you get the messages I left by the phone?"

"Yeah." And Kyle had thrown them in the trash. Lots of guys had been calling him, wondering where he'd been, wanting to "get together," "have a drink," or any of the other not-so-subtle ways guys had for asking to get laid.

"And I saw Ricky at the gym this morning," Evan said over the rustle of the take-out bag. "Guess he's been trying to get a hold of you all week. Said he was hoping to hook up."

Great. Kyle closed the empty document on his laptop. He didn't want Ricky. Or the delivery guy. Or any of the other guys he usually would've been anxious to follow through with. He'd never experienced a dry spell like this before. He was so horny, if Evan jumped him right then, he'd probably blow with one touch to his dick.

Evan walked into the living room with plates full of Castillo's specialty blue corn enchiladas. He set Kyle's on the coffee table in front of him. "Forgot to tell you. Guess who I saw at the restaurant yesterday?" Evan sank onto the couch next to Kyle, plate in hand. "Jake Gallagher."

"Seriously?"

"Yep. God, that man is gorgeous. You should've seen the waitstaff. Half the guys and all the women were drooling. You'd think we'd never seen a movie star before. I think Miguel was even a little taken with him." Evan laughed.

That laugh sounded good. Damn good. Evan was finally acting more like himself.

I could make him feel so good.

Kyle forced that thought away. "Hey." He bumped Evan's knee with the side of his fist. "How's it feel?"

"Damn." Evan laid his plate on his lap and leaned back against the couch. "I can't believe it. Or that I'm done at the restaurant. And that party… I can't believe Miguel opened late."

"That man has a soft spot for you."

Evan smiled, flashing a hint of a dimple on his right cheek. "I thought he'd be upset to see me go, but he's happy for me. Says I can come back if this doesn't work out."

"That's not going to happen."

"I hope not." Evan ran a hand through his blond hair. "'Cause going from writing for an Emmy-winning show back to waiter would royally suck."

Kyle laughed with him, but all he could think about was that hand running through his own hair, down his chest, his abs, wrapping around his dick.

Don't you fucking hurt him.

Evan turned toward Kyle. He smiled again. His blue eyes lit up. "I just want a shot. Some experience so people will take me seriously when I pitch my own stuff."

"They will. You'll see."

Evan looked like he wanted to say something else, but he didn't. He grabbed his fork and took a bite of an enchilada. "So what's up with you? If I recall, Ricky is one of your rare repeat fuck buddies."

"Nothing's up." Kyle cringed. Bad choice of words. Something was definitely making its way up. Watching Evan eat did that. Those full lips sliding over the fork. His tongue sneaking out to catch a drop of sauce on his lower lip. His throat working as he swallowed.

Evan took another bite and set his fork on the edge of the plate. "Come on. How am I supposed to live vicariously through your sexual escapades if you're not out there?" He waved an arm through the air. Indicating what? Did he think Kyle just had to step outside the door and he'd find someone to fuck?

Why wouldn't Evan think that about him? Hell, today's delivery proved he didn't even have to leave the apartment.

Kyle shrugged. *Just tell him. It's because I'd rather be home fucking you.*

Evan was biting his bottom lip. Kyle had to look away before he swiped his tongue over that same lip.

Quieter, Evan added, "You don't have to stay in and keep me company every night. Go out and live your life."

Kyle focused on his laptop screen again. He held his breath, too scared of what he'd do if he moved. He hadn't gone for the plate of food yet.

"Hey." Evan sounded excited. "Were you writing?"

"Trying to."

"Still nothing?"

"I don't know what the fuck is wrong with me."

Evan leaned in like he wanted to get a look at the laptop screen. God, he smelled amazing. Like the usual musky scent of his cologne and a hint of something more…Miguel's signature black bean and beer soup. He wanted to lick Evan's neck to see if he tasted like the soup.

Below all that was another scent. If Kyle hadn't known Evan had come from work, he would've sworn he'd just been jerking off. Was he imagining it or had Evan stopped off somewhere? That thought did not help take his mind off sex.

"Uh," Evan said, "it would help if you open a document."

Kyle laughed. "I suppose." Evan was so close, his lips mere inches away. He should just do it. It wasn't like he hadn't kissed him before.

After all the years since that motel room in Iowa, he still remembered the way Evan had felt in his arms. The way Evan had touched him. The way they'd kissed. How they'd stopped kissing and stared at each other, the room silent except for their deep breaths. Then they'd kissed with more heat and intensity, their bodies plastered together, legs and arms wrapped around each other so tightly one or both of them might have feared they'd fall off the edge of the world if they let go. No one had ever been as passionate, as sensual as Evan. No one had ever turned Kyle on so damn fast the way Evan did. Then or now.

But before they'd gotten their clothes off, Kyle had pulled back. He hadn't meant to be a jerk about it, but there was no doubt what the look on Evan's face had meant. To this day, it still stung to know he'd been just another asshole on the list of guys who'd hurt Evan.

A month later, Evan had met someone. It was supposed to be a fling, a college affair with an older man. It had lasted ten years, until six months ago when Dickhead, aka Dennis, had broken Evan's heart. Evan had just won the National Screenwriters Competition, which was how he'd gotten the chance to pitch to the network, and Dickhead thought it was the right time to screw him over. It should've been the happiest time of Evan's life. He shouldn't have been sleeping in Kyle's spare room, watching old black-and-white movies every night, looking like he'd lost his whole world.

And now…

It had been so much easier for Kyle to push aside his lust when Evan had been serious with someone. Well, it wasn't exactly easy, but he'd done it. Out of respect for Evan's relationship.

Now here Evan was, staying in his apartment and completely unattached.

If Kyle reached out, pulled Evan in for a kiss, they'd be in his bed and fucking the night away. He never got turned down.

This wasn't the same, though. He usually came on to strangers, barely asking them for a name first. He'd never asked a guy for more than a quick fuck or a long blowjob.

This wasn't just some guy.

Evan smiled. "I've got an idea."

God, that smile was sexy. Those dimples…

When the hell did he notice something like a guy's dimples? Or his smile? Or the color of his eyes, for that matter?

"What kind of idea?" he asked.

"More like a surprise," Evan said. "Sue Ann needs to read it soon, yeah?"

"She called last night. She wants it by New Year's."

Evan's eyes widened. "The whole book?"

"No. Thank God. The first five chapters. I can work on it over the holiday. And the flight there and back."

"But she still thinks you're finished with it?"

"Yeah. She thinks I'm polishing, being a perfectionist."

"Why don't you tell her?"

"They've already set the date, scheduled the promo. What the fuck am I supposed to say? I can't write one goddamn word?"

"You can write. You just need to relax. That's where the surprise comes in. Wait here. I left them in the kitchen." Evan jumped off the couch, animated in a way Kyle hadn't seen in a long time. He really was doing better. Evan stopped short of the kitchen and pointed to Kyle's plate. "Eat."

Like he should talk. He'd barely touched his food. Same as the night before. Kyle had just started noticing it and hadn't figured out what was up. In the last year or two, Evan had put on a few extra pounds, not much anyone who didn't know him well would notice. He'd already lost that, and then some.

Evan turned away, and Kyle got a view of his ass. No extra pounds there. Just round, hard muscle. Kyle adjusted the hard-on forming in his pants and pictured the seats on the plane, the two of them sitting so close for several hours with nowhere to go. Who was he kidding? He wasn't going to get any writing done.

It was going to be one hell of a long flight home.

Chapter Four

Evan stepped into the kitchen and picked up the envelope he'd left on the counter with the bag from the restaurant. He pulled out the tickets and hesitated. One room. Three days and two nights each way. Was this a good idea?

Kyle was a flirt, always goofing with Evan. He'd been comfortable with his sexuality since Evan had first met him. Kyle simply was who he was and made no apologies, no excuses. But lately, his casual flirty ways had become something more. Kyle was determined, focused. Serious in a way he'd never been before.

Or had Evan been seeing what he wanted to?

Over the last two months, the dreams of Dennis had disappeared, and every night Evan dreamed of Kyle, of the two of them together in Kyle's bed. Of the way Kyle would look lying on his back with Evan straddling him, watching that mouth take him in. The way his cock would feel sliding between Kyle's lips. How it would taste to sample his own cum from Kyle's mouth like he wanted to do with the frosting earlier.

After Kyle had left the party at Castillo's, Evan had come up with all sorts of things he could do with frosting that had nothing to do with decorating a cake. His favorite so far was to slather his dick in it, fuck Kyle, then lick the frosting from Kyle's ass when they were done. Of course that had him pondering the lack of effectiveness of frosting as lube.

The frosting-filled fantasy surprised him. He'd never been much of a top. Dennis hadn't liked anal sex, but he'd switch once in a while, telling Evan he wanted to give him everything he craved. It had felt forced, though. A part of Evan had held back, knowing it wasn't Dennis's favorite thing. He'd never let go like he'd been doing in his dreams with Kyle.

More surprising than that...he was left trying to figure out when the hell his fantasies had gotten so kinky. He'd always thought he'd been happy with his sex life, but it wasn't anything wild. Certainly nothing involving licking frosting from someone's asshole.

It had been hell concentrating during his shift at the restaurant. He'd carried the wrong plates to four tables before Miguel finally called him into the back for a break. Over the next half hour, they'd worked in silence as he'd helped Miguel unpack a delivery in the store room. The quiet had been nice. He hadn't wanted to answer questions about the visit from Hastings or what else had been distracting him.

Evan was going to miss the easy way he could be himself around Miguel. Unlike how he'd felt around Dennis, which was an odd realization considering he'd been with him for ten years, six of those living together. He had a lingering unease that too much had been forced between them. Something he'd never noticed until he'd moved in with Kyle. Until the dreams of Kyle had started.

On the drive to the apartment from Castillo's, Evan had to talk himself out of stopping off at the market for tubs of premade cake frosting.

He'd managed not to stop. Instead, he'd jerked off sitting in the car not ten feet from the stairs leading to Kyle's apartment, where anyone could've seen him. He'd used the McDonald's napkins from the glove compartment to wipe the cum from his hand and the steering wheel right as Mrs. Longley had walked by with her toy poodle in her arms. She'd waved at Evan. He'd waved back and waited in the car until she'd turned the corner at the end of the driveway, still carrying the small dog. Only then did he get out and race up to the apartment before the takeout from Castillo's got any colder, trying not to think about how he could've been arrested had Mrs. Longley seen him with his dick hanging out of his pants.

Never had he done something so stupid. He was losing it. Good thing he and Kyle were leaving the next day. Forty-eight hours on the train and they'd no longer be alone together. They'd be in Ohio with their families, where he could get a little perspective.

He was just lonely. Horny. He'd be an idiot to do anything with Kyle again.

He'd made a big enough fool of himself the first time around.

He crushed the take-out bag into a ball and shoved it into the garbage can under the sink. It slid off the pile of used coffee filters. He gave a hard punch with his fist to keep the bag from falling. When it stayed put, he punched again for good measure. Or maybe to make himself feel better.

Kyle didn't need the hassle of Evan coming on to him like some kid in love. Like Evan had probably looked when he'd first met Kyle. Of course, back then he had thought Kyle was straight.

He'd never forget that first day in their English class. Kyle had walked in, looking so confident, not like a guy who'd just transferred to a new school on the first day of their senior year. He looked at ease in his skin, his dark hair stuck up in a way that said he used product to purposely get that just-fucked look.

So damn sexy.

The way his jeans hung from his hips, the way his hands were tucked in his pockets to give him a casual, take-it-or-leave-it look as he smiled at Candace Grey, captain of the cheerleading squad. Just what Evan needed. To fall for another straight guy. Then their teacher had made a point of mentioning Kyle wanted to write mysteries. A guy who was into writing? That had Evan staring again.

Once Kyle had found out they were neighbors and that they both were into writing, they'd hung out every day after his football practice. It was two months before Kyle told Evan he was gay. Talk about shocking the shit out of someone. Evan could do nothing but stare and blink and stare some more.

Kyle had laughed and continued browsing the collection of vintage movie posters in Evan's bedroom.

When Evan could speak again, he'd asked if Kyle was seeing someone. Of course, Kyle hadn't been. He didn't do that, but he'd been going to a gay bar in Toledo for over a year. It was closer to where he used to live, near his grandpa's farm, but they could still make the drive on weekends. Kyle had insisted the bar was the perfect place for Evan's virgin ass to meet someone.

Evan had met someone. Several someones. A string of loser boyfriends who had used him and thrown him aside.

He wasn't that same naive kid anymore. He wasn't going to let anyone use him again. Not even Kyle. Because that would be the end of things—the end of their friendship.

He put the tickets back in the envelope and headed into the living room. Kyle was still staring at his computer screen.

Yeah, Evan had made the right call. It couldn't be easy knowing so many people were waiting for the final book in his debut series. The first book had been an overnight success, a runaway hit which resulted in a deal with a major studio for the film rights. The second book had brought Kyle even more readers. Now everyone was anxiously awaiting the final book that would reveal who the leading character, a gay amateur sleuth named Mac, was going to choose as a lover: his oldest friend who he'd slept with for the first time in book one, or the hot, leather-wearing cop he'd met at the start of the series and who had saved his life more than once.

Evan tried not to bug Kyle about it, but he was dying to know who Mac would end up with. He sat on the couch and handed over the envelope. "Surprise."

Kyle stared at Evan for a moment, then opened the envelope. "Train tickets?"

"Yeah." Evan showed him the brochure he'd picked up at the train station and pointed to the route marked with a meandering red line from San Francisco to Chicago. The major stops along the route were indicated with white dots and the names of each city. "See, the train makes a lot of stops. You'll have three days there and three days back to write."

"You got these for me? For our trip home?"

"Yeah." Although Evan was looking forward to it too. He'd been feeling down about his first Christmas without Dennis. The idea of taking the train with Kyle had him excited about the holiday again. It wasn't like he'd be alone. He never really was. Not since his senior year of high school.

He pointed to the map again. "First we catch a commuter flight to San Francisco. There we get on the train and head all the way to Chicago. It's supposed to be some amazing scenery. We'll go through the Sierra Nevadas and the Rocky Mountains." He paused. "I got a room in one of the sleeper cars so you can have privacy to write."

"Wow." Kyle flipped through the tickets for their connecting train in Chicago that would take them on to Ohio and the ones for the trip back to California. Did he notice they only had the one room? It seemed silly for them not to share. And the tickets weren't cheap. "This is great, Ev. Thank you." Kyle looked...relaxed, happy. Not stressed like when Evan had walked in earlier.

Now wasn't the right time to ask him about the journal. It could wait. At least until Kyle started writing again. At least until he finished the five chapters he needed to send to his editor. Hastings expected an answer by the first of the year. That was two weeks away.

Kyle was examining the map in more detail. Evan reached for his tickets. While Kyle wrote, he could work on the script ideas he wanted to pitch to the writers' room after he'd gotten his feet wet. That was if he still had the job.

"This is really cool, Ev."

That had Evan smiling. He wouldn't let Hastings or the uncertainty of his future ruin their trip.

"Hey." Kyle faced him and leaned his arm on the back of the

couch, resting his temple against his closed fist. "You're doing a lot more smiling today than you have in a long time."

"It's almost Christmas."

"It is." Kyle's eyes crinkled up at the corners as his smile widened. "And you've been a good boy?"

Evan loved this playful side of Kyle. He hadn't been like this when Evan had first moved in. It was like Kyle was worried Evan was too fragile. And that pissed him off. So he'd gotten dumped by the person he thought he was going to spend his life with. People got over that. Didn't they? He wasn't the same weak kid who'd been used and rejected over and over.

Then what was he so afraid would happen if he and Kyle gave in and slept together?

He folded the brochure, needing to do something with his hands. "I have been very, very good."

"Yeah, you have." Kyle's voice was lower, deeper, sexier than a moment before, if that was possible. "What do you think good boys get in their stockings?"

"Um..." Evan sat back and pressed his index finger to his lips. "Porn. Really, really good porn."

Kyle huffed out a laugh. "That can be arranged."

"Well, you're the expert."

It was an old joke from college. They'd had a fight one night when Evan had told Kyle he was sleeping around so much he might as well have done porn and gotten paid for it. Kyle hadn't been offended. He'd turned it into a joke, one they revisited from time to time.

Kyle said, "You just want me to teach you the industry secrets."

"Ha. What secrets do you know that I don't?"

Kyle slowly leaned in until his chest touched Evan's shoulder and their mouths almost came together. Evan's breath caught in a rush. In an instant, he was back in that motel room, Kyle on top of him, Kyle's mouth on his.

"It's not something I can tell you," Kyle said. "You have to experience it." He licked his lower lip in an exaggerated move.

Evan could not stop watching that mouth, the moisture left behind by the swipe of Kyle's tongue. He wanted to lean in and follow the action with his own tongue. His breathing picked up, and his cock responded. The intense way Kyle watched him was unnerving. Like Evan was the only opportunity he'd had to fuck anyone in weeks.

Which was odd. Kyle had never experienced a lack in that department. How long had it been since he'd hooked up with anyone? Without a thought on what he was doing, Evan raised his hand and ran his thumb over Kyle's lower lip liked he'd done in Miguel's office earlier.

No shocked reaction this time. Instead, Kyle drew his eyebrows up in a questioning stare. "Frosting?"

Evan couldn't speak. He shook his head. He longed to shove Kyle backward, straddle him, and kiss him with a fierceness—a possessiveness—that scared Evan in its intensity. He wanted to grind their bodies together, press Kyle into the couch, until they were panting and writhing, until they came so hard they'd be unable to move. They'd fall asleep right there, his body draped over Kyle's.

Just kiss him.

No. It would never be just a kiss. Just another fuck. Not for Evan. He'd probably end up confessing what he felt for Kyle. Then what? How awkward and fucked-up would their friendship get after that?

"I can't." He dropped his hand.

"It's okay, Ev." Kyle eased back to his former location on the couch. He focused on the tickets again. "Thanks for this. I think it'll help."

"You're welcome." Evan squeezed his eyes shut and sucked in a deep breath. He opened his eyes and nudged Kyle's shoulder with his own. "It'll be fun. Our last trip before you move."

Kyle started to say something, but Evan turned away. He didn't want to hear anything more about Kyle leaving California. Didn't want to think about what it would be like not to see each other all the time, not to hang out together.

He stood and picked up his plate. "I'm going for a run. I'll let you get more staring at your computer done."

"Thanks." The frustrated expression was back as Kyle rested his head on the couch behind him and stared at the ceiling.

"You'll come up with some great stuff on the train. You'll see."

There was that serious, intense look again as Kyle glanced at him. Could there be something to it? Something more than desire? Evan left the room before he did something stupid and asked what it meant. He headed down the hall to Kyle's spare bedroom, closed the door, and leaned against it.

Why had he touched Kyle again?

Because a part of him would always love Kyle, would always imagine what it would be like to have all of him.

He pushed away from the door and undressed. He was not going there again. He slipped on his shorts and T-shirt, headed into the hall, and stopped at the apartment door. "I'll be back in an hour." When Kyle didn't say anything, Evan faced him.

Kyle was staring at Evan's crotch, breathing hard, his mouth hanging open. Had he been checking out his ass? He finally lifted his head and met Evan's stare. Those serious dark eyes did shit to Evan's willpower.

There was no denying it. He could have Kyle if he wanted. For one night.

He turned away and fumbled with the door handle, then left the apartment before he lost all reason.

Chapter Five

Kyle stared at the closed apartment door. He couldn't get the image of Evan in those shorts and that tight black T-shirt out of his mind. Evan had been exercising a lot since he'd moved in, and his build was firming up even more than what was visible in jeans or his uniform.

Especially his ass.

God, what Kyle would give to take that ass in his hands, tongue the round flesh, then shove his face between the cheeks and proceed to lick every inch of Evan's body. Then he wanted Evan to do the same to him. Right before Evan fucked the hell out of him.

Should he just do what Lorrie said and pounce?

Evan deserved a night of pleasure. He deserved to let go and enjoy himself. Kyle could give that to him. There wasn't one thing he didn't want to do to Evan. Or have Evan do to him. Which should've been a giant red flag warning him not to advance.

If he let himself go like that, would they ever be the same again?

He adjusted his swelling cock through the jeans. His dick sure didn't care about friendship or right and wrong or hurting Evan. Jerking off sounded good, but he forced himself to wait. Later, in bed. After Evan came home. Or better yet, while Evan showered after his run.

Kyle breathed deep and rubbed the back of his neck. No sense trying to work any longer. He shut down his laptop, picked up the plates from dinner, and headed for the kitchen. He needed to do laundry and pack. He hadn't been prepared to leave the next day. According to the tickets, they'd be in Ohio for over a week, then head back on New Year's Day.

He cleaned up the dirty plates and stored Evan's dinner, almost a full plate, in the fridge on the off chance Evan would actually want to eat more later. On his way to his room, Kyle stripped down to his underwear and tossed his clothes with the rest of his dirty laundry, then threw a load into the washing machine. He went to his room and got his suitcase and backpack out. In his closet, he grabbed his gloves, a wool hat, and the red scarf his mom had knitted for him the year before. According to Lorrie, the temperature had been dropping in Ohio for the past week, with snow falling steadily. He folded several long-sleeved shirts and sweatshirts. As he cleared a spot on the closet rack, he pictured his bedroom filled with Evan's things. Would Evan keep renting the place and move into the larger bedroom after Kyle was gone?

Kyle wasn't sure what the hell was wrong with him that he couldn't write, but for the sake of his career, he had to do something soon. A change in scenery was long overdue. To be honest, he missed his parents, his sister, and her kids. Everything in him told him home—Liberty Falls—was the right answer.

But he had no intention of moving as long as Evan needed him.

Although Evan didn't really need him. Never had.

He amazed Kyle. It might not have been the life Kyle wanted, but he had to admire Evan for not letting his status as victim consume him. Evan never blamed Kyle for what had happened to him. Despite the fact that it had been Kyle who had taken Evan to that bar where he'd met his first asshole boyfriend. Then the next, and the next, finally ending up with the one who'd hurt him the most.

And after all he'd been through, Evan had still fallen in love with someone.

He'd do it again too. Lorrie had been right about that.

The thought of Evan with another man was worse than the years of watching him with his ex. Why? Because of the past six months living together?

Kyle threw a dresser drawer open and went for his warmest pairs of socks, tucking each under his arm as he searched for more. When he'd collected enough for the next two weeks, he went to close the drawer and stopped short. There, peeking out from under the pile of socks he'd rummaged through, was his grandpa's journal.

He pulled the leather book out and sat on the edge of the bed. The socks tumbled from under his arm and dropped one by one beside him.

Part of him wanted to connect to his past. To a time when his grandpa was alive. When it was easy to write. When he had dreams of selling his work. When he and Evan had been young and the desire was new, not something he'd waited years to follow through on.

He wanted to go back to that youth—that innocence.

Was that the real reason he'd been planning to move? Or was there more he hadn't thought about?

He slowly opened the journal. The leather spine creaked with the movement. The scent of dust and aging paper drifted up around him.

He needed to read this, as if the answers to his own problems were inside.

June 25, 1952

> *Today I left all I had known for months behind and*
> *began the journey home. I am ready. To see the end*
> *of death. The bombs, the guns, the blood. To never*
> *see such destruction again. A part of me, though,*
> *cannot face my family, the simplicity of the farm, or*
> *the strangeness of the world we left behind. I am not*
> *ready for civilization. Yet, I am not ready to be*
> *alone. He has a plan, and I know I must follow him*
> *in it.*

Kyle stopped reading.

June 25, 1952. The day his grandpa left Korea. The war continued for a year and so did his grandpa's travels. He hadn't come home to Ohio until one year later, four days after the armistice was signed. A few months after that, he'd met Kyle's grandmother.

Throughout Kyle's childhood, his grandpa had talked a great deal about life, about the things he'd seen when he'd traveled with his wife on family vacations, about the trials and tribulations of running a small family-owned farm, about hard work and commitment. The two times he'd never mentioned were the war and the year he'd spent traveling afterward. When Kyle was ten and he'd been studying World War I in history class, he started to ask his grandpa if he'd ever killed a man, but Kyle's mom had cut him off. She'd pulled him aside and whispered that he was not to speak about the war or the year after with his grandfather ever again.

So he'd never mentioned it. Not in all the conversations they'd had over the years.

Now, here he was, holding a journal from that missing time of his grandpa's life.

He continued on to the next entry.

> *We reached Chicago yesterday. Free men. Military*
> *life no longer dictating our every decision, our every*
> *move. The buildings were enormous, and the crowds*

rushed by so quickly. The sidewalks were packed at
all hours of the day, the city life loud even while we
slept. It didn't faze us. We had slept through worse.
To watch him sleep in such peace, and not amid the
bombs and foxholes, was a treat I cannot describe.
His face no longer held the pain and worry, the guilt
of a man who'd done things he never wanted another
soul to know. I ran my finger along the scar over his
right eye, down his cheek, then held him in my arms.
My head on his shoulder, I pressed my palm over the
rise and fall of his chest. It was like a dream, being
alone in a room, finally in a real bed with Joe
Morrison. I wanted to watch him sleep forever. I also
wanted to wake him, kiss him, and know what it was
to feel alive again and again. All night. All day. Until
I felt the same peace.

Kyle lowered the journal to his lap. "Grandpa." He wasn't sure why he'd spoken aloud, wasn't sure if he wanted his grandpa to hear him, if he wanted to speak to the old man, and if he did, he had no idea what he wanted to say.

He slowly closed the book and dropped it into the nightstand drawer as if holding the journal any longer, looking at it for another second, would make it more real.

The words written so long ago couldn't find a place to settle in his brain, and he couldn't understand how they made him feel.

All he knew was they reminded him of another time in his life. A night when he'd lain side by side with someone he had watched sleep. Someone he'd wanted to wake but couldn't bring himself to touch again. About the night he and Evan had spent in a motel room in Des Moines, Iowa.

They had called it quits to the fooling around after Kyle had freaked. He'd taken a shower, and by the time he'd finished, Evan had been asleep. There'd only been the one bed, so he'd slipped on his underwear and climbed in beside Evan. He'd forgotten the rest of that night until he'd read his grandpa's words.

He'd spent a half hour watching Evan sleep, watching his eyes flutter with his dreams, watching his chest rise and fall with each breath. He had learned every inch of Evan's face, taking in the details—the hint of blond facial hair along his jawline, the parted, full lips, the slight wheeze through his open mouth—until Kyle finally let sleep drag him under.

It hadn't been just about sex. Not then. Not now. He wanted to spend time hanging out with Evan, talk over dinner every night, joke around, watch TV, live together like they'd been doing for the past six months.

You're in love with him.

Fuck.

He dropped to the bed, bouncing when his ass made contact with the mattress. "I'm in love with him."

He fumbled getting his phone out of his pocket. Lorrie answered on the third ring, and he said, "Goddamn you."

She squealed. "I knew it!"

"What the hell do I do now?" He stood and paced the length of his bedroom.

Lorrie laughed. "Talk to him."

"About what?"

"What you're feeling."

"I don't know what I'm feeling, and I sure as hell don't know what to say about it."

"Oh, good Lord." She sighed. "Show him, then. Show him what he means to you, and see if he responds."

"You're a lot of help."

"Kyle, this is Evan. Just be honest. Don't hide from what you're feeling and go with it. He'll meet you halfway if it's what he wants too." When he didn't say anything, she asked, "Can you do this?"

"I have no idea." He ran a hand through his hair. "I...I've gotta go."

"Don't think too much."

Not thinking sounded good. He'd take this one step at a time. Start with what he did best. Get Evan in bed and go from there. He went to the nightstand and opened the drawer. He grabbed the lube and condoms. "Okay. I can show him."

She laughed again. "I love you, baby brother." Then she was gone.

He held the phone in one hand and the condoms in the other. The tension in his chest eased. He'd been doing too much worrying lately. About his writing career. About sex. About Evan. She was right. Why shouldn't he go with what he was feeling? Give them both what they'd always desired and see where it led.

He threw the lube and condoms into his backpack. "What the hell." He added another handful of condoms for good measure. He was tired of holding back. And from the way Evan had almost kissed him in the living room, he was too.

Kyle heard the apartment door open, then close. He walked into the hall.

Evan stood at the other end. He was breathing hard, his body covered in a fine sheen of sweat, his blond hair slicked back as if he'd just run his hand through the moist strands.

But what stood out the most was the intense way Evan stared at him, mouth parted like in his sleep. Kyle felt naked in only his briefs, not to mention the way Evan's gaze took in the sight of him.

He wanted to throw Evan against the wall and taste him, touch him, do everything he'd ever done with another man, but somehow do more. That probably wasn't the best way to do this. Or maybe it was.

But if he didn't give Evan a chance to think first like he needed to do about everything, what would happen the next morning? What would Evan expect? And what would he be able to give Evan?

That held Kyle still. He came up with only one thing to say. "I think my grandpa had sex with another man."

Evan took a step toward him. "What?"

"A lawyer sent me one of his journals."

"A journal?" Evan moved forward another step.

"It came today. Grandpa wanted me to have it. I didn't want to read it at first. I thought it would be too hard, but...I don't know, something told me to take a look tonight. And..."

Evan searched his eyes. "What?"

"He was in bed with a guy."

"When?"

"After he got back from the war. He was in Chicago."

"Maybe they were sharing a room."

"No. It was more than that. He was touching him."

"Oh."

"I'm, uh...kinda freaked."

Evan shortened the distance between them, the look on his face so calm, understanding. "Why?"

Just like Ev, always making him think. "I don't know. I guess I should be okay with it. Right? That's why he sent it to me."

"Yeah," Evan said. "Sounds like this was before he was married."

"Yeah. I haven't read the rest yet."

They were close enough now that they could reach out and touch each other. There was no missing Evan's blue eyes focused on him.

Finally, Kyle could move again. He stepped closer. "Ev..."

Chapter Six

Evan shivered. Which made no sense. He was still warm from the run, the sweat on his skin not even dry yet.

Kyle took another step. Evan wanted him to stop. He wanted to shout all the reasons why this had to stop, before it got started, wanted to tell Kyle not to move another inch.

He didn't.

And Kyle didn't stop coming at him until they were practically touching, Kyle staring down at him.

Evan tried to focus on Kyle's words, on the news about the journal and his grandpa, but all he could think about was what he'd seen when he'd walked into the apartment: Kyle, all skin and taut muscles, wearing only his tight-as-sin white underwear, the briefs stretched over his cock, and the way Kyle had looked at him in the dim light of the hallway.

Just once. He's leaving anyway. Evan closed his eyes and forced himself to concentrate on the conversation. He looked up at Kyle again. "Are you okay?"

"Yeah." Kyle said the word with a slight curve of his lips. He took a step back and reclined against the wall, looking casual, like he was about to flirt with a bartender for a free drink. "After I read it, I was thinking about that night in the motel room in Iowa on our first drive out here." He slowly swung his head in Evan's direction. "Do you remember that night?"

Evan nodded.

"Do you ever think about it?" Kyle's voice was barely a whisper.

Up until a few months ago, Evan hadn't let himself, but since he'd moved in with Kyle… "Sometimes."

"Like right now?"

"Yeah."

Kyle slid along the wall, traveling the last remnants of space between them. "Ev, I've been waiting ten years to finish what we started." He pushed off the wall and turned until they were face-to-face again, his dark eyes unflinching as he leaned in. He stopped before their lips touched. The heat of that mouth and body so close stoked the fire inside Evan.

His own body reacted, his cock pushing at his shorts. He wanted to shove Kyle against the wall and kiss him until morning, do everything he'd ever dreamed of when it came to touching Kyle, everything he ached to feel about the man.

The smile Kyle gave him next wasn't the usual cocky one he'd used with countless guys over the years. He pressed forward and slid his lips along Evan's skin from the base of his neck to his earlobe, leaving a trail of goose bumps in his wake. He lingered over Evan's ear and whispered, "You smell so damn good. I want to fuck you, Ev."

Evan shivered again. "We shouldn't…" He couldn't say more. Didn't want to. The time for talking was over. Kyle ran the tip of his tongue along the outside of Evan's ear, and Evan instinctively moved closer. His breath hitched with the touch of Kyle's bare abs against him. Why had he worn a T-shirt to go running?

Using only the weight of his body, Kyle turned them until Evan's back was against the hall wall, then flattened his palms to the wall on either side of Evan's head. He licked his lips and spread his legs until their bodies lined up groin to groin, then rolled his hips, putting pressure against Evan's cock. "God, Ev…"

With that movement, those two words, Evan groaned and let his head fall back to the wall. He couldn't stop himself. He rocked his hips in time with Kyle's. The feel of Kyle's body, his hard cock against him, drove Evan's own arousal higher.

Kyle spoke again, his voice even lower. "It could be so fucking good."

Evan lost track of the arguments he'd been telling himself since he'd left the apartment earlier. He raised his head, and their lips met, the softest brush of flesh until Kyle opened his mouth, seized Evan by the back of the head, and slid his tongue into the touch. The kiss deepened, and Evan thought he'd never be able to stop feeling Kyle's mouth on his, their tongues pressed together.

Kyle pushed forward with his entire body, pinning Evan against the wall. Evan wrapped his arms around Kyle's neck and held on. The feel of Kyle's tongue and lips was better than the dreams, better than he'd remembered. It had to be his imagination, but Kyle tasted like the frosting from earlier still lingered on his lips.

Kyle dropped his other hand from the wall and clutched Evan's hip, then slowly slid his hand to his ass and tugged him even closer.

All Evan felt, all he tasted, was Kyle.

This was anything but casual. Nothing had ever felt like this. Out of control. Intense. So fucking right Evan wasn't sure how he'd ever be with anyone else again.

This could not be happening.

He couldn't fall for Kyle again. He'd end up in the same place as last time—heartbroken and longing for more than he could ever have.

They broke the kiss, both breathless, and Kyle ran his lips along the skin of Evan's neck again, this time adding his tongue into the mix. Evan dropped his head to the wall behind him and gripped the back of Kyle's neck, dragging his fingers up through the dark hair. Kyle explored with tongue and lips and teeth until Evan was gasping, tugging on Kyle, pulling him even closer.

God, he couldn't get enough of him. They rocked, body thrusting against body. Another minute and Evan was going to come in his shorts. How embarrassing. But this was Kyle. He could always be himself with him.

A phone rang out from the living room. Kyle lifted his head. They stared at each other as the phone rang again.

Evan shook his head and let his arms fall to his sides. This was fucked up. "I can't lose you."

"God, Ev, that's stupid. You aren't going to lose me."

"Stupid? You're leaving."

Kyle ran a hand through Evan's hair and gripped the back of his neck again. "I'm here." His breath brushed over Evan's lips as he said, "Right now. Just us." He tugged him forward, and their mouths met again, the sweet slide of tongue over tongue. Kyle rocked his hips, rubbing their cocks against each other through the thin cloth of briefs and shorts. Evan wanted to tear off the clothes and fall to the floor with Kyle. He wanted to touch and rub and kiss and fuck until every doubt and fear melted into a moment of pleasure they'd waited too long for.

This could never be just one night of sex.

He already wanted more.

The phone rang again. Evan pulled back, but with nowhere to go, he banged his head on the wall.

Kyle slipped his fingers between Evan and the wall and cupped the back of his head. "Are you okay?"

"Yes. No. I don't know." He pushed Kyle's hand away. "I can't do this." Even if it would mean something to Kyle, in the end, Evan would lose him. "This isn't just sex for me, Kyle."

"I don't think it is for me either. I think…maybe I can do this."

Evan searched his eyes. "Wh-what?"

"Maybe I want to try."

"Try?" Try what? One date. Then what? Evan had never heard Kyle talk like this. About anyone. It was worse than not hearing it at all. "I can't go through that again. Not with you."

"Through what?" Kyle asked.

"Losing someone. Losing you. It's too big of a risk for me."

"You mean *I'm* too big of a risk?" The concern vanished from Kyle's face. A more pissed-off look replaced it.

Let him be angry. That proved Evan's point. He shoved Kyle backward with both hands on his chest. For a moment, he hesitated, uncertain he could take one step away. He had to, though. He turned, went into the bedroom where he'd been staying for months, and slammed the door shut, not meaning for it to sound so loud, so frustrated.

He sat on the edge of the bed. What had he done? But he could not let them fuck things up, fuck up their friendship. Kyle was his safe place. Always had been.

No matter how much he'd loved Kyle once—hell, still did love him—and no matter how much Kyle desired him, they wanted different things out of life.

Evan had understood the reasons without explanation. Kyle had watched his parents slowly settle into a lifeless marriage, watched his sister lose herself to every guy she'd ever dated, giving up all her dreams as she fell for one man after another, finally marrying the loser who'd managed to fuck up putting on a condom. Kyle Bennett had grown up thinking love and passion—or happiness, for that matter— didn't mesh. He thought relationships killed a person's soul, destroyed the fire inside them. The writer in him was determined not to lose the spark, the passion.

No matter what hints Evan had offered over the years that Kyle would end up alone, there was no changing his mind.

If they slept together, Evan would admit everything he felt, and Kyle would run.

Evan had to focus on something else. Anything. He spotted his script on the nightstand. There were brightly colored sticky notes stuck every which way on the loose pages, indicating the parts he thought might need reworking. He'd marked every page with at least five notes. Like that was going to help. He still couldn't decide if he even wanted to make changes. And really, why was he bothering? The network might pull the contract before he ever got a chance to show his ideas to anyone.

No matter what else was in the journal, Kyle would not want to exploit his grandpa's past on a TV show.

Evan should tell Kyle now about the network's interest in the journal, but he couldn't move, couldn't face Kyle right then.

A better option would be to call Hastings and tell him there was no deal. Evan didn't want to exploit Kyle's grandpa either. He'd always liked Victor Bennett. Since before the night Victor had helped him when he'd gotten into trouble for smoking a joint in the Liberty Falls Cemetery with a college boy he'd met at the gay bar in Toledo. Evan had called Victor, instead of his mom, to pick him up at the police station. On the drive back, Victor hadn't asked him anything about the pot or the boy. He'd asked what old movies Evan had watched recently and about the screenplay he was writing.

If Victor had secrets hidden in his past, Evan didn't want to be the one to betray him.

Tomorrow he'd figure out a way to tell Kyle the network wanted access to the journal. Because no matter what, Kyle deserved the truth.

One thing Evan knew for sure, he didn't want Kyle to know Hastings was using his new job as leverage to get at the journal. He wouldn't put Kyle in that position.

Evan leaned forward, rested his head in his hands, and remembered why he'd promised he'd never again go where he'd just been with Kyle in the hall.

That night in the Motel 6, Evan had pushed Kyle too far. The next morning, they'd driven all day in silence, finally stopping at a roadside biker bar for burgers and beers. After three games of pool, Kyle had walked out the back door into the alley behind the bar with some guy he'd just met. Evan had watched Kyle follow the guy out the door, then he'd drunk more shots of Jack Daniel's than he'd ever had in his life. While Kyle was doing God knows what in that back alley, Evan had ended up in the bar's bathroom, kneeling on the sticky concrete floor, staring into a stained toilet bowl. A tear fell from his face into the mix of vomit and rust water. He'd wiped the vomit from his chin, the tears from his eyes, and he'd known the truth. Friends was all he'd ever let them be.

Then or now.

He wasn't about to watch Kyle walk from his bed to another guy again.

* * * *

Kyle stood in the hallway and tried to catch his breath, the sound of Evan's bedroom door slamming shut still ringing in his ears. He smacked an open palm against the wall. "Fuck." He'd royally screwed that up.

Or, actually, not gotten them to the screwing part. Again. He charged into his room and slammed his door shut for good measure.

But this wasn't just about screwing. For either of them.

"This isn't just sex for me, Kyle."

Lorrie had been right. Evan Walker was falling in love again.

And he knew better than to trust Kyle with his heart. Kyle couldn't blame him. Then why had he gotten so upset in the hall?

Fuck it. He worked his underwear over his straining erection and slid them off, then shoved the open suitcase off the bed, not caring when all but one of the sweatshirts he'd packed fell onto the floor. He lay down, still breathing heavily, his cock aching.

That kiss…

He'd always wondered if he'd somehow distorted that night they'd spent together in the motel into an idealized fantasy. Turned out his memories hadn't come close to the kisses they'd shared in the hall.

The shower turned on in the bathroom next to his room. He pictured Evan naked, the water streaming down his back and over the curve of his ass. The blond hair darkening under the spray. The soap lingering at his nipples and the light hair above his cock.

Kyle gripped his dick and began a steady stroke. He planted his feet on the bed and thrust into the touch, moving his hand faster and faster as he imagined stepping into the shower with Evan. Pressing Evan against the shower wall, this time with no clothes in the way between them. Hitting his knees and sucking Evan off while he shot his own load on the tile floor.

A loud groan escaped him as he came. He didn't care if Evan heard him. Let him think about what they could've been doing together right then.

When Kyle could breathe normally again—could think again—another thought hit him. Lorrie had been right about something else. This was his last shot with Evan. And here he was fucking it up. He had no idea what to say, what to do next. How to prove himself to Evan. Should he even try?

He rolled over and spotted the train ticket on the nightstand. One sleeper compartment, cramped quarters, two nights alone. He smiled. He'd show Evan the passion between them was too intense to deny any longer. Either that or he'd drive Evan insane trying. Force him to spend the entire train ride hard, dying for a touch, a kiss, anything.

Evan was bound to meet someone new soon. Someone who wouldn't be able to resist that smile, those blue eyes, that amazing body.

Kyle grabbed the pillow next to him and punched at it twice before dropping his head to the surface.

Who the fuck was he kidding? Someone who wouldn't be able to resist the whole man. The smart, loving, determined, compassionate Evan. The one who had trusted him once.

That night in high school when Evan's boyfriend had physically and emotionally hurt him, he had come to Kyle. The asshole boyfriend had wanted to tape them having sex, and when Evan said no, they'd argued. The argument turned physical fast, and Evan had ended up gagged, tied to the asshole's bed, and videotaped anyway.

Evan had refused to go to the cops, so Kyle had taken the matter into his own hands. He'd found the son of a bitch "boyfriend," and after destroying the tape, he'd made sure he'd never go near Evan again. A week later, he'd given the guy a serious pounding as a reminder.

No matter how sweet the revenge had been, it didn't lessen Kyle's guilt. He'd been the one who'd insisted Evan keep going to the bar with him, keep meeting guys.

Evan trusted in their friendship. Always had.

Don't fuck that up.

Not again.

* * * *

Men were everywhere, dancing, kissing, but Evan couldn't hear the beat of the music, the noise of the crowd in the bar around him, or the rustle of their clothes as they swayed and danced and gyrated against each other. He couldn't hear anything. It was like some weird-ass episode of a gay *Twilight Zone*.

Evan moved through the crowd, weaving around one man, then the next. There was barely space for him to squeeze through the pack of half-naked bodies. The men were touching, talking, laughing. Their mouths moved, but nothing they said to each other registered with Evan. What was happening to him?

A tall, shirtless man came in close. He wore jeans, a cowboy hat, and boots. He had his T-shirt off and tucked into his back pocket. An urban cowboy on the prowl. His body was twice the size of Evan's. He was broad, all muscle, with dark hair and a goatee. Evan found men with facial hair hot as hell. So was the serious look on the guy's face. He planned to have exactly what he was after: Evan.

The cowboy reached out and grabbed Evan's ass. He yanked him forward and ground his massive body against Evan's. It felt good...to be touched again. To be wanted.

Then Evan was being pulled backward, away from the tall cowboy, away from the warmth, the feel of the big hands on his body.

Someone spun him around.

Kyle.

The expression wasn't a normal one for Kyle. He was pissed. He had a tight grip on Evan's biceps.

The crowd around them kept moving. Strobe lights flashed across the sea of skin and nameless faces. Kyle leaned in. His rough, low voice was all Evan heard.

"So you'll fuck anyone but me. Is that how it is now? Fine. But remember one thing..." He came in closer. His lips moved again, but Evan could no longer hear him. He thought he saw the word love on Kyle's lips, but not in his eyes. When Kyle finished speaking, he backed away, his angry expression focused on Evan.

This wasn't Kyle. He didn't treat anyone like this. Evan watched as Kyle backed all the way out the open door of the bar where a moving truck waited for him at the curb.

He's leaving.

Evan wanted to run after Kyle, wanted to stop him, but his legs wouldn't work. He couldn't move.

"No!"

* * * *

Evan awoke and bolted upright, breathing heavily. He wore a T-shirt and underwear and was in the living room, sprawled on the couch, loose papers across his chest. He'd been working on his script since he'd pushed Kyle away earlier, since Kyle had gone into his room, where he'd stayed for the rest of the night.

Was that how it would be on the trip? Awkward silence with Kyle pissed at him?

"What the fuck?" Kyle stood at the far end of the couch near the hallway leading to the bedrooms, wearing only his underwear and holding a baseball bat in his hands, ready to take a swing. His eyes were wide. He looked around the room, then at Evan. "What happened?"

"What do you mean?" Evan swung his legs off the couch, using the loose pages to hide his erection. "I fell asleep."

"I heard a noise, and you were moaning or something. I thought someone was breaking in. Thought they hurt you."

"Hurt me?" Evan stood, the pages falling from his lap. Why should he care if he sported wood? It wasn't like Kyle hadn't felt it pressed against his own cock earlier. Evan closed the distance between them and slipped the bat from Kyle's grip. "No one broke in. I was dreaming. Go back to bed."

"You scared the shit out of me."

"Do you always get a boner when you're scared?"

"What?" Kyle glanced down. His cock was hard and tenting his underwear. Well, as much as the fabric would allow, given the tightness of the briefs. Did he buy them two sizes too small on purpose? Kyle ran a hand over his hard-on. Trying to make it disappear or give it some friction? "I was in the middle of a damn fine dream when you woke me up. The kind I really didn't want to miss the end of."

"Sorry." Evan added raised eyebrows to go with the sarcastic tone.

A thud came from the other end of the hall.

Kyle faced the bedrooms. "I told you I heard something."

Chapter Seven

Kyle grabbed the bat from Evan's hand. "Sounds like it's coming from my room now." He stepped down the hall, not wanting to tangle with an intruder, but he was more pissed off and frustrated than he'd been in a long time. If someone had broken in, he might as well direct his anger at that asshole and not Evan.

"What are you doing?" Evan whispered.

"Going to see who it is."

"Let's call the cops."

"Go get the phone," Kyle said, although he kept creeping forward. He heard Evan move toward the living room and then stop.

"Get back here," Evan called out in a rough whisper.

Out of the darkness of Kyle's bedroom, a man charged forward and slammed into Kyle. His back hit the wall, and he dropped the bat. He gasped as the breath was knocked from his chest with the force of the intruder's weight pressed against him. The guy smelled of sweat and piss, and the T-shirt he wore was ratty and damp.

Evan ran toward them. "Get off him."

The guy shoved Kyle to the ground, picked up the bat, and faced Evan.

"No." Kyle stumbled as he tried to stand.

Evan stopped a few feet away from the intruder and withdrew backward into the living room, his hands out in a defensive pose. The guy advanced and raised the bat.

He was going to do it—was going to smash Evan's skull in. Kyle had seen it in the asshole's eyes. A junkie looking to score cash for his next fix. He probably had no idea what he was doing.

Kyle stood, his lungs filling again. "Evan, run."

He didn't. Maybe he didn't want to turn his back on the intruder. Evan kept his gaze locked on the guy. "I can give you money if you promise to leave."

The guy stopped. "Yeah, yeah. Get me some cash."

Evan pointed toward the couch. "My wallet's in my pants."

As quietly as he could, Kyle edged into position to jump the asshole from behind. The guy must have seen him. The asshole moved fast and took a swing, hitting Evan in the gut with the bat before Kyle could react. Evan went down.

"No." Kyle rushed toward them.

The asshole faced him, the end of the bat pointed at the back of Evan's head. "Stop, motherfucker, or I crack your boy's pretty head open."

Kyle stopped. "Don't. I'll get you the money." A vision of Evan on the floor, blood pooling beside his head, those blue eyes open and lifeless, filled Kyle's mind. He wanted to rip the asshole junkie's arms off. He held still. He had to keep it together. He had to get this guy out of the apartment.

Evan was conscious, but he wasn't moving. He held a hand to his stomach. How badly was he hurt?

"Here." Kyle slowly stretched sideways for Evan's pants on the couch. He slid the wallet out and removed the cash. "Take it and go."

The asshole's gaze darted to the money, to Evan, then to the door. He dropped the bat, swiped the cash, and took off running out of the apartment.

Kyle kicked the bat aside and reached down to Evan. "Are you okay?"

"Yeah." Evan pushed off the floor.

"Take it easy." Kyle gripped his arm and helped him stand. "Let me see." He lifted Evan's shirt and brushed the flesh with his fingertips. "We should get you to the hospital."

"No. He barely made contact. He just surprised me."

He'd surprised Kyle too. More like sent his heart thundering into his throat. He swiped a hand over the skin of Evan's abs again. There wasn't a mark on him.

"I'm fine." Evan shoved Kyle's hand away and pushed his shirt down. He let out a nervous laugh. "His swing was pretty lame. The bat hardly touched me. We should call the police, though."

"Yeah." Kyle faced the door. He wanted to run after the asshole and show him how a man swung a bat. He forced himself to calm down before he said, "I'll take care of it."

Evan sat on the couch while Kyle grabbed his phone and made the call. When he hung up, he said, "It might be an hour or more." He tossed the phone into the armchair, and it bounced off and onto the floor. Not caring if he broke it, he kicked the phone out of his way and walked the length of the room and back.

"Stop pacing."

Kyle stopped and glared down at Evan. "You shouldn't have done that."

"What?"

"Come at the guy. That was fucking stupid."

"Yeah?"

"Yeah." Kyle balled his fists, wanting to punch the shit out of something. He also wanted—needed—to do something else. "Come here." Neither made a move for a moment, then Evan stood, and Kyle went to him. He reached for Evan's shirt and lifted it again.

Evan swiped at his hand. "I said I'm fine."

Kyle ignored him and raised the shirt higher. No bruising. Nothing swollen. He poked at Evan's stomach in several places. Evan didn't flinch. He tightened his abs. Damn, all those trips to the gym were paying off. Evan had more definition than Kyle had ever seen on him. He dropped the shirt before he did something stupid like fall to his knees and press a soft kiss where Evan had been hit.

"Satisfied?" Evan asked.

"I guess. You still shouldn't have done that."

"Well, you're the one who went looking when I said we should call the cops."

"Are you saying you almost getting your ass killed is my fault?"

"I didn't say that."

"I'm going to have a look around." Kyle headed down the hall and searched each room, trying not to think about the vision he'd seen earlier of a dead Evan lying in his own blood on the floor of the living room.

He found the bathroom window open. There was a ledge outside that ran from under the window to the other end of the building. A staircase led to more apartments thirty feet to the right. It looked possible to reach the ledge from the steps, but only a desperate man would make the climb. They were four floors up, and the ledge was less than a foot wide. How had that strung-out loser who couldn't swing a bat managed it?

It didn't look like the asshole had gone through the bathroom cabinets or drawers, but he'd searched in Kyle's room. He must have made his way there after Kyle had gone to the living room. The closet door was open and a lamp on top of the dresser had been knocked over. The asshole had rifled the contents of the dresser drawers but had only made it through the bottom two. Then he must have heard Kyle coming down the hall.

Maybe the junkie would've gone back out the window if Kyle

hadn't startled him. Maybe he wouldn't have hurt Evan.

Kyle gripped the top of the dresser in both hands. He shouldn't touch anything, but he couldn't help himself. He kicked the bottom drawer in and cursed when his bare toes connected with the wood.

"Stupid fucker."

He wasn't sure who he meant. The asshole who'd broken in. Or himself.

* * * *

Evan resisted the urge to touch Kyle's hand as Kyle sat beside him on the couch and handed him a glass of water.

"Thanks."

Kyle grunted a reply, his elbows on his knees, his head hanging low.

Somewhere during the last hour, Kyle had gone from being pissed at Evan to stoic silence to what looked like pissed at himself.

It was two a.m., and they had just finished giving their statements to the police. The officers had said there were several other break-ins reported in the apartment complex that night. The two cops were now looking over Kyle's place to fill in the details of their report.

Evan tapped the side of Kyle's knee with his own. "Hey."

Kyle raised his head.

They held the stare for a moment, and Evan added, "Sorry you missed the end of your dream."

Kyle fell back against the couch cushion and huffed out a laugh.

Evan did the same. "It was a good one?"

"Yeah." Kyle smirked. "Jake Gallagher was in it."

"Yeah?" He bumped Kyle's knee again. "Share, man. No keeping that one to yourself."

"You and I were at a table in Castillo's." Kyle stretched out and lifted his feet to the coffee table, his hands tucked behind his head. "The place was dark and empty except us. Jake came in the front door and walked right to our table. He was wearing a sleeveless shirt and was packing some serious muscles, like in his last film. He looked determined. Then he said, 'There's something I forgot to give you.'" Kyle paused as one of the officers stepped into the hallway. When he didn't appear at the end of the hall, Kyle continued. "Then Jake leaned down and kissed you."

"Me?"

Kyle nodded and shifted his ass on the couch. He was getting hard, his cock starting to tent the shorts he'd slipped on before the cops got there.

"You were turned on watching him with me?"

"No." Kyle dropped his arms to his sides and shifted his weight to turn in Evan's direction. "It was the next part."

"We're finished here."

Evan jumped at the cop's voice. He stood. Kyle didn't. Which was a good idea. What with his current condition. There was no need to hide the fact they were gay—this was West Hollywood, after all—but sporting a stiff one was probably not the best way to talk to the cops after a robbery and assault. Unless they were in a porno and the cops were going to join them in bed. Would Kyle like that? Had he ever been with more than one guy at a time? Evan filed that away as something he'd never ask. He didn't want to know. No matter how hot Kyle would make it sound.

The cop finished writing in his notebook. "I don't think you'll have any more trouble. Probably a guy strung out, looking for cash. Most of the robberies in this neighborhood over the past month have been like that."

The second cop entered the room and glared at Kyle on the couch while Evan spoke. "We appreciate you coming by." When the officers headed for the door, Evan reached for one of the pillows on the couch and tossed it at Kyle's lap.

Kyle hissed with the weight of the pillow. "Thanks."

Evan tried not to laugh as he followed the officers to the door. "We're going to be gone until after New Year's."

The one who'd done most of the talking said, "Best we can advise is lock up tight and don't keep your valuables here while you're gone. These small-time thieves haven't been hitting the same places twice, so you should be safe from a repeat break-in."

Evan opened the door and thanked the officers again.

After they left, Kyle stood and threw the pillow to the couch. "I'm going to bed." His voice was gruff, and he moved down the hall in a stiff walk. Evan laughed again but let the sound die as Kyle closed the door to his room without a look back.

So much for speaking again. Evan picked up the pages of his script. He was done trying to work, even if he couldn't fall asleep right away. He wanted to know more about the dream, about what had gotten Kyle so turned on.

He headed down the hall and hesitated outside Kyle's door. He heard the sound of slick skin over skin, an occasional grunt, the bed shifting. Evan couldn't move. Either forward or back. He'd heard Kyle jerking off before. He'd always gone on about his business and given his friend a little privacy. Now...

Why couldn't he walk in there? Why couldn't he let them have this one night?

He leaned his forehead against the closed bedroom door, listening to the sound of Kyle's heavy breathing, the sound of his hand moving faster and faster.

Evan clutched the doorknob in his fist.

He'd just have to live with the fantasy. That's all he'd have.

Then what was he doing?

He twisted the handle, and the door creaked as he pushed in. Every sound from Kyle stopped. The room was dark. The low light from the hall didn't help Evan see Kyle on the bed, not even an outline of his body. Maybe he'd ask Kyle to wait a minute before he started jerking off again, at least until Evan's eyes adjusted and he could watch him come. Too bad he couldn't get his voice to work.

Despite the darkness, Kyle had to know Evan was standing there.

The sound of a hand moving over slick flesh started again. Slow at first, then picking up speed until it sounded faster than it had before he'd opened the door. Kyle's grunts of pleasure grew louder.

That had Evan undone. He ached and wanted nothing more than to touch himself, to come with Kyle. He spun around and sped out of the room, leaving Kyle's door open, then the one to the guest room he'd been staying in. He dropped the script to the nightstand, slipped off his clothes, and got on the bed. He could still hear Kyle through the open doors.

He grabbed a bottle of lube from the nightstand drawer and slicked his cock. Only it wasn't his cock he pictured his hand on. He was touching Kyle, stroking the hard, sleek flesh in time with the sound of Kyle's movements from across the hall.

He'd never had a chance to touch Kyle like that, never had that dick in his mouth. He pictured running his lips and tongue over Kyle's dick, his chest, his balls, his ass.

Evan's abs tightened, the steady rhythm of his hand giving way to more sporadic tugs.

A low moan came from the other room. Then, "Oh God, Ev."

That did it. Evan slapped the headboard above his head with his free hand as pleasure shot through him. Ribbons of cum spurted up and landed on his chest, his body jerking with the orgasm.

When he finally finished coming, all he heard in the darkness was heavy breathing. From himself. From Kyle.

How the hell was he going to make it in their small bedroom on the train? There had better not be a limit on how many showers he could take.

Chapter Eight

Kyle sat at the kitchen table, staring at his e-mail. One hundred and eight new messages. In the past twenty-four hours alone. He hadn't opened his e-mail since early the day before, hoping the focus would help him figure out where to start the new book.

So much for that idea.

He had less than an hour until they needed to get going to catch the flight to San Francisco. He scrolled through the messages as he drank coffee from one of the two mugs Sue Ann had sent him as an early Christmas present. Blue novelty mugs that were covered with white lettering, spelling out the names of famous authors, Kyle's name printed in larger letters amid the others. The note with the mugs had said, *I know how much you need your coffee to write.*

He sure as hell needed something. Coffee in a novelty mug meant to boost his ego but did the exact opposite probably wasn't going to cut it. Maybe she thought he was as easy as most guys found him and all it would take to get him going was his name in large print between more prolific authors like Stephen King and J.K. Rowling.

Almost all the e-mails in his inbox were from readers asking about the next book. Most indicated what they hoped would happen in it. If they were like the rest he'd gotten in the past year, half would want Mac with the cop, and the other half would want him with his old friend.

Kyle really needed to let his publicist deal with the e-mail. The messages were seriously fucking with him. No, that was a cop-out. His writer's block had nothing to do with the fans.

He scanned the inbox again and located a message from Sue Ann.

> As we discussed yesterday, I'm looking forward to your pages after the New Year. I can't tell you how excited I am to finally find out who Mac ends up with. Let me know how it's going. Sue Ann.

He scoffed and closed his e-mail.

Who Mac ends up with.

Yeah, he'd like to know too. The cop and the best friend had been flirting with Mac for two books, and Kyle still had no idea what to do about that.

Who the hell was he kidding? He had no idea what to do about any of the damn story.

He heard Evan approach from behind and pause in the doorway. Then Evan crossed the room and went to the cupboard next to the sink. He got out the matching coffee mug from Sue Ann and hesitated again, his back to Kyle. Finally, he filled the mug and turned around, his gaze on the coffee he held close to his lips.

Kyle shut down his laptop. Evan leaned back against the kitchen counter and sipped his coffee while he stared at the tile floor.

The silence was more annoying than going to bed alone rock hard the night before. "All packed?" Kyle asked.

"Yep." Evan took another drink of the coffee.

"Got all the gifts?"

"Yep."

"We should get going soon."

"Yeah."

"Want me to call a cab?"

"I took care of it," Evan said. "It'll be here in half an hour."

"Good."

More silence. Evan sipped his coffee again, still watching the floor. Kyle made a show of leaning over the side of his chair and looking at the floor beside him like he was inspecting the tile for whatever the hell made it so interesting. When Evan didn't respond, Kyle said, "We should've just fucked if it's going to be like this."

Evan finally raised his head. "Like what?"

"Weird like this." Kyle gestured with an arm through the air, indicating the space between them. "Like when you fuck a guy and accidentally fall asleep in his bed. You just know the next morning he's thinking it meant something you stayed. You want to take off but can't bring yourself to hurt his feelings." He didn't want to examine why he'd chosen that example. He stood and stepped into Evan's space. Evan flinched in response. "Wasn't listening to me jerk off last night good for you?"

"Believe me, I don't think last night meant anything to you." Evan spun around, shoving Kyle backward with his shoulder. He set the half-full coffee mug into the sink. More like dropped it. The coffee splashed against the sides of the metal sink, and the mug bounced four times, probably chipping all over. Maybe Kyle's name had chipped right off, leaving a gaping space between King and Rowling, erasing him from the world of fiction, and he wouldn't need to finish the book.

He gripped Evan's arm and forced him to turn around. "That's what I was saying. I think…it did mean something to me. You mean—"

"Forget it," Evan said. "Can we just drop it?"

"No." Kyle crossed his arms over his chest, stepped back, and leaned against the refrigerator. "I'm pretty sure I made it clear last night how much I want you. You're worried sex will fuck up our friendship? That I can't handle more? Well, I won't know unless we try." He didn't want to talk anymore. He ached to take Evan to bed and show him, like Lorrie said. He forced himself to continue. "If you don't want to, then I'm not going to be an ass about it. I'm not going to jump you or make a big deal about this. I respect what you think, what you want." He dropped his arms and slid his hands into the pockets of his jeans. Softer, he asked, "Okay?"

Evan met his gaze. "Okay."

"I'm not a fucking sex addict who can't have a friend he doesn't fuck."

Evan rolled his eyes. "I know that."

"Okay. So no more weirdness?"

Evan let out a quick, shaky laugh. "No more weirdness."

"All right." Kyle returned to the table and loaded the laptop into his backpack. A part of him wished he could leave the computer home, forget about the deadline.

"I need to talk to you about something else." Evan moved away from the counter and stood close at his back.

Kyle put the backpack aside and sat. "Okay."

Evan bit his lower lip. Not good. Something he didn't want to mention.

"Ev, sit your ass in the chair and say it."

Evan nodded. The move took longer than necessary, and he barely made a sound as he pulled the chair out and sat across from Kyle. He cleared his throat. "The guy who came by the party yesterday… He's the VP of the Entertainment Division at the network."

"Holy shit. Why was he there? To congratulate you?"

"I wish. He wanted something from me."

"What?"

"Well, not really from me. From you."

"Me?"

Evan stared at the table with as much focus as he'd given the floor tile. "They have a show they're doing research for, and they think you can help them."

"I don't understand."

"That's what I first said. Then Hastings told me you could help with *American Treasures*. They're working on a list of lost treasures for the show, trying to figure out which ones to use, where the clues are, that kind of thing." He raised his head and met Kyle's stare with a sadness in his eyes he hadn't had in weeks. "Well, I guess…"

"What?"

"They think you have something they need. It might have clues to some hidden money or something. He wouldn't tell me what they think is in the journal."

"Journal? My grandpa's journal?"

"I guess. He said you had a journal they wanted to look at. Said they are willing to pay you if it has information they can use for the show."

"For the show?" Kyle stood, stalked across the room, and ditched his coffee mug into the sink. The two mugs cracked as they collided. So much for the coffee to write by. Perhaps it was time for a change in more ways than one. He gripped the edge of the countertop in both hands. "I've only read two pages. How would they know what's in it? How do they know it exists? Grandpa said I was the only one to know about it. Just him and me. And he's dead." Kyle hated the way he'd spat out the word "dead."

"I don't know," Evan said. "Hastings wouldn't answer my questions."

Kyle paced the small kitchen, two strides in each direction before he had to turn. "I guess the law firm knew. They sent me the journal, and they must have kept it for him these last two years."

"Wouldn't that be confidential?" Evan asked.

Kyle stopped. "Nothing is confidential given enough pressure and enough money. People can get their hands on anything."

Evan looked away. There was something he didn't want to admit.

"Why did they come to you with this?" Kyle asked.

"They know we're friends."

"And a VP from the network just asked you to talk to me? Are they putting pressure on you?"

"I told him I'd mention it to you. That it was your decision."

Nice try, Ev. That didn't answer the question.

A knock sounded on the door.

Evan stood. "Cab. Must be early." He slid past Kyle and hurried for the apartment door.

"I forgot something," Kyle said. "You start loading up. I'll be right back." He went to his room and grabbed his grandpa's journal from the nightstand drawer. He hesitated. He had to read more, had to find out what other secrets it contained. Even if he wasn't sure he wanted to know.

He tucked it under his arm and headed out of his room. He froze. At the end of the hall by the front door was Evan's ex. Evan had his hand on the doorknob of the open apartment door. The two were silent, staring at each other.

Dickhead was over half a foot taller than Evan, and he was bigger than Kyle, all muscle and solid body. He wore his leather chaps over jeans and his big-ass biker boots. His black helmet with the green serpent coiled on the back hung from his hand. The dark stubble on his face was new. And sexy. Damn him. The smart, tough-looking, bike-riding professor who all the students, gay or straight, at the University of Southern California fell for.

Kyle couldn't read Evan's expression.

Dickhead moved closer to him. "I need to talk to you." He raised his free hand but stopped short of running it through Evan's hair. Least he knew better than to touch what was no longer his.

Evan shook his head. "We're leaving." His voice cracked with the words. He was still hurting.

Nice timing, Dickhead.

He'd had six months to realize what he'd given up. Maybe he wasn't as smart as the professor gig implied. Especially after what he'd said to Kyle when the breakup had first occurred and Kyle had gone to see him. He hadn't been sure what he could do to get them back together, but he had to try. Of course, when he'd gotten there, he'd just stood silently in the doorway of Dickhead's office. He'd planned to ask what the hell he was thinking and mention all Evan's qualities that made him one hell of a catch, but he'd been unable to force the words out. Maybe Lorrie had been right about what he'd been feeling, even then.

Dickhead had stood behind his desk and stared back at Kyle, then said, "Don't bother. I know what I'm doing." Kyle had wanted to say what he was doing was destroying Evan, but again the words escaped him. He'd simply turned and left.

Now here he stood, words failing him yet again as he watched the two men down the hall.

"I got your e-mail." Dickhead looked at the bags packed by the door. "You're still going to Ohio?"

"Yes." Evan's gaze was focused on the black helmet with the snake. Or on the huge hand of the man holding it.

"It's early to be leaving," Dickhead said.

"Might as well go now." Evan picked up one of his bags. "There's nothing keeping me here."

"Let me take you to the airport."

A surge of possessiveness slammed into Kyle. He strode to the end of the hall. "Hey, Doc, all that education and you can't figure out it's not possible to fit a man and all his luggage on your bike?"

Slowly, Dickhead looked Kyle's way. The expression wasn't filled with anger but sadness. Kyle wasn't about to apologize, but he did feel bad. Dickhead was obviously hurting, missing Evan. That didn't mean Kyle could stop his next words. "And we're leaving early because we're taking the train. Got our own private room and everything."

A car honked outside, and Evan said, "That's our ride."

"Can we talk?" Dickhead asked, his attention on Evan again.

Evan grabbed his other bag. "I don't have time for this."

"Wait." Dickhead clutched Evan by the forearm.

Kyle flinched but kept his feet planted. After the break-in the night before and with his current level of frustration, who knew what he'd do to Dickhead. Something about shoving the bike helmet up his ass was sounding a little too good. But it wasn't like Dickhead was being that rough. And it wasn't like Evan was pushing him away. *Like he did to you last night.* Kyle strode past them into the kitchen and got his backpack. He couldn't help himself. He looked their way again.

"I'll be here when you get back." Dickhead drew away from the touch in a rush, like he knew he had no right. "We need to talk."

"There's nothing to talk about," Evan said.

"Yes, there is." He forced Evan to look up at him with a hand on his chin. He ran a thumb over Evan's cheek. There was nothing rough about that touch. "There's our future."

"I don't think you understand the concept of breaking up with someone. That's you saying you don't want a future together."

"I need to explain. I need to talk to you." Dickhead made eye contact with Kyle, then focused on Evan again. "Alone."

Evan faced the door, but half of Dickhead was blocking the way. Asshole. Using his size against Evan.

"Maybe when I get back," Evan finally said.

"All right." Dickhead stepped aside and watched as Evan made his way down the four flights of stairs to the cab waiting below. Without looking Kyle's way, Dickhead said, "I still love him."

"Then what did you hurt him for?"

"I didn't mean to. I wanted…" He clutched his bike helmet in both hands.

"Whatever." Kyle shoved the journal into his backpack, grabbed his bags and the winter coat he'd need in Ohio, and went to leave.

Dickhead stepped in his way. "You'll hurt him more than I ever did. You know that, right?"

"I'd never hurt him. I'm the one person who hasn't." Well, that wasn't exactly true, but he damn well planned on never hurting Evan again.

"Sure, you haven't." Dickhead turned and made his way down the stairs. His bike roared a moment later; then the tires squealed as he drove off. *Dickhead.*

What did he think? He could show up and Evan would be waiting for him? Maybe that was what was supposed to happen. Maybe Dickhead's timing wasn't so bad after all.

Evan returned and locked the door behind Kyle. They didn't speak as they helped the cab driver put their bags in the trunk and then slid into the backseat.

Kyle had never been bothered by silence. He preferred the written word over talking, action over dialogue. Until now. "He wants you back."

Evan stared out the side window.

Kyle wanted to ask what Evan was going to do. Instead, he said, "I didn't know you two were talking again."

"We're not. It was one e-mail. Just 'happy holidays.'" He waved a hand through the air like it was nothing.

"I get it. You were baiting the hook. Looks like he took a bite."

Evan continued to stare out the window. Finally, he said, "I guess he did."

So much for something happening on the trip. So much for the small quarters of their sleeper compartment. For all the condoms and lube Kyle had brought. For everything he'd imagined the night before when they'd been jerking off.

He wouldn't get in the way of Evan's happiness. He'd back off, and everything would go back to the way it was before—

Evan turned toward him. "What if that's not what I want anymore?"

The concentrated stare from the usually reserved Evan Walker wasn't what Kyle had expected. The look was filled with lust and determination. Kyle forced down a stiff swallow. "What do you want?"

The silence stretched on until it didn't seem Evan would answer. Then he did. He slid his hand under the coat draped across Kyle's lap and gripped his thigh. He worked his hand higher, finally cupping the bulge at the front of Kyle's jeans.

"Oh God," Kyle whispered as he raised his hips off the seat. He'd never been on the receiving end of this bold, flirtatious Evan. He couldn't believe how much it drove him crazy.

Evan laughed. He continued to move his hand up and down, teasing, putting pressure in all the right places.

Remembering where they were, Kyle squeezed the edge of the seat beside him and forced himself to sit still, to breathe through his nose so he wouldn't let out an embarrassing moan usually reserved for virgins getting their first handjob. If he made a sound, if he moved, Evan might pull back. Like that night in the motel. Every ounce of Kyle's body urged him to roll over onto Evan, press him into the back of the seat, and lay a kiss on him neither of them would ever forget.

The cab driver cleared his throat, and Evan removed his hand in a flash. He pulled away until he was plastered to the side door, staring out the window again.

Kyle whispered, "You're such a tease."

"I am not." Evan's tone was defensive, but he couldn't hide the smirk. He fixed his gaze on Kyle again. "I'm not a tease."

How was Kyle supposed to be noble and let Evan get back to the life he wanted when Evan came on to him like that?

Was it too late to trade in those train tickets and get on a goddamn plane?

Fuck that. And fuck nobility. Hadn't Evan given him an answer on what he wanted? Kyle. Or more precisely Kyle's dick.

Thank God for the condoms and lube he'd packed.

Thank God for the train.

Chapter Nine

"Stop. Don't you move one more inch."

Kyle halted at the woman's request, his hand on the strap of the backpack slung over his shoulder, his winter coat tucked under his arm and a duffel bag in his other hand. He and Evan had gotten on the train at the wrong location and had to walk through the upper deck of more than one coach car to get to the sleeper cars. The seats were filling up as they went by, and Kyle had been meandering around a stream of passengers when the woman had shouted her command.

Evan laughed from behind him. "She didn't mean you." He pointed over Kyle's shoulder to the floor in front of them.

A little girl with dark hair and darker eyes stared up at him. Maybe six or seven years old. She giggled, then took off running in the direction he and Evan had been heading, her tennis shoes lighting up at the back with each step. The slew of passengers did nothing to slow her down.

"Rebecca Lynn! You get back here now." The woman's voice came from his right. A young woman, thin and short, maybe five feet tall, if that. She stood on a seat, bent forward to keep her head from touching the ceiling of the train. Her face gave away her age as older than her height suggested. Midtwenties, maybe older. She had her hair in a high ponytail that swung back and forth as she peered around the passengers. She had gorgeous dark eyes, and even with the frown, he knew she'd have a killer smile. If he had ever been straight a day in his life, he'd have been seriously interested. Trapped by the aisle full of passengers, she watched as the girl named Rebecca ran away. Definitely the expression made by a mom. Exactly like he'd seen his sis look at her kids.

A member of the train crew was gesturing at the woman. "Ma'am, please get down off the seat."

She pointed toward where the girl had run off. "My daughter…"

Kyle handed his coat and duffel to Evan and said to the young woman, "I'll get her." He took off toward the other end of the car, slipping around passengers and offering his apologies as he went. Rows of two seats on each side flanked the blue carpeted aisle that was wider than most airplane aisles but was still barely enough space for two people to get by each other.

He found Rebecca in the enclosed vestibule between cars. She was jumping up and down, trying to look out the window facing away from the passenger platform, her shoes lighting up as she landed with each jump, the twin braids of her hair flying in the air, then slapping against her back.

Kyle laughed. "What are you doing?"

She stopped and pointed to the window. "There are more trains over there. Bigger trains."

"Yes." He crouched in front of her. "But your mom wants you to get back to your seat."

She slapped her hands over her mouth.

He smiled and nodded. "I think you're in trouble."

She giggled again and said, "I'm not supposed to talk to strangers. Don't tell on me." Then, in a flash, she sprinted back the way they'd come.

He stood and followed her, apologizing to most of the same people on his way through the car. Evan and the mom were headed his way. He pointed toward the little girl in front of him, since the other passengers in the aisle blocked the short mother's view. Her face lost most of the tension she'd been sporting. She mouthed *thank you.*

Rebecca zigzagged her way through the crowd, crawling on the floor in between one woman's legs and under her skirt when she found no way around her. Most people were taking their seats as Kyle made his way after Rebecca, although he chose to wait for the woman blocking the aisle rather than crawl between her legs.

The young mother scooped Rebecca into a hug. "You are in so much trouble. You have to stop running away."

"I wanted to see the trains."

"Yes, but you have to wait for me." The mom spoke to Kyle as he reached Evan's side. "Thank you for stopping her."

"I didn't stop her. More like found her and sent her back in your direction."

"Well, thank you. I was trying to load our bags in the overhead compartment when she took off."

Kyle gestured toward her bags on the seat beside the one she'd been standing on. "Let me help you." He tried to step forward, but Evan was blocking his way, staring at him, his mouth hanging open.

"Hey, Ev, can I get by?"

Evan blinked and snapped out of the trance he seemed to be in. "Yeah." He turned sideways.

Kyle slid between Evan and the row of seats. He paused when they were face-to-face. Evan was still staring up at him, biting his bottom lip. Kyle wanted to bend down and give him a kiss, wanted to take a taste of those lips again. "I'll be right back."

Evan nodded and watched him walk away. Kyle could practically feel Evan's gaze on him as he lifted the woman's two bags into the overhead compartment.

"Thank you again," she said as she got her daughter situated in her seat next to the window.

"No problem." He smiled at Rebecca. "No more running off to see trains, okay?"

She pointed out the window. "I can see them from here now."

"Yeah, you can." He gave the mom a wink and stepped away. He didn't want to be the one to tell Rebecca once they started moving, they wouldn't be seeing too many other trains.

Evan had moved out of the main aisle into the space before an empty seat to let people pass, but he was still staring at Kyle.

Kyle took his coat and duffel bag from Evan and said, "Let's go check out the digs."

Evan snapped his mouth shut. "Sure."

What did that look mean? Now that they were on the train, about to be alone for three days, was Evan regretting his actions in the cab? Like the night before.

After moving through another section of coach seats, the observation car, and an empty dining area lined with booth-style seating, they reached the first car with private rooms.

"Happy holidays," a train employee said as he walked toward them. "Tickets?" They handed them over. The man smiled, revealing bright white teeth with a wide gap between the front two. It was the kind of smile that had you immediately smiling back. He wore a dark blue shirt and pants, both neatly pressed, with creases along the pants like a military uniform. He also had on a red Santa hat with a white ball at the end swinging back and forth as he moved. He was a huge man, taller than Kyle and three times as round. How did he navigate the train's narrow aisles without smacking into everything?

"You guys are in a sleeper," the man said.

"Yes." Evan sounded more excited than Kyle wanted to contemplate right then. Or maybe he did. Maybe Evan wasn't regretting anything. Maybe he was also imagining everything they could do together in their shared room all the way to Chicago.

"Well," the train guy said, "why are you coming from that way? You must have walked right by this car on the platform."

"It's our first trip on a train." Evan was smiling back at the train attendant. "We got on at one of the coach cars."

"They should've directed you back this way so you didn't have to walk through all that chaos."

"It's okay," Evan said, then his smile broadened, his dimples flashing. "Kyle made a new friend."

Kyle rolled his eyes and fought the urge to smack Evan on the ass. Or to lean in and brush his thumb over one of those adorable dimples.

He was losing it.

"That's what we like to hear," the train guy said. "The friendliest people ride the rails. I'm Oscar, your car attendant. I'll be taking care of you all the way to Chicago. Come on. I'll show you the way."

Oscar took one of Evan's bags and led them through the car, the ball on his Santa hat swaying as he went. They walked a center hallway lined on both sides with rooms large enough for only two seats in each, no space to stand and move around. Only to sit in the facing seats and stare out the window, or at each other. Good thing Evan had gone for a larger room. Oscar moved gracefully through the train, smiling at passengers and bowing his head as they went by, the ball on his Santa hat never still for long. Either it was a standard part of the uniform this time of year or Oscar was one of those rare customer service employees who enjoyed his job, as well as the Christmas season.

"So, your first time on the train," Oscar said.

"Yeah," Evan said. "I'm looking forward to it. We usually fly. This looks like more fun." He glanced over his shoulder at Kyle.

Fun?

After the cab ride, they'd barely talked on the flight from LA to San Francisco. They'd been in a two-seat row by the windows, and Evan had spent the forty-five-minute flight looking over the pages of his script while Kyle had faked a nap. After the grope in the cab, Kyle had hoped to avoid any accidental touches, sidelong looks, or conversation, for that matter. He'd never been reserved when it came to sex. Not even public sex. But his first time with Evan—maybe his only time now that Dickhead was angling his way back into Evan's life—was not going to be something that would qualify them for the mile-high club. He wanted more than a handjob while crammed into a public bathroom stall, their clothes on, no room to touch Evan like he wanted to do, like he needed to do.

"You boys'll like your sleeper," Oscar said. "Much roomier than those crowded coach seats."

They rounded a curve to another section where the hallway stretched the remaining length of the car with a bank of windows along one side and larger rooms lining the other. Each room had a sliding glass door with a blue curtain that could be pulled closed for privacy.

Oscar stopped at the other end of the hall. "This here's your room. Let me show you the place, and then I'll let you boys settle." He gave them a brief tour by standing in the center of the room, spinning around and pointing while he explained how the fold-down table, thermostat, and call button worked. Kyle and Evan listened in from the open doorway.

Roomier? Than those two-seaters they'd passed, but that word couldn't be used to describe the bedroom he and Evan would be sharing.

"I'll stop by later to see if you need anything," Oscar added. "And I'll check with you on dinner. You can give me your orders if you prefer to eat here, or you can head to the dining car as soon as I give the word." He stepped out into the hall. "I'll also come by tonight to set up your beds."

Kyle glanced at Evan, who had moved backward to the wall of windows facing the train platform.

Was he thinking about going to sleep that night? Or about the night before when they'd been lying in their own beds touching themselves at the same time?

Did he want something to happen on the train? It sure had seemed like it in the cab.

If he didn't, how were they supposed to spend three days and two nights together in the smallest bedroom known to man?

Kyle thanked Oscar as he left, then stepped into the room for a better look. "Uh, it's small but nicer than the ones at the other end of the car."

Evan nodded from where he still stood outside the door.

Maybe nothing would happen between them. Maybe there'd be no talking or joking or anything all the way home. Kyle set his bag and backpack on the long bench that took up one side of the room. On the other side was a single seat next to an enclosure that had to be their private bathroom. In front of the lone oversize window, there was a flip table that could be raised and lowered between the bench and the chair. The room was covered in blues. Blue carpet, blue bench and seat cushions, blue curtains pinned back from the window. Wasn't blue the color of tranquility? With that much blue maybe there was usually a need to keep passengers calm. Why? It wasn't like they were on a plane with turbulence or the potential for the engines to cut out, leaving them plummeting to the earth. What could go wrong on a train?

The rest of the room, including the walls, was devoid of color. He peeked into the open door of the bathroom. Also stark white. Small. No, minuscule. "You aren't going to believe this."

Evan didn't say anything.

"Ev?"

"Yeah." He finally stepped into the room and placed his bags next to Kyle's. "What am I not going to believe?"

"The bathroom *is* the shower."

"What?"

"The toilet's in the shower."

"No way." Evan walked the two steps it took to reach the bathroom and poked his head inside, trapping Kyle against the far wall. "I don't understand."

"They have to save space somehow."

"Yeah, I guess." Evan laughed. "It's kinda cool. I think the bench is one of the beds."

"Yeah. The other one folds down so they're like bunk beds." Kyle sucked in a slow breath. Evan hadn't moved from where he'd practically pinned him to the wall with his shoulder.

Kyle had thought sleeping in separate rooms in his apartment had been bad.

Evan finally stepped away and crossed the room. He picked up a magazine from the seat by the window and laughed again. "Look what they left for us." He held up the magazine. Jake Gallagher was on the cover. He wore a white T-shirt and jeans, his feet bare, his hands tucked into the front pockets on his jeans. His hair was disheveled, and he had a five o'clock shadow.

Kyle laughed with Evan. It felt good. Normal. Like them. "Nice of them to provide you with some one-handed material."

"Me?" Evan said. "You're the one dreaming about him."

Kyle couldn't stop the smile. Yeah, this was better.

Then they grew quiet as Evan stared at the magazine in his hands. Kyle pictured the night before. Evan in his running shorts. Evan lying on the couch in his underwear. The two of them kissing in the hallway, their bodies thrusting together, both of them tugging and clinging and coming so close to more.

Jerking off while Evan was doing the same, knowing they were each hearing the other, thinking of each other, had been one of the most erotic moments of his life, and it had involved nothing more than his own hand, and the grunts and slick sounds from Evan.

"The room's not bad," Evan said as he tossed aside the magazine and opened his bag. "At least it'll be quiet so you can write." Maybe his thoughts weren't running along the same lines as Kyle's. He slipped by Kyle and went into the bathroom, carrying a bottle of contact solution.

Speaking of writing…

Kyle moved away from the wall and tried to bury the thoughts about jerking off. About Evan's body. He opened his bag. He had to get to work. He spotted the journal tucked inside. He also had something else to take care of.

Writing would have to wait. He sat and read the next entry of the journal.

Chicago. September 1, 1952

The bar was one of those places I had only read about. Like nothing I'd seen in my youth in Ohio. I just knew every guy in the place had a gun tucked under his jacket. Joe understood I was nervous. I didn't have to say anything. Neither did he. He smiled and held the door open for me. It was stupid to be scared. I'd been through a war. I'd carried a gun slung over my shoulder for months. I'd killed men. Walking into a mob-run bar should not have been a big deal.

I stepped inside, and Joe followed close behind. I felt him at my back. Normally such close proximity out in public would have bothered me. I didn't want anyone to jump to the right conclusions about us. But at that bar, at that moment, I needed his strength at my back. I needed his reassurance. I had a very bad feeling about the next couple of hours.

The bar and what we were going to do inside was only the first entry on Joe's list of adventures. He wanted to feel alive after all we'd seen in the war, and I wanted to give him everything he desired.

We headed to the door that led to the back rooms we'd learned about the night before at the Gold Star Casino. A man sporting a scowl and a scar that ran from his forehead to his chin and cut through one eye stood guard at the door. It reminded me of Joe's scar and how lucky he'd been he hadn't lost his eye. How lucky we both were to come home from the war.

Joe gave the code word and handed over the cash. Without speaking, Scarface led us inside and down the long hallway to the last door before the rear exit. The sounds of live music, conversations, and the clinking of glasses from the bar were gone as we stepped inside the silence of the small room and Scarface shut the door behind us.

One man stood in the corner next to a rolling cart that held bar glasses and bottles of liquor. His hands were clasped in front of him. He didn't move a muscle. A round poker table took up the bulk of the room. Five men were seated evenly around it.

No one spoke. Their faces gave nothing away.

They all sat so still they looked dead.

Kyle dropped the journal to his lap. *That's it.*

He grabbed his backpack and slid out his laptop. He turned it on, opened a blank document, and began typing.

They were all dead.

I had thought seeing a dead body was bad. Seeing five, all posed around a poker table with cards in their hands like they'd expired in the middle of a game, was beyond bad.

There were no bullet wounds, no slashes where a knife had decimated their arteries. No signs of a struggle anywhere in the room. All their eyes were open.

It was the creepiest thing I'd ever seen. And I'd seen some creepy shit in the past two years.

I wanted to turn around, sprint out the door, and phone the police, but I couldn't. It was like I was witnessing something important, and my body knew better than to run away. This was the ultimate accident along the road for a guy like me, and I didn't want to miss the details.

Evan stepped out of the bathroom, and Kyle halted his typing. Evan was squinting, his right eye squeezed shut.

"What's up with your eyes?"

"I lost my contact lens."

"Just now?"

"Yeah. It was bugging me, so I rinsed it off and then dropped it."

"Let me look for you." Kyle set his laptop aside and went to the bathroom.

"Forget it." Evan sat on the bench and pulled out papers from his bag. "It's gone."

"I can give it a try." Kyle squatted for a better view of the tiny sink. He ran his hand gently along the surface. Nothing.

"I said don't bother. It's not worth your time." Evan sounded angry, frustrated.

Kyle poked his head out of the bathroom. "It's not a bother. I want to try."

Their gazes locked. Were they talking about a contact lens? He wasn't about to ask. When had he become such a coward? But the idea that Evan would push him away again had his confidence waning. He returned to his search for the contact. Five minutes later, he had to give up. He left the bathroom. "I can't find it. Sorry."

"It's okay." Evan was still doing a funny blinking thing, trying to read his papers.

"Do you have another pair?"

"I thought I packed them, but I can't find the case." He squinted and held the papers closer to his face.

"Put your glasses on."

"I hate wearing them." Evan scrunched up his forehead, then went back to reading. And squinting.

Kyle grabbed Evan's bag and searched through it. He pulled out the glasses case and handed it to Evan. "Put them on."

It took a minute of Kyle standing there with the case held out between them before Evan finally reached for it. He removed the remaining contact lens and slipped on the glasses. Kyle sank to the other end of the bench. He had forgotten how damn sexy Evan looked in his glasses. He hadn't been wearing them at all around Kyle. Not since he'd moved in.

"Dennis said I should get new ones. He said these make me look too geeky."

Sounded like something Dickhead would say.

"You look hot."

Evan wouldn't look at him.

"What did you see in him? I mean he's fucking gorgeous, but—"

"Don't."

"I know he's not a horrible guy, but he was nowhere near good enough for you."

"Kyle, just…don't, please."

He still loves him.

Evan went back to his reading, and Kyle tried to ignore the churning in his gut. He wanted Evan to be happy, to have everything he deserved. What if that was Dickhead?

Kyle spotted his grandpa's journal on the table and reached for his laptop again. He didn't give it much thought. He put his fingers to the keyboard and let the words flow.

The poker game victims had been murdered, and Mac had to find out why and who had done the deed.

Kyle had work to do.

Chapter Ten

Ten pages in, Kyle stopped typing. Out the window, an open field sped by, row after row of alfalfa, then an orchard with trees he couldn't name, another flat field, then evenly spaced houses in a subdivision beyond that in the distance. "Hey, we're moving."

Evan laughed. "I told you that an hour ago. How did you not feel the train moving? Or hear the horn at every intersection?"

"I guess I did, but I was too focused to pay attention."

"I saw that. I knew this would be a good idea."

"It was." Kyle picked up the leather journal and waved it in the air. "I've had a little inspiration too." He wanted to read more of his grandpa's words, wished the old man was there for him to talk to. To ask about that poker game. About the man named Joe and what had happened between them. "Hey. You got those small sticky notes?"

"What?" Evan asked.

"The ones you use for marking your scripts. Did you bring some with you?"

"Sure." Evan dug in his bag and handed over a small pad of yellow paper. "What are you doing?"

"I want to make notes." *And I want to ask my dead grandpa some questions.* He didn't want to admit that. Evan would get it, but Kyle had never been one for sharing the personal stuff. Not even with Evan.

"What kind of notes?" Evan asked.

"My reactions to stuff. Things I want to come back to later."

Evan slid closer. "Are there clues about a treasure?"

"Not yet. I haven't read very far, though."

"You'll have time. After you get your pages done." Evan sat back but didn't move as far away as he'd been sitting before. "I'll let you write more, or read, whichever you want to do."

He should be doing both, but all Kyle could think about now that Evan had moved closer was everything they hadn't had a chance to do yet, every place on Evan's body he hadn't had a chance to run his tongue yet.

He wanted to say fuck Dickhead and make another move. See if Evan would continue with what he'd been doing in the cab. See if he'd meet Kyle halfway like Lorrie said.

Before he could move, Evan stood, rolled the pages he'd been reading, and shoved them into his back pocket. "I'm going to go check out the observation car. Make a few calls. See if I can find out what *American Treasures* is working on."

"You think that's common knowledge?"

"No, but I know someone I can ask. You remember Roy? I went to school with him. The one who told me about the screenwriting contest. He's an assistant producer in the reality show division. He might know something. Or he might know who to ask."

"Ev"—Kyle took a moment to find the right words—"no matter what the journal says, I have no intention of giving it to anyone. He trusted me with his secrets."

"I know. You should at least know why they want it." Evan turned to leave.

"Thanks, Ev. For everything."

Evan hesitated a moment at the door. He nodded and left.

There was still something he wasn't saying. About Hastings and the journal. Or maybe what had happened between the two of them. Maybe about Dickhead.

One thing Kyle had always been good at was getting Evan to talk. Did he want to hear it this time?

* * * *

"Are you telling me you don't know anything or you can't tell me anything?" Evan was seated in the middle of the upper deck of the observation car, trying to keep his voice low so he wouldn't bother the handful of other people nearby enjoying the panoramic view via bench-style seats facing the wall of windows on each side of the car. The train was passing through the foothills of the Sierra Nevadas, and the oversize windows made it seem like there wasn't anything between the seats and the wilderness beyond.

"I'm telling you the truth," Roy said. "The network keeps a tight lid on that show. No one not directly involved has a clue what each episode is about until the promos air."

"But you know something." Evan had heard it in Roy's voice the minute he'd explained he was trying to find out what projects were currently in development for *American Treasures*.

"Just a rumor. It sounded ridiculous, so I never believed it."

"A rumor about what?"

Roy didn't respond.

"Say it. About me, right?"

Another moment of silence, then Roy said, "When your script was selected as one of the finalists, I overheard some talk you were a shoo-in to win the contest."

Evan swallowed around the lump in his throat, knowing what was coming but needing to ask anyway. "Why?"

"They said you had a connection to *American Treasures*, and the network was going to guarantee your cooperation."

"By what? Fixing the competition? Giving me the job?"

"I doubt that's the case, but yeah, that's the rumor I heard."

With the visit from Hastings on the same day Kyle had received the journal, Evan had no doubt the rumor was true. He felt like someone had punched him in the gut harder than the asshole who'd broken into Kyle's apartment had hit him with the bat. He couldn't come up with a response. It was like he was free-falling, like he'd been shoved out an airplane without a parachute, and his brain didn't want to accept the inevitable.

"Listen," Roy said, "I have a friend who might know more. She was an assistant with the show until last week when Hastings fired her. She admitted to me she was pissed about the tactics she'd been forced to resort to for the show, and when she spoke up at a meeting, she was fired the next day. The official reason was incompetence, but there's nothing incompetent about Amy."

"I need to talk to her."

"I can't guarantee she'll say anything to you. Like all of us, she signed a confidentiality agreement with her contract."

"Can you give me her number?"

"I'll give her a call. If she's willing to talk to you, I'll have her call you."

"I appreciate that."

They exchanged good-byes, and Evan hung up.

It was snowing now. Large flakes stuck to the pine trees and uneven terrain. He'd been looking forward to the cool weather, to seeing everything in Liberty Falls covered in a layer of white. He loved passing through the dozens of Christmas tree farms that made up the perimeter of the community. He loved the moment they drove into town and spotted the first of the two-foot-tall lighted stars hanging on every streetlamp and the engine at the local fire department decorated in Christmas lights and flanked by plastic light-up reindeer.

The view outside the train was breathtaking, more beautiful than his memories of Liberty Falls, but he was too numb to enjoy it.

A man bent forward and rested his elbows along the back of the seat beside Evan. He let out a long whistle. "It's really coming down. I didn't think this area got much snow." He was a big guy with a deep voice and forearms as large as Evan's calves. He had short gray hair and moved with a precision that reminded Evan of the cop who'd given a guest lecture during his Writing the Dramatic Series course at USC.

"They're officially calling it a blizzard south of Truckee," another man said from the far end of the car. "Supposed to be the nastiest one in a long time. Been snowing there for days. The weather forecast said the worst will stay south of our route, but my guess is that's changing as we speak."

"We're going to go through a blizzard?" Evan asked.

"Don't worry about it," the large gray-haired man next to him said. "A little snow doesn't stop the train."

"Good." He just wanted to get to Ohio. To forget about Hastings, the job, everything except seeing his mom and celebrating Christmas.

And Kyle.

Evan wanted to believe Kyle was ready for something to happen between them, desperately wanted to trust Kyle's words, his touches. Evan was so close to having what he'd dreamed of for years, he wasn't sure he could keep away no matter the inevitable outcome. That was the only way to explain why he'd reached for Kyle in the cab.

His phone rang.

"Excuse me," he said to the man still watching out the window. He stood and headed to the end of the walkway but stopped short of pushing the button to enter the vestibule between cars where the squeak and clank of the train would be too loud to hear.

He leaned against the wall at the end of the line of seats and stared out at the snowy ground along the tracks, which looked like it was moving past them at a rush instead of the other way around, reminding him of his life lately: out of his control and not at all what he thought it'd be. He answered his phone.

"Evan? This is Amy, Roy's friend. He said you wanted to speak with me."

"Thank you for calling so quickly. You used to work on *American Treasures*?"

"Yes, but I'm not at liberty to discuss the show."

Right. If she didn't want to talk, she wouldn't have called. She was probably aching to bad-mouth her old bosses. He said, "I know they fired you because you expressed concern with how the show was being run. I'm being blackmailed. A friend of mine has information they need."

She said nothing for a moment, then let out a long sigh. "I'll deny it if anyone asks if I talked to you. I don't need to get sued over this."

"I won't mention your name."

"I know about your job offer. I know about your roommate, Kyle Bennett. About the book they're after. All of it. It's why I was fired."

Evan gave up on the snow-covered ground and let his gaze settle on his reflection in the glass. He recognized the disappointed look. He'd seen it too many times lately. "What do you mean?"

"The network has been making payments to an assistant at an Ohio law firm for two years. Three months ago, I was given her name when someone else left the show. I was to be the assistant's new contact. Only I never knew what she'd be contacting me about. Last week she called me to say the package was being delivered. When I pushed her for more information, she told me the whole story."

When Amy didn't continue, Evan said, "I'm listening."

"All right. A man at the network approached her two years ago. He bribed her into telling him about the estate of a deceased veteran named Victor Bennett. The network knew there was a book that was not part of the rest of the estate. She told the man she'd seen a book labeled with Mr. Bennett's name in the law firm's safe and that it was going to be delivered to his grandson sometime in the future. She didn't know when. The network paid her every month so she'd tell them as soon as she knew when that package was set to be delivered."

"So they've known this entire time. I *was* hired to get Kyle."

"I think so."

"Do you know what's in the journal?"

"No. I didn't know it was a journal. I reported back to the network the book was about to be shipped to Kyle Bennett along with my concerns about paying off people for confidential information. Well, that was my last day." Her words ended abruptly, and then she said, "Can I give you some career advice?"

Career? He was pretty sure he was about to lose the one shot he'd had in ten years to get his career started. He pressed his forehead to the cool glass of the window in front of him, his reflection disappearing as he tried to focus on the world outside, on anything other than his dream slipping away. "Sure," he said.

"Don't mess with them. Give them what they want and take the job." She paused, then more softly added, "I'm never going to work in this town again."

"I'm sorry."

"Forget it. It's done."

"I appreciate you telling me the truth."

"Sure. Good luck. You'll need it." She hung up.

Her final words left a chill on his skin, colder than the glass of the window against his forehead.

All of it—his entire future—all a lie. Nothing in his life was real anymore.

No, that wasn't true. Kyle was real. And Evan wasn't about to screw him over. Not even for the career he'd been working his ass off to achieve. Some things were more important than success or a single moment of bliss. No matter how good it would be to give in and be together, he was not losing Kyle's friendship.

The blare of the train's horn sounded unusually loud as they passed through an intersection. Another small town. How many more until they reached the end of the line?

A woman sitting in the seat next to where he stood smiled up at him.

He tilted his head toward the window to indicate her view. "Am I in your way?"

"Not at all," she said. "It's just snow. There'll always be more."

Was that true? At some point in every person's life, they'd have a chance to watch their last snowfall. Only, most would never know it was their last at the time. Was this his last chance with his career? With Kyle?

The woman was still watching him. She was around his mom's age with warm, kind eyes and wild, short hair a shade of red unlike any he'd seen on another person. She held knitting needles, a green ball of yarn resting in her lap along with the folded piece of whatever she'd been knitting. A blanket or a scarf, something thick and warm for the winter season. That reminded him of Kyle's mom and her endless knitting projects, reminded him of winter in Liberty Falls and his own mom. Maybe Kyle had the right idea. Maybe it was time to move back to Ohio.

The red-haired woman returned to her knitting and said, "If you need to make another call, go right ahead. You're not bothering me."

"Thanks." He did have one more call to make.

He got out the business card from his wallet and dialed. When a woman answered, he said, "Mr. Hastings, please."

"He's in a board meeting and can't be disturbed. May I take a message?"

"Tell him Evan Walker called."

"Mr. Walker, I've been instructed to put your calls through. One moment."

What the hell was in that journal?

There was more snow coming down, and the wind had picked up. What would it be like when they got higher into the mountains? How bad would it have to get before the train stopped at the next station and stayed there? As much as he loved snow, he didn't want to head into a blizzard, but he couldn't stop the inevitable. Like the rest of his life. There was only one track and no crossroads ahead. He had to ride it out.

Hastings came on the line in less than a minute. "Mr. Walker, I'm glad you called."

"I'm not sure you'll be glad when you hear what I have to say."

"I hope you'll say you have every intention of helping us."

"I talked to Kyle, and he is not interested in a deal."

"That's disappointing, but frankly this is where we'd hoped you'd do some friendly convincing on behalf of the network."

"Or what? The job offer is pulled?"

"I believe I was clear on how this game is going to be played. You get us that journal, Mr. Walker, and your career moves forward. You don't, and we'll be reconsidering a number of things."

"Then I guess you'll be doing some reconsidering. Good day, Mr. Hastings."

Chapter Eleven

Evan ended the call and clenched the phone in his hand. What did he just do?

The big man talking about the snow earlier passed behind him and pushed the button to open the door to the vestibule between cars. The metallic clank of the train along the tracks startled Evan as the rush of colder air slammed into him. It felt good against his heated skin but did nothing to ease the tension in his gut.

The observation car was filling with passengers. Before long, it'd be standing room only to watch the train roll through the storm. He needed space, some air to breathe. He wished he could open the window, get off the train and head into the desolate wilderness, disappear for just a little while.

He focused on the line of snowcapped pine trees rushing by the window.

He wanted to be home.

Where was that? Ohio? The house where he'd lived with Dennis? Kyle's apartment in West Hollywood?

Where did he belong?

"Are you okay?" the red-haired woman asked.

He tried to answer with a nod, but he wasn't sure he'd moved his head.

"Have a seat." She scooted to make room.

"Thanks." He took a seat on the bench beside her, and she returned to her knitting, which was good. He didn't have it in him to make small talk. He felt a lump in his back pocket. The script. He yanked it out.

All that work to get to this point. How stupid of him to think his talent had been what they'd wanted.

It didn't matter.

He'd done the right thing. He'd done what Kyle wanted—what Kyle would've done for him.

Hell, Kyle went out of his way for strangers. The young woman and her daughter on the train earlier were just another example. He was a conundrum. Never getting close to anyone—an ass about sex and relationships and love—but he was the best man Evan had ever known.

Someone brushed a hand along the back of Evan's neck. He lifted his head. Kyle stood beside him, his backpack over his shoulder. The observation car had cleared out somewhat, and the red-haired woman beside him was gone.

Kyle took her seat. "Check out that view. Lots of snow. Just like you like."

Evan had already seen the snow. He'd rather focus on Kyle, on how much he wanted to get back to what they'd been doing in the cab earlier. Focus on what it would be like to drop to the floor right there and swallow the man's cock, to feel his own dick ramming into that firm ass, to see Kyle sweat-soaked and covered in cum. Anything but the phone call he'd just had. Instead, he said, "They say there's a blizzard in the mountains."

"Really? Are we going through it?"

"Supposed to be south of us, but it already looks bad out there."

Kyle nodded. "You hungry? The dining car is open, or I brought my laptop in case you were working on your screenplay."

"Nah. I'm not working." Evan stood, folded the pages of his script in half, and shoved them in his back pocket again. "Let's go."

They headed to the dining car, where a line had formed, stretching out into the vestibule between cars. Neither spoke as they waited. Evan needed to tell Kyle about the call with Hastings, but he couldn't break the silence. He wanted a more definite plan in place for his next move with his career before he mentioned it. No way would he let Kyle feel responsible.

Ten minutes later, they were next in line. The dining car was flanked by panoramic windows and booth-style seating with linen tablecloths and full place settings at each seat. The lighting was dimmer than the other locations on the train, and the dark carpeting, faux wood accents, and slightly tinted windows beside each booth gave the car a romantic vibe. The conversation was muted, and low instrumental music played overhead.

"Nice," Kyle said.

"Yeah." Evan's palms were moist. He dried them down the front of his jeans, hoping no one would notice, especially Kyle. Why the hell did this feel like a date? They'd been out to eat together a thousand times before.

A woman approached. "Just the two of you? We like to fill the booths when we can. Another couple said you can join them."

Another couple? Maybe they did look like they were on a date.

"Sounds good," Kyle said.

She led them to a booth with a man and woman seated on the far side. The same red-haired woman who'd talked to Evan in the observation car. She smiled at him as he sat across from her.

Kyle slid his bag into the booth before he joined Evan. With the bag in the way, there'd be no chance they'd brush against each other while they ate. Maybe Kyle had changed his mind about wanting him. Maybe he'd freaked sooner than Evan had imagined. Or maybe he was pretending nothing had happened in the cab earlier and was honoring what he'd said to Evan in the kitchen that morning.

"Hello again," the woman said. "I'm Penny, and this is my husband Nate."

"Evan. And my friend Kyle."

Nate was reading his menu, and Penny smiled wider as she elbowed her husband in the side.

"What?" He snapped his head up and threw his wife an annoyed look. The broad smile on her face and the tilt of her head must have given him a clue. He faced Evan and Kyle. "Oh, hello. Nice to meet you."

Nate's hair was white and thick, with a matching full beard that made him look like a man in his late sixties or older, but a closer inspection revealed a much younger face. Nate shifted slowly in the booth like someone who'd worked hard all his life and whose body was beginning to protest the push past middle age. He was forty pounds overweight, all of it settling in his middle. When he smiled, his eyes crinkled up at the corners in a way that said he'd made that expression a lot in his life.

Like Kyle's eyes were starting to look. Would he have the same deep lines at Nate's age?

Evan didn't want to think about the future. He joined Nate in looking over the menu. There were several entrée selections, as well as an assortment of beer, wine, sides, salads, and desserts including a description for a *decadent chocolate cake topped with creamy white frosting*. Just what he needed. To be this close to Kyle and, yet again, thinking about frosting and its unrealistic potential as lube.

Kyle nudged Evan's arm. So much for not touching. "That cake sounds good. You getting it?"

"No!"

Both Penny and Nate peeked at them over the tops of their menus.

Evan felt his face flush. He set his menu down and asked, "Are you two on vacation?"

"We are," Penny said. "Nate was offered an early retirement package, so we are seeing the countryside."

Evan glanced at Nate. "You're not old enough to be retired."

"I like you, kid." Nate smiled, then grew serious as he stared at his menu again. "We shouldn't be doing this."

"Yes, we should," Penny said. "He thinks he should be working. Says he could be one of those door greeters at Walmart. I told him he's too grumpy." Nate glared at her, and she laughed. "See? You can't even be nice to your wife."

"It's easier to be nice to strangers."

"Well, we needed this. It was a good idea." She tapped the back of his hand, and he gripped hers in his. The unexpected affection surprised Evan. The tenderness in that simple touch between two people who had spent a life together moved him.

"We almost had to cancel," Penny said. "Our granddaughter's been real sick."

"I'm sorry," Kyle said in a low voice as he set his menu on the table. The compassion in his tone, the sympathy in his expression. It was those little glimpses of the man inside that drew Evan to him. God, there was no denying it. He loved Kyle. He had never really stopped.

"Thank you," Penny said. "It's actually been fun watching this little girl on the train. She's so full of energy and has been giving her mama all sorts of trouble."

Kyle huffed out a laugh. "I'm sure I know exactly which little girl that is."

"But it makes me sad too." Penny pursed her lips and shook her head. "Our little one's been stuck in bed for a while now."

Nate slammed his menu on the table. The force of it rattled the salt and pepper shakers at the opposite end. "We should be home, not off traveling around like this."

"No," she said. "It was right to book the trip. We needed this." They exchanged another touch of their hands, so brief but full of love and support. There was an ache in Evan's chest just watching them. A reminder of how different his life goals were from Kyle's.

How many disappointing blows would he have to take today?

Their server arrived. Penny gave her order, selecting the only chicken entrée available. Evan didn't want to eat, but he ordered the same anyway. Then Nate gave his selection, going for a steak, baked potato, and broccoli.

"That sounds good," Kyle said. "I'll have the same. Oh, and I'm definitely going to want some of that cake."

Great. Maybe Evan would suggest they slip out before the dessert arrived, and Kyle would forget all about the cake. Or else Evan would end up with a boner he'd never have a shot of hiding on the trek back to their room. Unless he walked directly behind Kyle. Like that would help. If he had his dick that close to Kyle's ass, he'd never get rid of the hard-on.

Kyle asked the server, "Can we also get a bottle of Cabernet Sauvignon for the table?" He'd never ordered wine when they'd dined out before. In spite of the couple sitting across the way, this sure as hell felt like a date.

The server nodded, and before he left, Penny said, "Can my husband switch the broccoli for a salad?" She looked to Nate. "You know how it affects your system. I'm not sleeping there with you all night if you eat broccoli."

Nate threw her another annoyed expression, his white eyebrows scrunching together to form a single line. He stroked his beard twice, then said, "Guess you better do what the wife says. I'm not sleeping on top of the train." He handed the server his menu. "One time she actually made me sit outside the RV for two hours in the middle of the night before she'd unlock the door and let me back in."

The server took off in a hurry. Evan bit his lip to keep from laughing.

Penny asked, "Where are you boys headed?"

"Home," Kyle said. "For Christmas."

"And home is?"

"Liberty Falls, Ohio."

"Never heard of it. How long have you lived there?"

Kyle didn't respond. He unrolled his silverware from the linen napkin. It should've been an easy question to answer. They hadn't lived there in a long time.

"It's where we grew up," Evan said.

"So, returning home, then," she said. "That's lovely. We live in the same small town where I grew up in Illinois, so I'm always home."

Always home. Had Evan ever felt like that anywhere? "Did you take the train all the way to San Francisco?"

"Actually, we drove on the way out. This is our first time on the train. Nate grew up in San Francisco. He doesn't like to visit, but everyone should return to the place where they came from once in a while. It's how you remember who you are and what's important."

Nate leaned across his wife's lap, pressing her against the back of the bench.

"Hey," she said.

He ignored her. "Check out the snow."

They were heading through a thick wooded area, farther into the mountains, and the drifts of snow alongside the tracks illustrated how much it had been snowing there.

"It's really coming down now," Penny said. "I'm surprised they didn't stop us at one of the earlier stations to wait this out."

"Nah," Nate said as he returned to his section of the booth. "Trains keep on going. They don't have to stop like cars. And planes cancel for anything. Or they gotta delay you while they deice the wings. Not with the train. They keep on going. Riding the rails is a much safer way to travel too."

Penny's eyebrows rose. "Like you know what you're talking about. You're not a world traveler. We've only ever gone places we could drive to in the RV. And what do you know about trains? You sound like you used to drive trains for a living. You worked in a sleeping-bag-and-tent factory."

"There's nothing wrong with a hard day's work."

"I didn't say there was."

Evan startled as Kyle moved in close and pointed to the window. "Check it out. There are cabins out there."

The scent of Kyle's cologne overwhelmed him. He forced himself to turn and look out the window. The blowing snow made it difficult to see. Nate and Penny continued discussing Nate's former occupation and his lack of knowledge when it came to various forms of travel.

"There," Kyle whispered, moving in closer.

Evan almost missed the cabins, what with the blowing snow and the scent of the man beside him, and then he saw them. Two cabins fifty feet apart, each a hundred yards from the tracks. A plume of smoke billowed out the chimney of one. He pictured a log fire, hot cocoa, a blanket to curl up under. "Wouldn't it be cool to live out there?"

Kyle leaned over him the same way Nate had done with his wife. His shoulder brushed against Evan's chest, and he placed a hand on his thigh. Evan jumped with the touch, and Kyle turned his head until they were eye to eye. He said, "There's no Starbucks."

This close, the scent of his alluring cologne, and the man underneath, was even more pronounced. Evan wanted to breathe in more of it, lose himself in that scent. He had never considered how to describe that cologne, but it came to him now. Like being outside in the fresh winter air in Ohio. Like sledding and ice skating and snowball fights. Like escaping from the world and feeling free and alive. Had Kyle put on more before coming to get Evan in the observation car? Maybe he did see this as a date.

Evan couldn't resist. He grabbed Kyle's hand and slowly slid it up his own thigh, stopping only when they came close to a destination they could never reach at the table with their dinner companions. "But a cabin out there in the wilderness, alone, just us. It would be a nice way to spend the holidays." He swallowed, his throat suddenly tight with emotion.

Kyle licked his lips and stroked Evan's thigh, moving their hands as one. "Yeah, it would."

"How long have you two been together?"

Penny's voice startled Evan. When had she and Nate stopped their bickering? Kyle sat back but didn't remove his hand from Evan's thigh.

Nate tapped the back of his wife's hand. "Now, don't embarrass them. What they got going on is their business."

Was anything going on? Evan shook his head. "We're not together. I mean, we are, but…not…like that." God, he needed to shut up. He'd practically moved Kyle's hand to his dick in a public dining room. If that wasn't "together," what the hell was?

Kyle was still staring at him. A slight curve of his lips had formed as Evan had fumbled with his words. The server arrived with their wine and food, and only then did Kyle slowly remove his hand from Evan's thigh. Maybe he was okay with people seeing them like that, thinking they were together. Evan stared at the flecks of rosemary covering the chicken on his plate. He sucked in a long breath and tried to remember how to work a knife and fork.

They ate the first few bites of their dinners in silence. Then Nate talked about the upcoming Donner Pass and the train that had been stranded there during a 1952 blizzard, mentioning the three days the passengers were trapped in the frozen train and how they had to be rescued by cars once the nearby highway was dug out. "Donner Pass is also where all them people traveling west in the 1800s got stuck and had to eat each other."

"Nate!" Penny smacked his arm. "We're trying to enjoy our dinner."

"It's our history."

"History no one wants to talk about." Penny laughed, a sound of exasperation and humor. "Only you and your perverse mind."

Evan laughed with her. Under Penny and Nate's harsh words and admonishments, there was sincere affection, years spent together, one knowing the other so well they could talk without complete sentences, could predict the other's thoughts and actions.

Kyle poked him in the side. "Why aren't you eating?"

"What?"

"You barely eat enough to stay alive."

"I eat."

"No, you don't. I thought you were depressed or something, but that doesn't explain the exercise. Depressed people don't go jogging every night and to the gym every morning."

"I just wanted to lose some weight. Gain a little muscle. It's not a big deal." Evan turned away again. In the glass of the window was the reflection of the enclosed life inside the train, including Kyle's stern expression aimed at the back of his head.

Nate and Penny were watching them. He didn't want Kyle to ask about this. Not now.

Chapter Twelve

Kyle clenched his fists in his lap under the table. He knew it.

Since the breakup six months ago, Evan hadn't been acting like himself. He was more insecure than ever before in his life.

"What the hell did Dickhead say to you?"

"What?" Evan spun around. "Nothing."

"That fucker." Kyle glanced over at Nate and Penny. "Sorry."

Nate said, "We should go."

Penny grabbed his arm. "No way."

Kyle didn't care if they stayed. He and Evan were talking about this.

Looked like Evan didn't like that option. He glared at Kyle. "Dennis didn't say anything. Why do you always make him sound like such a horrible person?"

"He's not? Prove me wrong. Why all this concern about how you look?"

"Like you should talk. You spend more money on clothes, hair products, and skin care shit than anyone I know. Even my mother."

"That's not what—"

"God forbid you miss an opportunity to impress some guy. Who'd suck your dick every night? Couldn't possibly be the same guy as the night before, right?"

"Oh my," Penny said.

"We should go," Nate said again, but neither made a move to get up.

Evan continued. "That would be so boring, wouldn't it? So like all the hets of the world."

"Yeah," Kyle said. "'Cause getting my dick sucked by a guy is just like what straight guys do."

"You know what I mean."

"I don't know what the hell you mean. What is wrong with you?"

"Nothing. You're the one asking rude questions." Evan looked at

Penny and Nate as if he just realized they were still there. He gave them a subdued smile.

Penny reached across the table and patted his hand. "There must be a reason you're so concerned with your appearance. Sounds like it was a recent change. Talk to him." She scooted closer to her husband, shooing him to the end of the booth. "Come on. Move. We'll give these boys some privacy." When Nate made no attempt to get up, she nudged him again. "Let's go already."

"I wanted to get a piece of that cake."

She held perfectly still, her gaze locked on him until he sighed and slipped out of the booth. He waited for her to stand and then held her arm as they made their way to the other end of the dining car.

Evan didn't face Kyle as he spoke. "I just... I think he wanted someone younger, someone...better."

Kyle forced down the usual impulse to hold back on the touchy-feeling stuff. It didn't take much effort. The words came more natural than breathing. "There's no one better than you." When Evan didn't respond, Kyle asked, "He didn't tell you why he broke it off?"

"Not really."

"Did he meet someone else? Is that what this is about?"

"No. He said he needed a change. That's all he kept saying." Evan picked up his fork and pushed a piece of chicken back and forth across his plate.

When it seemed like he wasn't going to stop, Kyle stilled his hand. "Talk to me."

"You know what's funny?" Evan set the fork down. "I was asking him to change our entire lives. I think I pushed too hard."

"Pushed? About what?"

"I thought he was into it." Evan shook his head as if he couldn't say the words. "He used to say he wanted the same things."

"Into what? What things?"

Evan looked him in the eye. "I don't want to talk about it. Not with you."

What the hell did he want?

The server came by the table and cleared the empty wineglasses and plates where Penny and Nate had been sitting. Evan made like he was going to get up. No way. Kyle was getting answers. He didn't move to let Evan out of the booth.

"Take your time," the server said. "There's only two more in line. If you don't mind, I'll have them join you."

"That's fine," Evan said before Kyle could answer.

The server gestured for the other passengers to step forward and take the seats vacated by Penny and Nate.

"Evan…"

Rebecca bounded onto the bench across the table. "Hi, you." Her mom sat beside her.

Kyle forced himself to relax and gave a smile to Rebecca. "Hi, you."

"Hello again," the mom said. "I'm glad I have another chance to thank you. I'm Sasha, and this is Rebecca, as you know from my screaming earlier."

Kyle introduced himself and Evan, and Rebecca waved. He gave a smirk and waved back. She was adorable. Probably how she got away with so much. No one could resist those wide, innocent eyes and that sweet smile. "There's no need to thank me. I'm just glad nothing happened to her."

"Me too. She's quite a handful. I'm too easy on her most days, but with her dad gone—"

"Daddy's not gone," Rebecca said. "He's in the army."

"Yes, hon." She ran a hand over her daughter's hair and looked back at Kyle. "He's serving overseas."

"That must be hard. Tell him thank you."

Sasha nodded with a smile, and Rebecca looked up at him at the same time Evan did. "What did Daddy do for you?" Rebecca asked.

"Not just for me. For everyone. He's serving his country for all of us."

"Oh." She held up the linen napkin until the silverware wrapped inside fell to the table. Then she rolled the napkin into a long thin log.

"Where's he stationed?" Evan asked. It was the first time he'd spoken since Sasha and Rebecca had joined them. His voice was quiet, reserved. Different than he'd been since they'd gotten on the train. What was it he wanted? And was that the real reason he thought the two of them couldn't take a chance together?

Rebecca set the napkin aside and hijacked the salt and pepper shakers from the end of the table. "We're not supposed to say where he's at."

Sasha said, "He's Special Forces."

"Can I show the picture, Mommy?"

"Go ahead."

Rebecca reached into her back pocket and tugged out a tiny photo album covered in sparkly stickers. Flowers, unicorns, and butterflies. She flipped to the first photo and pointed. "That's my daddy." A young man in the standard army dress blues, close-cropped hair, a serious expression on his face, a sparkly heart sticker pasted above his right shoulder.

"Handsome," Kyle said. "He has kind eyes."

She pulled the picture back and stared at it like she was seeing it for the first time. "He does!"

Sasha said, "We're going to spend Christmas with his family in Chicago. She adores her grandfather."

Rebecca gave a last look at the picture and stuffed the album back into her pocket, then set to stacking the salt shaker on top of the pepper and using the folded napkin as a moat around the tower of spices. She talked while she worked on getting the salt to balance just right so it would stay on its own. "Grandpa used to be in the army too, so he says he knows how much Daddy misses me while he's gone." She gave up on the salt shaker and let it fall to the table. The napkin moat kept the salt from tipping onto its side and spilling its contents. She turned and plastered her hands to the window. Nightfall was fast approaching. "I wish we'd stop right here."

"We cannot get off the train," Sasha said in a tone that sounded like she'd already repeated it a thousand times in the last hour. "See how we keep moving? This train is for traveling, not for stopping to look around."

"But I want to see those little houses." Rebecca pointed to another cabin off in the distance, the light streaming out through its windows. "Do people live out there?"

"I'm sure they do."

She faced her mom. "They must get bored. There's no playground. No school. Nothing."

"They probably have a TV and books."

"I wanna see." Rebecca pressed her nose to the window as if she could get closer and look inside the next cabin they passed. Her breath fogged the window, and she sat back to examine the effect. With her finger, she wrote a message in the condensation using slow deliberate swoops. Everyone was watching her, but she didn't seem to notice, or care. It took her a minute to write out *I luv u*. With a quick swipe of her hand, she wiped away her message.

"Was that to your dad?" Evan asked.

She held a finger to her lips. "Shhh. It's a secret. If anyone else reads it before I wipe it away, he won't get the message." She stared back out the window.

Kyle watched Rebecca for a moment more, then looked to Evan again. He was also staring out the window, his reflection visible in the glass, the expression on his face as miserable as he'd looked when

Dickhead had first broken up with him.

What did Evan want? Something to do with sex? Was he into some kind of kink? Pain? Multiple partners?

No, not Evan.

What did he want, then? He wanted his career to take off. That was happening, wasn't it? Or maybe the network was putting more pressure on Evan than he'd made it sound.

Kyle's chest ached at that. There had to be a way for Evan to get everything he'd been dreaming of, to be happy again.

As happy and alive as he was in your arms last night.

Chapter Thirteen

They walked from the dining car in silence, and Kyle had had enough. They were having a discussion when they got back to the room, and Evan was going to explain what he really wanted.

A large man stood in the hallway of their sleeper car, staring out the window, his arms crossed over his chest like he was guarding their room. He had a dominating presence, his body tense and on alert. His hair was short, buzzed so close to his scalp it was hard to tell it was gray. He was good looking, younger than his hair implied with an intense gaze and snug jeans stretched over his ass, as well as the sizeable package up front. He turned and headed toward them, moving in a confident, sexy saunter that would've had Kyle seriously interested had it been six months earlier, had he not been so uneasy about the conversation with Evan in the dining room.

Had he not been falling for Evan.

The man coming their way wasn't focused on Kyle, though. He didn't take his eyes off Evan as he passed by them, the look on his face one of lust more than anything else. He gave a quick nod to Evan before he was gone. Nice to know they weren't the only gay men on the train.

Or maybe not so nice, what with the way the guy had looked like he wanted to devour Evan.

Kyle couldn't keep from asking. "You know him?"

"I talked to him about the snow earlier in the observation car."

No doubt the man had been just as focused on Evan then.

That was how it always was with him. Evan was definitely good-looking, but there was something else about him that drew most guys in. Hell, most women too. Only, Evan didn't get it, didn't know he had that power, that allure. He still thought of himself as the scrawny, geeky kid he'd been when he was a boy. The one everyone knew was gay before he did, the one kids made fun of, the one who didn't have any close friends until Kyle had moved to town.

Evan slid open the door to their room and stopped suddenly in his tracks.

Kyle ran into the back of him. "Sorry." He didn't want to step away—his groin was smashed against the top of Evan's ass—but something was wrong. Evan hadn't moved. "What are you doing?"

"Someone was in here."

Kyle looked around Evan. Their duffel bags were open. So was Evan's backpack. Good thing Kyle had taken his pack with the computer inside with him when he went to find Evan in the observation car. "Was your laptop in here?"

"Yeah." Evan stepped inside and went to his bag. "It's still here."

Kyle searched through his stuff. "Nothing of mine was taken."

"This is too weird. First the apartment. Now here." Evan snapped his fingers. "Your grandpa's journal. Where is it?"

"It was with me, in my backpack. What? You think they sent someone here to get it?"

"I called Hastings and told him you weren't interested in his offer."

"When?"

"Before you came to get me for dinner."

"You think they had someone following us in case I said no?"

"I think they'll do quite a lot to get their hands on it."

Well, fuck that. Kyle wasn't going to sit back and find out what. "I'm reporting this. They can't get away with this shit." He punched at the call button, then dropped to the bench and pulled the journal from his bag.

Evan sat beside him. "You haven't read what they could be after?"

"No, but I'm not even halfway through it. Grandpa and this guy Joe bought a car and traveled the country doing stuff Joe wanted to do. Sort of like a bucket list. The first was to play a high-stakes poker game. They ended up in a mob-run bar playing in a back room. Joe won several hands, then this mob guy drew a gun and told them to take their winnings and get the hell out. They sprinted out the back of the bar, and before they made it out of the alley, Joe grabbed Grandpa and kissed him. They were...together, right there behind the bar."

"Oh."

"I uh, kinda skimmed that part." It had been odd, to say the least, reading about his grandpa's intense desire for someone. "They drove all over the country. They learned to sail on Lake Superior, walked across the Golden Gate Bridge in San Francisco, and worked on a cattle ranch in Wyoming for five weeks.

"They did all that together?"

"Yeah. And more. Some of the stuff scared Grandpa too."

"Sounds like he loved Joe."

Love? Sex and desire did not equal love. "Why would you say that?"

Evan sat back and stared across the room, a serious look on his face like he was remembering something. "It's sort of obvious. I mean, why was he doing all that? To make Joe happy?"

"I guess."

Oscar arrived out of breath in the open doorway. He leaned against the door, and the glass rattled with his weight. "Whew. When it rains it pours." He pulled a handkerchief from his pocket, lifted the Santa hat, and wiped his brow. "What do you boys need?"

Evan spoke first. "Someone was in our room."

"While you were at dinner?" Oscar asked.

"Yeah."

"Well, that makes it all of you. Seems all the empty rooms in this car were searched while everyone was in the dining car. Did they take anything?"

"Not that we can tell," Evan said.

"No cash?"

"Mine's all in my wallet, and that was with me."

"Mine too," Kyle offered. "There was a man in the hallway when we got back from dinner."

"What did he look like?"

Like someone too interested in what wasn't his. "Gray hair but young-looking. Tall. A big guy. Muscular. Like he could take on just about anyone."

"And gorgeous," Evan added under his breath.

A surge of anger overwhelmed Kyle. He couldn't stop glaring at Evan. Or wanting to punch the hell out of the older guy who Evan thought was gorgeous and who could probably kick his ass without lifting a finger.

Jealousy.

He'd never been jealous of anyone before. Or had he been? It wasn't like he'd ever been Dickhead's biggest fan.

Oscar looked between Kyle and Evan. He smirked and then grew serious again. "I'll let my boss know about your room. Whoever it was, it looks like they were after money. They left behind computers and phones but took everyone's cash. Best be on the safe side and not leave your valuables or cash lying around. Whoever this is has the means to get into the rooms. Which means I'm the most likely suspect." He smiled again. The gap between his teeth and the playful expression made him look ten years younger. "I love it when the cops are after my ass. Reminds me of my youth. All right then, you boys stay safe. Let me know if you think of anything you're missing." He stood straight like he was about to salute and spoke in a formal tone. "I'm sorry for all the inconvenience, and I hope you enjoy the rest of your travels with us." He winked. "That's in the handbook, for when stuff goes wrong." He turned and left, the ball on the Santa hat swinging as he went.

Evan dropped his head and laughed, his face more relaxed than he'd looked all day.

The sound of that laughter washed over Kyle. "So maybe not about the journal."

"I guess." Evan leaned back against the bench, and his expression grew grim.

"Ev, what did Hastings say to you?"

"Can we talk about it later? You need to keep writing, and then I think we need to know what else is in that journal."

The urge to press the issue was strong, but Evan was right. They needed to know what the network was after. Kyle opened the journal.

"You're not going to write first?" Evan asked.

"No. I need to read this. Before someone really does come looking for it." *And I want to know how Grandpa decided to walk away from love.*

"It's your choice," Evan said, his tone abrupt.

What the hell did that mean?

Evan pulled out the papers from his back pocket. His script again. It was crazy of him to keep going over it. The ideas he'd put together for *The Agency* were fantastic. He didn't need to rework them yet again.

Maybe Evan agreed. He tossed the pages toward his bag on the floor by the bathroom. Kyle almost changed his mind and forced Evan to talk about what Hastings had said, but did he want to know what Evan had given up for him? Or what it meant? Because if the situation were reversed, there wasn't a person in the world who could force Kyle to hurt Evan. Not again.

Chapter Fourteen

Kyle read one more paragraph, then closed the journal and reached for a bottle of water on the table. While he'd been reading, the train had made another scheduled stop and had stayed at the station so long it seemed like they might not start up again. They had to be running more than two hours behind schedule now. Perhaps they were trying to determine if it was safe to head into the worsening storm, which didn't look like it was doing such a good job of staying south.

It was getting late. Evan was moving around the room, taking clothes out of his bag, then putting them back. He'd found his spare contacts earlier and had swapped those out for the glasses. What was he looking for now? Or was it nervous movement? He'd been as anxious to know what the network wanted from the journal as Kyle.

Despite reading to the halfway mark, Kyle still hadn't read anything that indicated his grandpa had known about any treasure or money or anything like that. The last twenty entries he'd read had detailed the weeks after his grandpa and Joe had met up with four men in a bar in Denver, Colorado. Vern, Henry, George, and Charles were all veterans from the Korean War. They'd been living off the land in a remote region outside Denver for several months, and they had no intention of returning to civilization. Except for a quick beer and a stopover at a boarding house where they could find four local girls who, with a cash exchange for incentive, would agree to spend the night at their campsite.

In that bar, they'd drunk their way through several beers as they'd shared war stories, and eventually the four men had invited his grandpa and Joe to join their fire at the campsite. It turned into a more permanent residence than they'd planned when they postponed leaving Colorado and settled into a tent next to their new friends.

His grandpa had felt comfortable there, around those men. Like he was finally home from the war. Which hadn't set well with Kyle. He'd thought the farm had been his grandpa's home, his sanctuary, the place that made him who he was.

Kyle had set the journal aside on his fourth yawn. He'd barely gotten any sleep after the break-in the night before.

"I'm gonna hit the sack."

"Yeah, me too." Evan zipped his bag shut and pressed the call button. He didn't say another word, not even to ask what Kyle had read.

A knock sounded on the door. Evan slid it open, and Oscar poked his head in. "Ready to turn in? Just step out for a sec, and I'll get you all squared away."

Evan nodded and moved into the hall. What was up with the silence?

Before Kyle could join him, Oscar asked, "You need both beds?" He pointed to the bench. "Once it's pulled out, the bottom bed is big enough for two if you boys prefer to go that route."

Kyle glanced at Evan, but he was in the hall staring out the window into the darkness beyond.

"Could you set up both, please?"

"Sure thing." Oscar set to work on the beds, and Kyle went into the hall to wait with Evan. They didn't talk and instead watched the snow zip through the path of light seeping out the windows of the train. What would Evan have done if Kyle had told Oscar to skip the second bed?

How was he supposed to show Evan he could trust him if they couldn't touch? How was he supposed to find out what was wrong if Evan wouldn't talk to him?

After Oscar left, Kyle grabbed his bag and threw it onto the bottom bed. "Looks like everyone thinks we're together."

Evan didn't respond. He removed something from his bag and slipped into the bathroom. A minute later, he came out wearing a white T-shirt and flannel pajama pants. He tossed his clothes toward his bag, climbed onto the top bed, and lay down, his back to Kyle.

What the hell? "That must have been some contortionist act?"

Evan rolled onto his back. "What?"

"Getting undressed in that small fucking bathroom." Kyle hadn't meant to sound like such a prick, but Evan's silence and avoidance were pissing him off.

Another pause. Then Evan faced the wall again.

Kyle got undressed and slid under the covers in his underwear. He reached for the light switch and flipped it off, trying to pretend it was the sway of the train and the clanking as it rolled along the tracks making his head hurt. They weren't traveling as quickly as they had in the lower elevations. Was that typical? Or were they going slower because of the weather? How long until they were home? It was going to feel twice as long with Evan's current mood. The cramped seats and stale air of an airplane were sounding good.

A half hour later, Kyle was still awake. He heard Evan's uneven breathing. He wasn't sleeping either. Maybe they should do a replay of the night before. No matter how pissed off Kyle was, he was sure he could give himself a few strokes, picture fucking Evan up against the wall of windows out in the hall, and get hard in an instant. Despite their lack of sexual experience together, he knew Evan would like being pressed face-first against the glass so he could watch the snow fall, feeling like they were out in it, while Kyle rammed into him from behind. That image had his cock perking up.

Evan shifted on the bed above. "Kyle?"

Perfect timing, Ev. "Yeah." The simple word sounded more like an exhale.

"Are you really moving to Ohio?"

The words flew out of his mouth before Kyle could stop them. "Would you be upset if I did?" He held his breath, knowing the answer now but needing to hear it anyway.

Too bad Evan had another question. "What about your writing?"

"I can do that anywhere." Or not. It wasn't as if he'd been writing much the past year. Although he'd been writing a lot in the last few hours. Since he'd started reading the journal.

Without warning, Evan climbed off the top bunk and headed for the door. "I'm going for a walk."

"A walk?" Kyle threw back his blanket and jumped in front of him. "Where to? We're on a fucking train."

Evan stared at Kyle's chest. He didn't answer, but he also didn't make a move to leave.

"Why are you mad at me?" Kyle asked.

"You have a career, and you're fucking it up."

He'd have been less shocked if Evan had taken a swing at him. "What?"

"You have a chance, and you're tossing it away because you're scared. Do you know what I'd give to be where you are with my career?"

Kyle took a step back. "I'm doing the best I can. It's called writer's block."

"Sure. You've got too many people interested in your work now. It's not just for you this time, so you're running away. It's what you always do. Never let yourself feel anything. Never allow yourself to do anything that means making a commitment, an emotional connection."

Kyle moved into Evan's space, backing him against the far wall. "What the fuck—"

Evan shoved him, both hands on Kyle's chest. "I was there for you when you hit it big. I celebrated with you and cheered you on. I listened when things got tough. Now it's my shot, and you're taking off? I should've known I could never count on you."

"What's that supposed to mean?"

"You worked on those two books for years. You can spend weeks writing and rewriting one scene, but you cannot commit to anyone."

"Bullshit." Kyle raised his hands and smacked his palms against the wall on either side of Evan's head like he'd done when they'd been in his apartment the night before. Everything was getting out of hand. He took a steadying breath and moved in closer, their foreheads almost touching. "I have always been there for you." He couldn't hide his shock, his anger at Evan's words, but he also hated Evan being mad at him, hated Evan sounding so lost. He wanted to make promises he couldn't find the words for.

There was a low rumbling sound. The train lurched. Evan fell against Kyle, and they tumbled onto the bottom bed, Evan on top. They were breathing heavily, staring at each other.

Evan's weight on him felt right. Like every fantasy he'd been having. He wanted the rest of those fantasies to come true. He wanted all of Evan.

Too bad words hadn't been his friends for a long time. He had no idea how the hell to ask for any of it.

Chapter Fifteen

Evan bit his bottom lip and stared down at Kyle. He hadn't meant to hurt him with his words, but he hadn't felt so alive in the past six months as he had telling Kyle how he felt.

Or lying on top of him.

He slowly rolled his hips, putting more pressure against Kyle's body, the fabric of Evan's flannel pants sliding along the bare thighs below him. He wanted to rip the damn pants off. He wanted what they'd done in the hallway at the apartment. He wanted everything he'd been dreaming about.

The train lurched again, and that pulled him out of the lust-filled daze. Only then did he notice the pull of the brakes working against their forward movement. Now if only he could find the brakes for his body. "The train's stopping."

Kyle's voice was low when he finally spoke. "Pretty fast too."

"Maybe something's wrong."

"No." Kyle thrust his groin upward against Evan, creating friction in all the right places. "Nothing's wrong."

"Okay." Evan shifted his hips again, caressing Kyle's body with his own. "Probably just need to wait out the storm."

Kyle sucked in a sharp breath as Evan kept moving. "Best to stop before it becomes serious."

Right. They had to stop this. Evan stilled.

Maybe that wasn't what Kyle had meant. He grabbed Evan's hips, his grip tight, demanding, and he forced Evan to move again. Evan sat up and straddled Kyle's thighs, pressing his ass against the hard cock underneath him, blocked only by the thin fabric of briefs and the flannel of his pajama pants.

Maybe it was too late to stop anything.

There was a commotion in the hall, and then a knock sounded at the door. Oscar's voice rang out. "Are you boys okay in there?" The train was nearly stopped.

Kyle hadn't looked away from him. Evan could make out his features in the low light seeping in around the curtain covering the door to their room. Kyle's dark eyebrows were drawn in, and his expression was a little too serious, too concerned, for Evan's comfort.

Oscar knocked again. "Hello."

Evan climbed off Kyle and went for the door. Oscar looked like he'd been woken up from a deep sleep, still in his uniform, but he no longer wore his Santa hat.

"You boys all right?"

Evan glanced back at Kyle. He hadn't moved, hadn't covered himself as he lay in only his briefs. He was still staring at Evan just as intently as before. Evan spoke without looking away from Kyle. "We're okay."

"Good." Oscar let out a long whistle. "That was one hell of a stop."

Evan forced himself to focus on Oscar. "What happened?"

"Avalanche. Everything seems to have settled, so we're not in immediate danger, but we've got snow and debris piled on the tracks ahead. It buried the snowshed. We might not be able to get through. The engineer is checking it out now."

"A snowshed?"

"Covers the tracks to protect it from snow. You know, in case of an avalanche." He laughed. "Guess they needed to make it just a tad longer. We're okay, though. That's the important thing." Oscar leaned against the wall and pointed at the windows directly across the hall from their room. "This is one horrible storm we've gotten ourselves into. Well, I'll keep you boys posted. I need to check the rest of the car." He went down the hall and knocked on the door of the next sleeper compartment. A moment later, Evan heard the words, "I'm sorry for all the inconvenience, and I hope you enjoy the rest of your travels with us."

Evan stepped out of the room to get a better view out the wall of windows. The wind was howling, the train swaying. The snow drifts were piling up around them and more was blowing off the mountain. The howl of the wind sounded louder than the train had when they'd been speeding along. Under normal circumstances, he would've been more worried about the storm, about being stuck out there, about missing Christmas in Liberty Falls, but he couldn't get how Kyle had looked at him out of his head. Evan rested his forehead against the window. His breath fogged the glass, and he had the urge to run the tip of his finger through it to write a secret message, then wipe it away like Rebecca had done earlier. He raised his hand.

"Jesus."

Evan jumped at the sound of Kyle's voice. He rubbed the side of his fist through the condensation, destroying any chance of leaving an embarrassing message. How stupid that he'd almost done it. He wasn't a kid falling for the new boy in school anymore. "You heard what happened?"

"Yeah." Kyle was standing beside him, looking out the window, wearing only his jeans, the top button undone. "This isn't good."

More people came out of their rooms and stared out the windows farther down the hall. The wind surged louder, and the car rocked. Evan gripped the railing below the windows, and Kyle placed a hand against the opposite wall. They were facing each other, blocking the hallway.

Kyle's voice was low when he spoke. "Ev—"

"It's okay. I knew the minute I met you you'd never be mine."

Kyle moved toward him. "I am."

"Don't." Evan squeezed his eyes shut. "You don't mean that the way I want you to."

"I think I do. This isn't just sex for me." The same words he'd said to Kyle the night before in the apartment. Not that they'd gotten to any actual sex. Yet.

Another gust of wind rocked the train. Evan clutched the railing tighter and shook his head.

"Why are you fighting me on this?" Kyle asked.

Just because every kiss, every touch had been as intense as ten years ago did not mean anything. "We want different things."

Kyle scoffed. "Sounds like that's a common problem for you."

So what if he knew what he wanted out of life? Why shouldn't he have it? Why should he settle for less?

"All right, folks," Oscar said as he came out of the room at the end of the hall holding a radio in his hand. "Just got word we're blocked in and there's more snow behind us. They're checking it out now. We might be here for a bit until we can get the tracks cleared, so go on back to bed and get some sleep. Shouldn't take too long, and we'll get going again." He walked the length of the hall, shooing guests back into their rooms.

Kyle and Evan hadn't moved.

"What if we have another avalanche?" Evan asked. Seemed stupid to sleep through what might be left of their lives.

"Guess that's a possibility, but it sounds like we're stuck here."

"Yeah."

"All we can do is wait it out. No sense worrying."

Oscar approached and pointed to their room. "Go on, boys."

Evan went inside. He heard the door slide shut behind him, not the angry rattle of glass he'd expected, but a slow closing off of their room. He turned around. Kyle was staring at the floor, his hands in the pockets of his jeans. The frustration was gone, but Evan couldn't read the look on his face. His instincts told him to go easy on Kyle, make this easier for both of them. Although it would never be for Evan. "Guess we should get some sleep."

Kyle nodded. Neither made a move for the beds.

The advance was quick, and Evan had no time to prepare. Or to stop it. Kyle came at him and planted a hard kiss on his lips. It wasn't a passionate kiss. It was frustrated and possessive and didn't seem like it would ever end. Then Kyle pulled back, not letting go of Evan. "No matter what, I will be there for you. Whatever you need."

Evan slowly wrapped his arms around Kyle's waist. "I know that."

"Do you?" The words were spoken into the hair above Evan's temple.

Their relationship had always been important to both of them. They cared for each other. They were attracted to each other. That didn't mean they could find a future together as more than friends, but that also didn't mean he had to lose Kyle. Sex or no sex.

"I do."

They stood locked in that moment, holding each other. They'd never done anything like this before. This push and pull between them was going to kill Evan by the time they reached Ohio.

Kyle stepped back and leaned against the closed door. "What is it you want?" His voice was low, tense.

Might as well lay it all out. "A home. A partner."

"You had that. So what freaked him out?"

"Children. I want a family." He sighed, then hurried to say the rest. "I want to be old and retired and still with the same person, traveling together on the train, bickering over broccoli, worrying about our grandkids."

"Oh."

Yeah. Nothing Kyle Bennett wanted. Just as Evan had been thinking in the dining car.

He hadn't expected the fall from the high he'd been on when they'd been touching earlier to make him feel so sick. Hell, he hadn't expected the fall at all. Was that how it was for junkies like the guy who'd broken into Kyle's apartment? Did they ever think about what it would be like after they came down from the high they were after?

Evan forced himself to look at Kyle again. He was still leaning against the door, sporting a frown and frustrated lines across his forehead.

"Let's just get some sleep."

"Yeah," Kyle said. "Okay." He moved slowly. Like a man who'd had too much to drink. He lay down on his bed over the blankets, still wearing his jeans. Evan took a deep breath and turned away to climb back on the top bed. A few minutes later, Kyle was asleep on the bench below him. How could he be so free, so able to touch and then stop and go on as if nothing had happened? As if an avalanche hadn't just rained down around them? In more ways than one.

That proved Evan's point. If they started something, he would be the one putting his heart on the line.

Then why did he still want to?

Chapter Sixteen

"You'll send me those pages after the holiday?" Sue Ann asked.

Kyle shifted the phone to his other ear, tucked the end of the towel in at his waist, and tried not to snap at her. He'd just stepped out of the shower when she'd called. Since heading into the mountains, the signal on his phone had been spotty at best, so he'd figured it was a good idea to talk to Sue Ann before she sent out a search party for his manuscript. Despite learning the train was stuck, she'd gotten right to the point of her call.

"Consider it done," he said as he ran a hand through his wet hair to shake off some of the water. He had written twenty pages so far, but since the argument with Evan the night before, since Evan had told him what he wanted for his future, the muse had taken another train. Kyle had tried to write more that morning, but he was stuck again.

"All right," Sue Ann said. "Be safe out there, and do what you can to stay focused on the manuscript." The call cut out before he could make another promise he wasn't sure he could keep.

He threw the phone at his bag. It missed, bounced off the carpeted floor, and smacked into the steel rod that connected the chair to the floor. With his current level of frustration, he'd be breaking his phone, his laptop, everything he'd brought with him before long.

It had taken every ounce of self-control not to walk back into their room after the interruption the night before and fuck Evan like mad, avalanche or no avalanche, but Evan needed something else then. Maybe Kyle did too. Which was the craziest part of the whole trip. He never put talking before fucking. Not that he'd ever put it after either.

He dropped to the bench. Not a bench this time, though. A bed. After sleeping in that morning, neither of them had bothered to call Oscar so he could return their miniscule bedroom to its original state. The guy probably had more important things to worry about, a lot of unhappy passengers to appease since they were still stuck on the tracks in the same location as the night before. The mussed sheet and blanket reminded Kyle how little sleep he'd gotten. He'd lain still at first so Evan would relax and get some rest, but once he'd heard Evan's slight snore, he'd tossed and turned all night, unable to rid his body of the tension. Or the erection.

He was beginning to think his writer's block had a lot to do with his dick's happiness, or lack thereof, to be more precise.

Guess he'd have no chance of writing more before getting off the train. Time to get his mind on something else.

He picked up the leather-bound journal, and his thoughts went right back to what he'd been trying to avoid.

Kyle had spent much of the summer before they left for California with Evan on the farm, an hour drive from Liberty Falls, working with the horses and stacking bales of hay, and spending their nights in a tent his grandpa had set up behind the house. If he could only go back and kick his eighteen-year-old ass into gear, he could've had Evan's dick years ago. But even then, Evan longed for more than sex from the guys he was with, and the eighteen-year-old Kyle wanted none of that.

What about now? Could he have a relationship? Did he even know how?

He needed to stop this before he came to a conclusion he didn't like. He needed to read the rest of his grandpa's words, needed the answers to more questions than just what the network was after. He opened the journal and got lost in a life lived sixty years earlier.

A road trip to play craps in Las Vegas. Rock climbing near Colorado Springs. Hiking through the Rocky Mountains. Some of the trips they'd made with their new friends. Some his grandpa and Joe had taken alone, making love in the backseat of their car parked along dirt roads or spread out on a blanket after they'd watched the sun set.

They had felt comfortable on the back roads of America, between small towns and farmlands, away from civilization and in their own private world. As if nothing and no one could burst the bubble they had been living in since they'd left Korea.

Kyle read another passage. Joe had called home for the first time in months and had learned the news of his brother's marriage and new baby.

Today Joe told me he wants to go home to visit his brother's family, to see the child, to introduce me to everyone.

That's when I knew. He wants a life with me. I can't give him that. No matter how much I love him. No matter what I'd like to have.

I know now things are going to change between us. We can't stay in this place forever. We have to grow together. Or apart.

But I can't walk away. Not yet.

Kyle's chest tightened as he read the words on the aged paper before him. A surge of emotions overcame him. They battled with his rational, logical thoughts, like a swell pushing against the side of a sailboat, forcing it to turn. The sails lose the wind for a brief moment before catching again, bringing the vessel back on course, creating questions where there had been none a moment before. Do you stay on course? Or ride the waves and see where they take you?

No answers. Only questions.

Kyle turned the page and read more from the journal.

We returned to the campsite outside Denver today. It has become a home for us. A place where we can be with people again but also be together—sleep in the same tent, be gone for hours on long walks, just the two of us, and no one seems to know or care if we are more than friends.

As we drove down the dirt lane toward the campsite, everything became clear. I know now, this is the place where I will leave Joe. I have no idea how I will walk away, but the time draws near that I will go. I want these final moments to last as long as possible.

Kyle turned the page to the next entry.

Everything changed tonight.

We heard on the radio the armistice had been signed the day before, ending the war where we'd both lost and found so much. Hearing the news finished things for me. It was time. Maybe Joe knew that. He'd been different all day.

As the sun set, he and I sat alone by the fire.
Everyone else had spent the day in Denver. They
must have had something planned because that
morning the four of them had been excited like we
hadn't seen since Joe and I had returned from our
last trip south. We didn't ask questions. We had our
own secrets to keep.

I was sitting between Joe's legs, leaning back
against him, watching the light dance in the fire,
trying to work up the nerve to talk to him about our
futures, when Vern's car barreled into the campsite,
kicking up dirt. It came to a sudden stop, and the
doors flew open. Vern, Henry, and George jumped
out. Charles was not with them. The three were
cursing, shoving at each other, kicking up more dirt
with their quick movements. We bounded to our feet
and tried to stop whatever was about to explode
between the three men.

We were too late. The curses turned to accusations,
to fists slamming against cheekbones, to bruised
knuckles, and blood spat onto the ground.

An hour later, after the storm of anger and violence
had passed, Joe and I learned the secrets our new
friends had been keeping. The four of them had
robbed the Denver Bank and Trust, apparently not
their first bank job, but the first time one of them had
been caught. The first time they'd fired their
weapons. The first time someone had died.

Kyle lowered the journal. That was it.

A bank robbery.

The door to their room opened, and Evan walked in carrying a tray of food. He set the tray on the table. Kyle dropped the journal to the bed beside him and stood. The towel fell from his waist and landed on the floor. His body was dry, but with the swift movement, his hair dripped water to his chest.

Evan sucked in his bottom lip and sank his teeth into it, like he'd done on top of Kyle the night before. Slowly, Evan knelt before him and picked up the towel. That put his head at the right location, at least according to Kyle's dick. It was filling, growing hard and thick. He shifted on his legs, unable to stand still. Evan paused at Kyle's cock. He licked his lips. Those lips were so damn close to his balls.

The swell of need and something more powerful slammed into Kyle, and he was off course again. He couldn't stop himself. He ran his hand through Evan's blond hair, cupping the back of his head, feeling the urge to force his mouth forward but holding still, his legs shaking with anticipation.

A slight shift and Evan's lips would be on his dick. Kyle wanted Evan to suck him. He wanted things he'd never wanted from another man—for Evan to bury his face in Kyle's ass, lick him, fuck him with tongue and lips and spit until he was writhing and panting and dying for more, then he wanted Evan to just plain old fuck him. Although there'd be nothing plain or old about that. Too bad he had no idea how to get them from Evan kneeling on the floor before him to Evan's cock buried in his ass. He sounded like a nervous virgin. Every guy he'd ever been with would've been laughing his ass off right then.

Evan leaned into his touch until palm met cheek.

Kyle forced Evan to look at him. "I…" He breathed deep and tried to will his cock, already standing at half-mast, to calm down. "I don't want to hurt you."

"It's okay." But maybe Evan didn't mean the words the way they sounded. He wrapped the towel around Kyle's waist, tucked in the end, and stood. He sat on the other side of the table and unloaded the tray. "You should look out the other side of the train. The drifting is getting worse." His voice was uneven, shaky, but growing stronger with each word. "We might be stuck here for a while longer."

Kyle squeezed his eyes closed until he caught his breath. When he could walk without making a fool of himself, he went to the corner of the small room and dressed, keeping his back to Evan as he resisted the urge to stroke himself and instead tucked his half-hard dick into his underwear.

Evan kept talking. "They need to send another train with equipment to clear the tracks and a new engineer since each can only be on duty so long, but nothing could get through before now. I guess there are more storms heading our way too." By the time Evan finished speaking, he sounded normal, casual.

The least Kyle could do was try for the same. He sat across the table. "Thanks for the food." There was a burger and fries for him and a salad for Evan. The fucker still wasn't eating enough.

"No problem," Evan said. "They're already serving lunch. Guess we slept in pretty late." He picked up a carrot stick and took a bite. He pointed the uneaten half at Kyle. "That's going to be your last shower. They're starting to conserve supplies. Water, food, fuel for the heat."

"Really? Shit." Kyle ran a hand through his drying hair.

"They're hoping help can get here before the next storm moves in, and that we can get moving this afternoon." Evan looked out the window and nibbled on the rest of the carrot.

Kyle couldn't stop watching that mouth, the tongue licking his lips, the throat muscles working as he swallowed. Maybe Evan had been right about the sex messing with them. Just in different ways. Being this close and not getting what his body was begging for was torture.

"Hope we don't miss Christmas," Evan said.

"We won't miss it. It might just be us, though."

Evan nodded but hadn't looked away from the line of snow-covered trees along the tracks.

Kyle gave up on thoughts of what Evan obviously didn't want to do right then—or maybe ever. He didn't want to fathom that last part. He picked up two fries and shoved them in his mouth.

"I talked to Oscar," Evan said. "That good-looking guy from the hallway last night after dinner has an alibi. When we saw him, he'd just come from another passenger's room. A married man on a business trip who he'd spent an hour alone with."

"Oh." So, yes, he was gay. Which also probably meant he had been checking out Evan. Without a thought on why he was changing the subject, Kyle said, "I found out why Hastings wants the journal."

Evan set his fork down, a hunk of lettuce still stuck to it. "Why?"

"My grandpa knew a group of men who lived in the Colorado wilderness. They were all vets from the war who robbed banks. I'm guessing it has to do with the money from one of their jobs in Denver."

"Holy shit." Evan gave a long stare, then his eyes widened. "The Denver Bank and Trust in 1953?"

"Yeah."

"There was a movie made about that. They never found the money."

"I thought it sounded familiar. Did you see the movie?"

"No. Was your..." Evan shook his head. "Never mind."

"Was my grandpa involved?"

"I'm sorry."

"Don't be. I don't think he was. One of the others had gotten caught, and that's how Grandpa found out about the robbery. I haven't read anything more yet." He paused, trying to decide if he should direct the conversation back to the one they'd left hanging the night before. "I want to know what happened with Hastings."

Evan took another bite of his salad before he spoke. "It was an ultimatum. The journal or my job."

"They fired you?"

"I guess I technically quit."

"You can't do that."

"I already did."

Kyle pointed a finger at Evan. "You call him back."

"No way. First of all, I don't want the job that way or to work for someone like that. Most importantly, the only way to keep the job is to sell out your grandpa. No matter what else is in the journal, I'm not doing that."

Evan's words shouldn't have surprised him, but the rush of pride slamming into him did. Kyle reached across the table and grabbed Evan by the back of the neck. Good thing the table was small because there was no stopping him. He leaned in and pulled Evan forward until their lips met. A simple kiss that said so much more.

Or maybe not, because Evan asked, "What was that for?"

"You being you." Kyle stood and paced the room. "Fuck them if they don't want you. You can find another writing job. A better job. Or you can do this on your own. You can produce your own show. You can take it to the web. You'll get your break, Ev, and you'll prove to everyone how talented you are. You'll see."

Evan was still seated, staring up at him, his mouth hanging open. His phone rang, and he scrambled to get it out of the front pocket on his jeans. "I couldn't get a signal earlier. I better take this. You read and find out more about the bank robbery. I'll, uh… I'll be back." He left the room in a rush, tripping over Kyle's bag on the way, catching himself palm out on the glass door.

Kyle held back the laugh. Evan was not acting like himself, and not in a good way like Kyle had been dreaming of, and that wasn't funny at all.

He glanced at the journal on the bench. Sometimes relationships had to end. Didn't they? Maybe before they got started. Wouldn't his grandpa have been better off if he'd never started things with Joe? Wasn't that what he'd said in the letter to Kyle? *I hope you learn something from my mistakes.*

Sounded logical.

Despite that, Kyle grabbed a pen and the pad of sticky notes and added a note to the journal.

Sometimes you have to do anything you can to hold on to what matters, despite how far off course you sail.

Chapter Seventeen

Evan leaned against the wall beside the door to their room.

"You'll get your break, Ev, and you'll prove to everyone how talented you are."

He'd never lose Kyle from his life. No matter what they did or didn't do when it came to sex. He knew that now.

His phone rang again. He'd forgotten he had it or why he'd stepped out into the hall in the first place. He checked the display. Dennis again. The fifth time. And that was with his signal going in and out. He'd let all the calls go to his voice mail the day before.

It felt colder on the train. Probably would grow even colder if they didn't get moving soon. He shivered as he looked at the display again and the one name he'd have given anything to see on his phone five months earlier. Now? He didn't want to answer it. He couldn't avoid life outside the train forever, though. "Hi, Dennis."

"Evan. It's good to hear your voice. I saw on the news a train was stuck in the mountains."

"That's us."

"Are you okay?"

"Yeah. So far it's the same." The same? Nothing was the same. "We're just stopped."

"When can they get you going again?"

"I don't know. Why did you call?"

"I want to come see you."

"Now?" He stared at the blue curtain covering the door to the room he and Kyle shared.

"In Ohio. I thought maybe… I want to see you for Christmas." Dennis paused, and when he spoke again, his voice was that low sexy tone that drove Evan crazy. "I want you back."

Of all the times Dennis could've said those words, he chose now. Seriously?

"Can I come so we can talk?" Dennis asked. "Face-to-face." When

Evan didn't say anything right away, he added, "Can you think about it? I can call you later."

Evan didn't bother to tell him it might be hard to get through later, what with more storms moving in and his phone's signal already shitty in their remote location. He needed to tell him the truth. But what was that? What were he and Kyle doing?

"Evan…"

He forced the words out before Dennis could say more. "I have to tell you something."

"Not over the phone. I want to see you." Maybe he knew Evan was going to say he'd made a mistake e-mailing him in the first place. "You think about it, and I'll call you later. I still love you, Evan. I always will."

That left him speechless. The words he wanted to hear more than anything. Only they hadn't come from the one he'd waited ten years to hear them from. He managed to say, "Okay, call me later," then hung up the phone. If Dennis still loved him, maybe it was right to tell him about Kyle in person, to apologize for getting back in touch after he'd fallen for Kyle again. He owed Dennis that. As soon as he called again, he would arrange to meet with him after the holidays.

Evan didn't feel like heading back into their room to finish his lunch. He should at least go in and get a sweatshirt, but he couldn't do that either.

He moved through the train to the observation car, took a seat on an empty bench, and watched the snow fly through the air with the wind, moving in no discernible patterns, as if each snowflake was alive and on its own journey toward a destination it was in no hurry to locate, blowing in the breeze until finally finding its way.

He shivered, leaned back, and wrapped his arms around himself. He wished he could walk off into the wilderness and be alone for a while. Just live and be and not think so much. Not feel so much. Not have so much hope.

He sank farther into the seat and closed his eyes. Who was he kidding? He wanted to hold on to that hope for as long as he could.

* * * *

Kyle hung up his phone and lay back on the bed. He might not have enough clout to make this work, but the call had sounded promising. No way was he saying anything to Evan yet. He'd wait until Sue Ann called him back with their response first.

He raised his arms above his head and pictured the night before with Evan on top of him. He wanted more. So much more.

Could he do this? Could he be who Evan deserved?

His gut told him no. He just wasn't sure he wanted to listen to it anymore.

He needed a distraction. He picked up his grandpa's journal and sat in the chair.

I shouldn't have been as surprised as I was they'd been robbing banks. With their lingering anger toward the government and their hatred for institutions of capitalism, their interest in the banks was more about a statement of power than the money itself. Yet we hadn't wanted to see who they really were. We had wanted a safe place to hide.

All I could think of in that moment was Charles. Would he turn on the rest, lead the police to the campsite? Would he mention Joe and me?

When the group of men settled down and all were quiet around the fire, George spoke. "We run. Now. Everyone goes their separate ways. But first..." He turned to Joe and me. "You two take the money and hide it until we can guarantee the police aren't after us."

Joe stood and said, "No. We're not getting involved in this. We're leaving." He gripped me by the arm, and we headed toward our car. George's next words stopped me cold.

"If we get caught with this money, we'll tell them you helped us. And we'll be sure to tell everyone who the two of you really are to each other."

I don't know why I was surprised. Of course they knew. We hadn't been all that careful around them.

Joe may have wanted that, may have wanted this moment to force it to the surface, so we could find someplace to settle down, rent an apartment, and live together for as long as I'd have him. I couldn't do any of those things. I couldn't even let this thief

*tell the police about us. Even if we were cleared of
any involvement in the robbery, the truth about us
would be in the papers. My family would find out.*

*With one look Joe knew what I was thinking. Without
taking his gaze off me, he spoke to George. "Okay.
What do you want us to do?"*

Kyle laid the journal on his lap. With each word he'd read, each moment he'd spent with Evan, he was getting closer to so many truths he wasn't sure how to live with.

Or how he had lived without them.

*   *   *   *

The bar was dark, smoky. Men were everywhere, dancing, touching, gyrating, but Evan couldn't hear the beat of the music or the noise of the crowd around him.

He moved through the bar, weaving around one man, then the next. The heat of their bodies and the air around them should have warmed Evan, but still he shivered. Snowflakes rained down from the darkness overhead, and his skin grew colder with each splatter of icy snow to flesh.

A tall, shirtless man came in close. A cowboy twice the size of Evan. His mouth moved as he spoke, but there was no sound.

The man grabbed Evan's ass and yanked him forward. He ground his body against Evan's. His touch was cold, and that brought out another shiver.

It was all wrong. Evan didn't want this man's hands on him. He tried to get free of the cowboy's grip.

Then Evan was being yanked backward, and the tall cowboy disappeared into the crowd, a vanishing special effect usually reserved for TV and movies, not reality, not even his dreams. All Evan felt were the hands on his hips, the warm body pressing in close behind him.

He spun around.

Kyle.

The crowd around them was gone. They were alone. In Castillo's. The restaurant was dark and quiet.

"You can't give up," Kyle said. "You are creative and talented, and fuck them if they don't want you. You are going to make it. You can do this." He leaned in close. "We can do this. I want you, Ev.

Want you more than I've ever wanted anyone." Then his lips were on Evan's.

Color and light and sound rushed back to Evan. He closed his eyes and gave in to the kiss, pressing his weight against Kyle. Warmth engulfed him. The sway of their bodies felt like a dance they'd done before but also like nothing they'd shared—like a promise.

Then Kyle pulled away.

Evan seized him by the waist. "No. You are not going anywhere."

Kyle smirked. "No, I'm not." He backed Evan to a wall and whispered in his ear. "Been dying to get you inside my ass." Without delay Kyle spun them around until his back was against the wall. Then he faced it and tugged Evan against his ass.

Evan heard the zip as Kyle opened his jeans. He reached for his own...

* * * *

"Sir, wake up." A train employee was tapping Evan's shoulder. Evan sat taller on the bench and blinked away the haze of sleep.

"I'm sorry to wake you," the train guy said. "But we are going to have to close the observation car. We need to conserve power."

Evan nodded, and the train guy stepped away. Which was good. Evan couldn't stand right then, and if he did there'd have been no hiding what sort of dream he'd been having. All he could think about was what Kyle had said. About sex. The network. And his writing.

Kyle was right. Evan wasn't going to walk away from his career. He was going to have to start over. Pitch to other networks. Write something new.

Even if the network bad-mouthed him to everyone in Hollywood, he'd find a way. He'd do what Kyle said and produce his own work. No matter how small he had to start out. He had lost too much, had given in to so many things over the past ten years. He was not giving up on this.

He was also not giving up on something else.

Surged into action by will and desire and hope, he stood and strode through several cars, the other passengers and train personnel a blur as he made his way. He was determined like he hadn't felt in months. Years.

Hell, like never before in his life.

Chapter Eighteen

Evan slid open the door to their room. Kyle was sitting in the chair by the window, his grandpa's journal on his lap. He closed the book and asked, "Where have you been?"

Evan shut the door behind him and approached. He yanked Kyle from his seat and tugged his shirt up to his armpits, revealing the gorgeous expanse of firm chest. He had to have a taste. He leaned forward and ran his tongue over one nipple, then along Kyle's chest to the other, savoring the crisp scent of cologne, the brush of fine chest hair against his cheek, the warm flesh under his tongue.

"Oh God." Kyle wrestled his shirt the rest of the way off. He dropped it to the floor and grabbed the back of Evan's head. "Come here." He dragged him up, and their mouths met in a slow, long kiss, all tongue and light touches of lips, like Kyle had no plans on stopping.

Or maybe he did. He pressed his forehead to Evan's. Their heavy breaths mingled in the space between them. "Are you sure?"

Evan laughed. "Shut up." He popped the top button on Kyle's jeans and unzipped them, purposely letting the backs of his fingers brush over Kyle's stiffening erection. This was a chance worth taking. He kissed Kyle again, mouth open wider, tongue more insistent, and Kyle barreled forward into it with as much intensity. When they pulled apart again Evan said, "We are doing this. No stopping this time."

"No stopping." Kyle kicked his shoes and pants off.

When Kyle was down to his underwear, Evan grasped him by the waist and drew him backward, then spun them around and pushed him onto the bed. Kyle's eyes widened, and he bounced as he landed on his back. Evan followed him down until they were exactly like they'd been the night before, his body straddling Kyle's, Kyle staring up at him, a pleading look in his eyes this time.

Yet, even with their promise of not stopping, Evan had to tell Kyle one truth before they went any further. He leaned in close, his T-shirt-covered chest pressed to Kyle's bare one, and spoke with his lips against Kyle's ear. "I want you to fuck me, but please don't touch me if you're going to freak after and leave. Don't walk out that door to find someone else to fuck. I can't watch you walk away from me to another guy again."

"I…" Kyle clasped him tighter and bucked his body against Evan.

Evan sat up and pressed his palms to Kyle's bare abs, restraining him to the bed. "You what?"

"Ev…I…" Kyle rolled his head to the side and tried to move again, but Evan had him sufficiently pinned in place. He wouldn't look at Evan.

He wasn't getting away with that. Evan cupped Kyle's cheek and forced him to make eye contact. "You what?"

"I don't ever want to leave this room. This bed. You. You're all I want." In a rush he flipped them and rolled on top of Evan.

The weight of Kyle's body and the touch of warm lips to his own lit up every nerve ending, and when Kyle opened his mouth and pressed his tongue into the kiss, Evan gave in and let himself feel it all.

Hard, intense, like no other kiss he'd ever had. They grabbed at each other, clutching, stroking any flesh they could reach.

Another minute of that kiss, and Evan had to move. He flipped them so he was on top again. He'd never felt so driven, determined. Like an express train with one destination. "I want you." He slid a hand inside Kyle's underwear. "I want you inside me."

Kyle's abs quivered with Evan's words, and his eyes widened as Evan finally held what he'd longed to for years.

He stroked the length of Kyle's cock, feeling it firm more at his touch, exploring the head with his thumb, pushing at the slit. Kyle moaned. Evan wanted more of that sound. He leaned over Kyle, and using one hand, he forced Kyle's arms above his head and held his wrists together on the bed. Evan gave him a soft, slow kiss and said, "I'm going to ride you until you scream."

"Fuck!" Kyle bucked up again.

Evan pulled back until he was kneeling over Kyle, their bodies no longer touching. He tugged on the edge of Kyle's underwear, letting the fabric snap back to skin. "Get these off." He swung off Kyle and stood beside the bed to undress. His shoes and T-shirt off first, his pants and underwear next, and then he was naked, every inch of his skin tingling, feeling so alive, waiting for Kyle's touch. He stroked his erect cock at the thought of getting back on the bed, of learning every detail of Kyle's body, and of finally having Kyle's dick in his ass.

Kyle hadn't moved. He lay on his back, mouth parted, his gaze roaming up and down Evan's naked body, his arms still lying overhead, the head of his cock sticking out the top of his briefs. Evan wanted a taste, wanted to feel his lips slide over that dick, wanted for it to finally be his mouth that was making Kyle explode with pleasure.

Like an instinct that could never be denied, he was on the bed again—on Kyle—and had his tongue gliding over and around the head of Kyle's dick, taking in the first taste of him.

"Oh God, Ev."

Hearing those three words repeated in the same way Kyle had shouted them out when they'd been jerking off at the apartment, and Evan was lost. To the sensations, the tastes, the sound of his own slick mouth working Kyle's cock, the ragged breaths pouring out of Kyle. He swirled his tongue, sucked and kissed, worshipping the tip of Kyle's dick, wanting more—so much more.

He clasped the waistband of Kyle's underwear. "You were supposed to take these off." He sucked his cock in again, moving down the shaft, sliding the underwear out of the way as he revealed each inch of that gorgeous dick, as he worked his mouth farther down.

"Ev!" Kyle jerked his hips forward, pushing more of his cock into Evan's mouth. "Sorry."

Sorry for what? This was exactly what Evan had been waiting for. He planned to take his time. Explore and taste and lick and suck until Kyle's cum coated the back of his throat.

"Not going to last," Kyle said as he thrust upward again.

That would never do. Because Evan also wanted something else. He let go of Kyle's dick and stripped the underwear over his hips. As Evan lowered the briefs, Kyle raised both legs in the air to aid in the task, but at the same time presenting his ass in a "please fuck me" pose that surprised the hell out of Evan. He gripped his own cock again at the thought of fucking Kyle.

God, he wanted it all.

No need to decide, though. Kyle took care of that. The underwear off and on the floor, Kyle lowered his legs and dived to the side of the bed, rummaging around in his backpack. He came back with a condom and lube, the condom package already torn open, the lid to the lube popped up. His dick, looking thick and red and ready to explode, slapped against his abs as he flopped back to the bed. He was going to feel amazing inside Evan. Kyle dropped the lube to the bed and rolled the condom on himself. He reached for the lube again.

"No." Evan grabbed for it. "Let me." He fumbled with the bottle and squeezed out far more than they'd need for three rounds of fucking.

Kyle laughed. "That's the good shit. You don't need that much."

"You afraid we'll run out?" Despite the confident tone of his voice, Evan's hand shook as he spread the slick lube on Kyle's dick. Kyle moaned again, and Evan couldn't resist. He kept stroking and leaned forward. "We're going to need a truckload of lube for how much I plan to do this before we get off the train."

With the words barely out, Kyle captured Evan's mouth in a fierce kiss. He ran a hand through Evan's hair, the touches soft and slow and in contrast to the intense kiss, to the way Kyle was moving, fucking Evan's hand.

Evan let go and sat back. A ton of lube still coated his right hand.

Kyle laughed again, but this time the sound was shaky, edgy. He scrambled to reach something on the floor beside the bed and threw Evan a pair of underwear. "Here, wipe it off on that."

Evan caught the briefs—Kyle's briefs—and cleaned his hand. He gave Kyle a measured, teasing smile. "You know what I did last week?"

Kyle shook his head. Maybe he couldn't form words any longer.

"You left a pair in the bathroom. I stole them and jerked off with your underwear wrapped around my cock and balls.

"Shit." Kyle made a move to roll them again.

"No." Evan squeezed his thighs around Kyle's legs. "I'm riding you."

Kyle sank back to the bed, and Evan forced his arms above his head again, then gripped Kyle's cock and positioned himself over it. Kyle squirmed under him, and Evan laughed. "You want this?"

"Fuck yes."

"Then lie still." He worked Kyle's cock between his ass cheeks.

Kyle groped above his head on the bed. With no headboard, there wasn't much for him to hold on to. Right as his cockhead entered Evan, Kyle clasped on to the top edge of the mattress, or cushion or whatever it was called when a bench on the train became a bed. "Ev!"

Evan had been right. About so many things.

About how perfect Kyle would feel inside him. About how good it would sound to hear Kyle call out his name in bed. About how much he'd want to keep doing this. Again and again.

He shifted up and down until he had every last inch of Kyle's dick buried inside his ass.

Oh God. Kyle...inside him, spreading him open. He'd waited so long for this.

Kyle had his eyes squeezed shut. He was breathing through his nose, his teeth clenched.

Evan stilled. "Hey."

"What?" Kyle's eyes flew open. "What's wrong? Why'd you stop?" He barely unclenched his teeth to speak.

"Nothing's wrong." Evan moved again, pausing with the full length of Kyle's dick buried in his ass, loving that it was his body making Kyle barely able to speak. He rolled his hips, and Kyle grunted out another sound of pleasure.

"Shhhh. Train. Rooms. People." That was all Evan could manage. Every movement of his ass dragging over Kyle's dick had his own cock on fire. He needed… "Kyle…"

In a rush, Kyle let go of the bed and took Evan's dick in his hand. He didn't bother with slow and steady. He planted his feet, pumped his hips off the mattress, and plowed into Evan while he stroked Evan like crazy, like he had to drive them both to the edge right then or die trying.

Evan clutched the bar that ran the width of the bunk above them. He wanted to take hold of Kyle and kiss him, but he didn't dare move for fear they'd lose this moment.

Or that he'd wake up.

If this was a dream, he didn't want it to end until Kyle exploded inside him, until he came too, covering them both in his cum.

His brain couldn't settle on any one sensation. The press of their naked bodies together for the first time. Kyle's hand working his cock. Kyle pumping inside him. It was all more intense than he'd imagined.

The silence left in the wake of the halted train and the wind dying down between storms was gone. Their sounds filled the room. The slap of skin against skin. Kyle's grunts. Evan's own little moans as Kyle took his ass again and again.

The upward thrusts picked up speed, and Kyle's hand stilled on Evan. He gave one last slam and groaned as he came. His eyes squeezed shut, and heavy breaths poured out of his open mouth.

A minute passed, maybe two, and Kyle's breathing slowed. His hair was more disheveled than usual and sweat beaded along his hairline. He looked like he'd flown a world away, then back and knew every last secret to happiness. He looked delectable. His eyes opened, and he smiled at Evan. "Come here." He pulled Evan forward by the hip and gripped the base of the condom as his cock slipped out.

Evan went to move out of the way so Kyle could get rid of the condom, but Kyle held on to his hips and kept pulling until Evan was straddling his chest. He seized Evan's cock again, slowly working his hand up and down the shaft. "I want to watch you. I've never seen you shoot out a load. Never seen those gorgeous blue eyes while you come."

The words were almost as good as the feel of Kyle's hand on him again. The two together had him ready to burst. He forced his eyes to stay open as Kyle kept staring at him. Kyle's hand moved faster, and that was it. Evan's orgasm shot out from his middle and exploded throughout him. His toes curled, catching the thin blue blanket in the grasp of his right foot. His cum splashed onto Kyle's cheek. The next spurt landed in the hair above Kyle's ear. After all the jerking off lately, he didn't think it was possible to come that long or that hard. He collapsed forward, his chest pressing against Kyle in the process, the cum smearing between them.

Kyle let out a long breath. "Oh man."

"Yeah." Evan laughed and lifted up so Kyle could breathe. The laugh felt like his first real one in months. Years.

"Why…" Another long breath surged out of Kyle. He threw his arms above his head like he'd been lying when Evan had taken his dick in. "Why the hell did we wait so long to do that?"

Evan rolled off him and smacked Kyle on the arm. "I was practically married." The bed was small for two people. Too small. Oscar must not have ever tried to lie in one with his wife, unless she was one-tenth his size.

"Oh yeah," Kyle said. "I forgot." He got rid of the condom and faced Evan. He had cum drying on his cheek. "You weren't practically married that night in Iowa. Or for the past six months."

Evan threw a hand over his face. "God, we were stupid."

"Uh-huh. So stupid." Kyle sounded relaxed like he hadn't since Evan had moved in with him.

"It was dumb of me to worry so much."

"Yeah, it was. You know what else I think?" Kyle stretched, looking even more content. How long had it been since he'd had sex? For Kyle, going two weeks was probably a record. Evan forced that thought away. He didn't want to wonder how what they'd just done compared to anything—or anyone—else Kyle had done before.

"What?" he asked.

"We are doing that again," Kyle said.

"Oh yeah. We are."

"Come here." Kyle reached out for him. Evan was about to ask if he really thought he could get it up again that fast, and then Kyle tugged on him until Evan's head lay on his chest.

Evan heard Kyle's heartbeat, smelled his own cum, could practically still feel Kyle in his ass, but what stood out the most, what he hadn't expected, was the intimate, tender way Kyle touched him, one hand in his hair, the other sliding along his bare back. Evan squeezed his eyes shut and tried to mentally capture every caress, everything about the past few minutes. The way Kyle had sounded when he came. His smile afterward. The words he'd said when he'd made Evan move closer so he could jerk him off. Evan ran a hand down Kyle's chest and abs, needing to memorize the body he'd dreamed of for so long. He slid his hand lower, over the flaccid cock and balls.

"You can play with it all you want, but I am not getting it up again right away. You wrung me dry."

"I'm not trying to get you up again." Evan lifted his head and rested his chin on Kyle's chest. "Not yet. But soon."

"Oh yeah? I believe you said something about a truckload of lube."

Evan felt his face blush. He never said things like that. Never.

Kyle stroked his cheek. "There they are."

"What?"

"Your dimples. Fucking adorable. They only show up when you make a certain smile."

Evan dropped his head to Kyle's chest again. "Shut up." He hated his dimples, and he didn't think his heart could take Kyle talking to him like that. Who the hell was this, and what had he done with Kyle Bennett?

Although this had to mean something to Kyle too. He wouldn't be cruel, not on purpose. Evan didn't want to think about that right then. He was always thinking too much. Time to enjoy the moment, the quiet, the peace. "Uh, the train's still not moving."

"Yeah," Kyle said. "I don't fucking care."

"I thought I felt it start again while we..." Kind of stupid of him not to be able to say the words.

Kyle huffed out a laugh. "Yeah, me too." He ran his hand down Evan's back again. "I haven't felt this good in a long time."

"Me either."

They lay in the quiet for another minute, and then Kyle broke the spell. "Ev...I..." He hesitated, then sat up and swung his legs off the side of the bed. His back to Evan, he said nothing for a long moment. He ran his hand through his hair and stood. "I'm gonna hop in the shower quick before they cut off the water."

After Kyle stepped into the small bathroom, Evan rolled to his stomach and tried not to think about what Kyle had been about to say. Or why he hadn't said it. About what he might be thinking or feeling. The pillow smelled like Kyle's cologne. He closed his eyes and breathed in more of that scent. A minute or two later, he heard the bathroom door open.

"Ev..." Kyle stood naked beside the bed, his hair wet from the shower. "What you said before about me leaving. I don't want this to be a one-time thing. I meant what I said—"

Evan sat up and reached for Kyle. He pulled him down to lie on the bed and planted a long kiss on him. Sometimes Kyle thought too much too. "You want me again?"

"Hell, yeah." Kyle flashed a smile. "That was amazing."

"It was." There was a knock on the door. "Oh shit." Evan bit his bottom lip and tried not to laugh. Had they made too much noise? Had the entire car heard them going at it?

"Hang on a sec," Kyle called out. He scrambled off the bed and pulled on his pants. "I'll get rid of whoever it is." He grabbed Evan's shirt and jeans off the floor and tossed them to him.

Evan stood and worked on his pants and T-shirt. He was going to kill whoever was at the door. Who knew when Kyle would ever be like this again?

Kyle opened the door, and Oscar gave a nod. If he hadn't known what they were doing, he would soon. The room still reeked of sex. "Sorry to uh"—he coughed into a closed fist—"bother you, but we've got a situation here. We're looking for a lost little girl. We believe she slipped away while her mom was taking a nap this afternoon."

"Oh man," Kyle said. "I bet I know which little girl that is. Sasha will be lucky if that kid makes it to fifteen."

"Tell me about it," Oscar said. "We're searching all the rooms. Can you boys step out for a minute? I need to check every bathroom and storage space."

Kyle moved into the hall, and Evan followed him out while Oscar looked over their room.

"I hope she's okay," Kyle said.

"Me too." Evan tried to dampen the huge-ass smile, but despite the news about Rebecca, the avalanche, being stuck in the mountains, and the seriousness of everything going on around them, he couldn't contain the excitement.

They'd had sex. And it didn't look like Kyle was freaking. He'd said he wanted more, that it was more than sex for him too. Maybe Kyle wasn't ready for everything, but with time...he might be. Evan couldn't walk away from that.

Sure, there were sacrifices he'd have to make. Kyle might never be ready for the family Evan wanted.

Could he live with that? What about in five years? Ten? Would he resent Kyle?

"Are you okay?" Kyle asked. Those dark eyes were studying him.

"Yeah. I just… I can't believe this." And he didn't mean Rebecca.

Kyle took a step closer. "Me too." Didn't look like he meant Rebecca either.

Oscar came out into the hall. "Thanks, boys."

"Can I help you look for her?" Kyle asked.

"Thanks, but no. Best thing you can do is stay in your room and let us search."

"Can you let me know when you find her?"

"Sure. I'll stop back. Now, please wait in your room."

Evan stepped inside first. Kyle entered behind him and closed the door. He stood motionless, his back to Evan, his hand on the doorknob.

Finally he turned around and was across the room in two large steps. He backed Evan to the far wall. "I want you again." He grabbed Evan's wrists and shoved him against the wall, Evan's hands above his head. Kyle ground his body against him. "I have never been so turned on again this fast. Never wanted anyone more in my life. Can't get enough of you."

Desire thundered through Evan's body, his cock waking up and taking notice of Kyle's proximity, his words. Evan longed for Kyle's mouth on his dick. He hadn't had a blowjob in six months. One thought raced through his mind. *Tell him to get on his knees and suck you.*

He never acted on thoughts like that, never telling any man what to do to him.

Kyle threw his shirt off, then raised Evan's over his head and to the floor for the second time in an hour. He ran his hands over Evan's chest. "You feel so fucking good." He moved his hands lower to his abs. "But you need to eat more. You're too thin." He dropped to his knees and kissed Evan's stomach. One light brush of lips after another, the soft kisses covering Evan's midsection.

It was as if the incredibly kind man Evan had always known had collided with the passionate one from Evan's dreams. He raked his fingers through Kyle's dark hair. Where had this Kyle been all his life? "Are you always such a talker?"

Kyle lifted his head. "Hell, no. You're driving me crazy."

Chapter Nineteen

Kyle stood. He cupped Evan's cheek and brushed his thumb over the moist lips. "God, I love your smile. This mouth." He needed to shut the hell up. At this rate, he'd be caught up in no time for all the years of not saying much of anything to the guys he fucked.

Evan's face flushed. He shook his head, then dropped to his knees. He opened Kyle's pants, slid a hand in, and pulled out his dick. If Evan was trying to distract him from talking, that did the trick. Evan stroked Kyle's cock, his hand moving slowly, feeling achingly fine against Kyle's skin as he hardened and lengthened more. Then Evan moved the pants down and slid his mouth over the top of Kyle's dick. The heat, the suction, those lips, those blue eyes looking up at him. So goddamn perfect.

He ran his hand through Evan's hair, wanting to somehow get closer, touch more than mouth to prick but without giving up that one touch. Evan gripped the base of his cock and set to a rhythm of suck and pump with mouth and fist that had Kyle close before long. He knew Evan would be great at this. He wanted to come inside that sweet mouth. He was close too.

"Gonna come." He grunted out the words, but Evan didn't back off. Another few bobs of his head, and Kyle came, forcing his eyes to stay open so he could watch Evan suck and swallow throughout his orgasm.

When Kyle had given over everything left in his balls, Evan sat back on his heels and looked up at him. "I've wanted you to come in my mouth for so long."

"You have?" Kyle swiped a finger along Evan's lower lip, wet with moisture and remnants of his cum.

Evan nodded, eyes wide, breathing heavily. He leaned in to the touch and licked Kyle's finger. "Better than frosting."

The wave was once again crashing against Kyle. He kicked off his pants, dropped to his knees, and pushed Evan to his back on the floor.

He kissed him everywhere, wandering his tongue over every inch of Evan's upper body, breathing in his scent. Evan made a noise, a whimper. It sounded amazing. Kyle brushed his hand over Evan's cock still trapped inside the jeans, and Evan whimpered again.

There was more where that came from—and Kyle wanted it all.

He buried his face in Evan's abs and breathed deep as he undid the jeans. He needed to feel Evan's cock in his mouth for the first time. Apparently, he wasn't the only one.

"Suck me," Evan said, his voice rough and stern but low, almost a whisper.

Kyle lifted his head. "Say that again."

"Suck me." Evan grazed the pad of his thumb over Kyle's lips like he'd done at Castillo's when he'd wiped the frosting from Kyle's mouth. Had that only been two days ago? Evan traced Kyle's lips again. "I want to fuck this beautiful mouth."

Kyle had no words. That was okay. He could do nothing except exactly what Evan wanted—needed—from him. He stripped off Evan's pants, gripped his cock in his hand, and pressed his mouth to the tip. He opened wider, ran his tongue around the crown, getting Evan good and wet, letting his saliva drip down the length. Then he worked his way along the shaft to Evan's balls, wetting them just as much, teasing, tugging.

He wasn't sure if he pushed at Evan's legs or if Evan lifted them first, but there was his ass. Kyle couldn't resist. He wandered his tongue behind Evan's balls and rimmed the hell out of him, licking, flicking, stabbing his tongue inside, the sensations so new and hotter than he'd ever imagined. The wet slurps mixed with Evan's sounds of pleasure. When the begging started, Kyle went back to Evan's cock and sucked him all the way in.

Evan touched Kyle. Ran his hand through his hair, over his shoulder and back up, along his jaw to his mouth where they were connected cock to lips. "Oh God...Kyle." Evan whimpered again. Then he let out a long moan as Kyle took him in deep.

It was only then Kyle remembered where they were. The top deck of a passenger train. Not the most soundproof walls and floors. He pulled off and laughed. "Shhhh." He reached up with one hand and covered Evan's lips.

Evan sucked Kyle's fingers into his mouth. That spurred him on. He took Evan deeper, moved his mouth faster.

With each upward drag of his lips, Evan pounded a hand on the floor. The people in the sleepers below wouldn't miss that. Kyle slipped his fingers free of Evan's mouth and placed his hand under

Evan's. Evan clasped it in his. Kyle had never done anything with a guy while holding his hand. The intimacy of that one touch should've scared the hell out of him. It didn't. This was Evan.

He was going to make this a moment Evan would never forget. But this was more than something he was doing for him.

Kyle liked touching a man's cock with his hands and mouth, but he'd never gotten off on sucking dick like a lot of men did. Some guys were content with going at it from that angle, then jerking off in their own hand after the blowjob.

Then there were the assholes who didn't give a shit about what the other guy wanted. They were polite about the condom and lube when it came to the fucking, but when it came to the sucking, they'd grab the back of a guy's head, ram their dick inside, and choke the shit out of him until they came down his throat. Most continued to grunt their pleasure as the other man gagged.

But this…this was Evan, and it was a total turn on taking his cock in, tracing every vein, learning what made him unique, what made him squirm. Kyle was hard again, dying to come just having Evan in his mouth, and with every slight jerk of Evan's hips, every slide of his own mouth on Evan's cock, Kyle's body was aching and feeling more alive than he had in…forever.

He wanted more.

He pulled off and flipped them so Evan was straddling him. "Fuck my mouth, Ev."

Evan stared down at him, wide-eyed. Then in a flash he moved up and guided his cock to Kyle's mouth. It didn't take long before Evan was pumping his hips and moaning in concert with the slick sounds of their bodies coming together.

In another rapid move that startled Kyle, Evan rolled to the side and gripped him by the arm.

"What? You want to stop?" No one ever stopped. Not once a mouth was on their dick.

"No." Evan leaned forward and kissed him, the hard, uncoordinated kiss of a man about to come. He drew back again. He was breathing heavily, his expression so serious. "I love you."

Kyle's chest tightened. Three little words he'd never wanted to hear from a man. He yanked Evan on top of him, their naked bodies touching all along their lengths, Evan's hard, wet cock like a brand against his skin. "Say it again."

The tension in Evan's features softened. "I love you. Always have."

Kyle brought Evan to him and pressed their foreheads together. "I can do this, Ev. I know I can."

Evan didn't say anything right away. Then he slowly flashed a teasing smile. "You can give a blowjob?"

"Fucker." Kyle poked him in the side. "That's not what I meant, and you know it." Evan returned the playful touches. They laughed and rolled around on the floor, turning it into a wrestling match. In short order, Evan was getting the better of him. Kyle said, "If you don't stop, I'm not going to suck you off while I have my finger up your ass."

That did it. Evan stopped. He lay perfectly still on his back.

Kyle crouched over him. He looked into the bluest eyes he'd ever seen and said, "I can do this." Then he slid down Evan's body, sucked him into his mouth, and ran a wet finger along the crease of Evan's ass. The first time he nailed his prostate, Evan cried out with his loudest response yet.

At this rate, they'd be lucky if they didn't get an official letter banning them from ever taking the train again.

Chapter Twenty

Kyle snored softly, and Evan muffled a laugh. Kyle had always been able to fall asleep quickly. No matter where. No matter what else was going on. While Evan had been lying beside him for fifteen minutes, staring at Kyle, imagining what it would be like to go to sleep with him every night and wake up next to him every morning. Which made him feel like the teenager with a crush he'd once been.

He forced himself to focus on everything that had actually happened in the past few hours.

The sex had been so intense. He couldn't remember it ever being like that for him. Explosive. Primal. Like he was able to finally let go—to be himself—to give and take, to love and fuck and laugh. He hadn't known sex could be like that.

He needed to think. How do you keep the most promiscuous man you'd ever known from walking away?

How do you make a life with someone who didn't want the same things?

Maybe it wouldn't be so bad not to be a father. Kids were a lot of work, after all. Sasha had to be going nuts worrying about Rebecca. Oscar hadn't come by to tell them they'd found her yet. Were all kids so dang difficult?

Yeah, maybe it wouldn't be so bad. His family might be smaller than he'd been thinking, but he'd have Kyle.

He sat up and took in the sight of Kyle again. The thin, blue blanket was barely covering his ass, leaving his back and arms and broad shoulders on display. Evan wanted to touch him everywhere so there was not one inch of Kyle's skin he didn't know by heart. But that had him back to feeling like his former teenage self with daydreams of a boyfriend taking him to the prom and telling him he loved him.

Kyle's dark hair was sticking out all over. It had a more disheveled look than normal. Evan slid his fingers through the dark strands above

Kyle's ear, loving that it was he who'd given Kyle his signature just-fucked look this time.

The growl of Evan's stomach distracted him. The dining car would be opening soon. Dinner in bed followed by more sex sounded good.

He carefully slid off the bed, washed up, got dressed, and headed out. At the end of the hall, Oscar and another train employee were talking. Oscar stood with his shoulders hunched forward, no toothy smile, no Santa hat. He looked exhausted.

"We need to stay calm," he said. "If she did get off, you probably shut the door, and she's waiting outside. Have you checked yet?"

"That's where I was going," the other man said. He headed for the door at the far end of the car. "Like this isn't already the train ride from hell, being stuck out here, running low on everything. Now this kid."

"Rebecca?" Evan asked as he hurried toward the two men.

Oscar jumped at the sound of Evan's voice.

"She's still missing? Did she get off the train?"

"Someone spotted her five minutes ago," Oscar said. "She was running down the aisle of one of the coach cars, but we haven't seen her again. I'm sure she's fine. We're just trying to think of everything. We'll find her. Don't you worry." He turned back to the other employee and said, "You have to go look. Now."

"I know. Damn, I liked this job." They moved into the vestibule, and Evan followed through the dining and observation cars. They reached the first coach car and stopped. Sasha was in the aisle. Two train employees had a hold of her by the upper arms. She was screaming to be let go, trying to make her way to the stairs that led to the nearest exit.

The train's conductor, a short, round man wearing a blue blazer and matching tie with the standard conductor's hat, was speaking to her. He had his hands on his hips, a phone and two-way radio hung from a belt visible under the blazer. "Ma'am, I'm here to help you, but she could not have gotten off the train."

"I know she got off. She wanted to see if there are more cabins out there. She's been talking about them since we stopped."

"I assure you, she couldn't have gotten the door open on her own."

"Well…" the train employee next to Oscar said.

The conductor looked his way. "Well what?"

"I had the door open right after she was spotted. You said to check the drifts along that car. I was distracted for a moment, and I think…"

"What?"

"She could've slipped by me."

"Dammit. Did you check outside?"

"It just occurred to me she might have gotten out. I was on my way to look now."

The conductor pointed to the steps that led to the main door for the car. "You and Oscar go. Look for footprints."

The two men left, and Evan went farther into the car, passing Nate and Penny who were seated two rows in front of where Sasha stood in the aisle. Penny gave a slight wave, but she didn't flash her usual smile. Evan nodded and went to Sasha. He didn't like the way the train employees had their hands on her. "Sasha…"

She let out a panicked sigh when she saw him. "Rebecca is outside. I know she is."

"They went to check."

Oscar returned and whispered to the conductor. "There are footprints at the bottom of the steps. They look the right size."

"Oh God." Sasha gripped Evan's forearm.

"Can you tell which way she went?" the conductor asked.

Oscar shook his head. "There are several sets of her tracks, like she ran back and forth along the train. If she walked off, I can't tell where she went. The wind's blowing like crazy."

"I have to go find her." Sasha lunged for the stairs. "She's not wearing her coat."

The two employees stopped her again.

"You need to wait here," the conductor said. "I'll call for help and send my crew out to search for her." To Oscar, he said, "Tell everyone to get their coats on. Kitchen staff too." He headed for the door leading to the next car.

"I'm not staying here," Sasha cried out.

Evan wrapped an arm around her shoulders. "It's going to be okay." She leaned in and cried against his chest. "I've got her," he said to the two men, and they let go. Sasha wouldn't do any good outside in her current state. He patted her on the back. "You need to be here for when they find her and bring her back to you. I'll go help them look."

She lifted her head, tears in her eyes.

"We'll find her," he said. "I promise. You be here to take care of her."

She nodded.

Evan gave her shoulders a final squeeze and helped her into her seat. Then he jogged after the conductor, catching him before he reached the door. "I'd like to help with the search."

"Just take your seat and let us handle this."

The gorgeous gray-haired man from the observation car the day before, who still could be a thief if he was lying about his alibi, stepped forward. "I'm retired law enforcement. If she's outside, you need to find her now. I'll help with a search."

"I'll help too," another man said, then a couple of women in their early twenties stepped forward.

Nate stood to join the volunteers, and Penny seized his arm. "You cannot go out there."

"I can too."

More passengers stood, and murmurs filled the car.

Evan clutched the conductor's arm before he turned away again. "It'll be dark before long. Even with every employee you've got on this train, you need help, and you know it."

The conductor sighed. "I'm going to be fired for this."

* * * *

Kyle awoke, and for a minute, nothing odd registered. He hadn't been asleep for long. Extending the nap sounded good. He rolled over, and then it hit him. Evan had been beside him when he'd fallen asleep. He sat up and scrubbed his face with his hands, unease settling over him. A series of lies ran through his mind before he landed on the truth. He would have liked waking with Evan in his arms.

Especially after what they'd spent the afternoon doing.

"I'm going to ride you until you scream."

He'd heard horny guys say all kinds of shit when they were fucking, but no one's words had ever had such an effect on him. No one had ever shown him being the bottom didn't have anything to do with giving up control. Or maybe they had. He just hadn't cared to notice.

The best sex of his life, and he'd lain there on his back, watching Evan sit on his cock, letting Evan boss him around.

Who was he kidding? He'd loved Evan like that. So confident. So sure of what he wanted. It was a side of Evan he'd never seen—a side he wanted to see a lot more of.

Would he get that chance? Evan loved him, always had. Then why hadn't he ever said anything? *Because he can't trust you. He thinks you're going to hurt him. Again.*

The wind howled outside, and the train rocked. A new storm had moved in, and their room was colder than before. He got up and went to the window. It was getting close to dusk. Would they be spending the night stuck on that mountainside? Evan had probably gone for food. Man could not live on sex alone. Even fantastic fucking sex.

Kyle pulled clean clothes from his bag and got dressed. He grabbed his phone. Not a great signal, but he dialed anyway.

Lorrie answered. "Kyle?" She sounded alarmed. "Are you guys still stranded?"

"Yep. They can't get us moving until some equipment gets here."

"I'm glad you called. Everyone is freaking out." Her voice was cutting in and out.

"Why?" he asked.

"The folks don't think you'll be home in time for Christmas. You're still so far away. Whose brilliant idea was it to take the train?"

That would be Evan's brilliant idea. The man had never had a better one.

"I'm sure we'll get moving soon. All we can do is wait it out."

"Waiting?" she asked with a lilt to her voice. "Is that all you've been doing? You and Evan haven't—"

"I think I broke his heart." Of all the things he could've told Lorrie, why that?

"Already? What the hell did you do?"

"Not now. Ten years ago. He's scared." What had Evan said? *I can't watch you walk away from me to another guy again.*

Like he'd done in that bar in Iowa. He'd hurt Evan more than he'd known, given it had been ten years and Evan still used that as a reason they needed to keep apart. Although, they hadn't done so well at keeping apart.

He'd told Evan he didn't want to leave him, and he'd meant it too. Could he keep that promise? Evan would expect him to be faithful. Monogamy. One person. Forever? "I don't want to be another asshole who hurts him."

"Then don't be an asshole. The world is filled with those."

"So, then avoiding it is probably easier said than done."

"Kyle, don't think so much. Just let yourself go with the flow, with what you're feeling." Her voice turned serious. "Travel the high of love and sex and see where it leads you."

The door to their room opened, and Evan's reflection in the window stared back at him. The expression on his face said it all. Something was wrong. "I have to go, Lorrie. I'll call you later." He hung up and faced Evan. "What happened?"

"Rebecca's still missing. She got off the train a few minutes ago."

"What? How?"

"She slipped out while someone had the door open. Probably went looking for more cabins. They're putting a search party together. I figured you'd want to go too."

"Hell, yes."

Evan dug through his bag. "We have to hurry. I just came to get my coat, and you." He pulled on a sweatshirt, then got out his hat and gloves.

Kyle grabbed his own winter gear, including the red scarf from his mom. "You should take my coat. It's warmer."

"That's stupid. What the hell would you wear?" Evan picked up his coat. "Let's go."

When they reached the lounge car, the room was full, people standing everywhere, all talking. Evan pointed to a man conversing with what looked like a group of kitchen staff in the corner, all dressed to head out. "The conductor," Evan said. "I guess he's running the show."

The men and women with the conductor looked scared shitless at the idea of going out into the storm. Kyle couldn't blame them.

The gray-haired potential thief approached the conductor and exchanged a few words with him. Evan indicated the man with a nod. "That guy we thought broke into our room is a cop. Said he was retired law enforcement."

So maybe not their thief.

Oscar stood near the conductor too, dressed in a long coat, the Santa hat gone, replaced by a wool cap with flaps over his ears. He spotted Kyle and gave a nod.

The conductor faced the crowd and spoke. "Okay, here's the deal. We've called for a search chopper, but they can't take off in this weather. So we're on our own until an official search-and-rescue team can get here. We go out in groups of two. All passengers are to be teamed with a train employee. Some employees are here in the lounge car. The rest are already searching the immediate area around the train. We have several two-way radios and a few compasses. We'll hand those out to as many as we can. Other than that, each team be sure you have a phone with you. Every employee has my number. No one is getting much of a signal right now, but at least try to call if you find her or you get lost. Each team will head out in a straight line for fifteen minutes, then turn around and come back to report in. You are to stay within sight of your search partner at all times. No exceptions. The little girl's name is Rebecca. She has on a pink sweat suit and is not wearing a coat or hat. As best we can tell, she's been out there for"—he checked his watch—"fifteen minutes now. If you find her, get her as warm as you can and get her back here fast. We have a passenger who is a retired physician who will be standing by. Any questions?" The room remained silent. "All right. Let's move."

Oscar and a woman Kyle had seen working in the lounge car quickly headed their way. The woman stood five foot nothing and looked like one strong wind would knock her over. She wouldn't be much help in carrying the little girl, let alone assisting someone larger back to the train in an emergency.

"I'll head out with one of you," Oscar said.

Kyle liked that idea. "Go with Evan."

Before Evan could speak, Kyle gave a nod to the woman. "That means you're with me. I'm Kyle."

"Diane." She pointed toward the west side of the train. "We're going this way."

Oscar indicated the opposite direction for him and Evan. Everyone was in a rush to get outside before it was too late to help Rebecca.

"Wait," Kyle said before Evan walked away. He seized him by the collar and kissed him, a quick, hard press of lips, then released him and said, "Take this. My coat's collar comes up higher." He wrapped the red scarf around Evan's neck, tucking it into his coat. He met Evan's gaze. "Be careful." Then he turned away to head out into the storm.

Chapter Twenty-One

Five minutes away from the train and Evan had a sinking feeling in his gut. No one would last long out here. His face stung from the bitter cold wind that came at them from every direction. It whipped the branches of the monstrous pine trees around like they were miniatures from a train set. He had snow caked on his pants from dragging his legs through the drifts piling up all over the uneven terrain.

How had Rebecca gotten two steps away from the train? She sure was a determined little shit.

It would be dark soon. He looked back the way they'd come. They hadn't gone far, and it had only been a fraction of their fifteen minutes, but through the trees and the blowing snow, he could no longer see the train.

Oscar stopped and raised the sweatshirt he wore as a makeshift scarf higher to cover his mouth. He glanced Evan's way, and they exchanged a look. If they didn't find her soon, this would not end well.

"Let's keep moving." Evan had to holler to be heard over the wind.

Oscar nodded and tipped his head forward as he hiked on.

The wind died down for a moment, and Evan heard rushing water, possibly a river. It sounded far off. Then the wind picked up again, and the sound of the water was gone. She'd only have minutes in this weather if she'd gotten wet. If there was a chance she'd fallen into the river, he hoped someone's search path was close enough to find her before it was too late.

He continued forward. With the snow-covered trees, the vast expanse of the wilderness, no houses, roads, or power lines, it was picturesque. He'd have thought it was beautiful, if Rebecca were safe beside her mother in their seats and he and Kyle were still on the train, looking out the windows from the warmth within.

Another two minutes and they hadn't made it much farther.

It was far enough, though.

There, under the shelter of a fallen tree, the pine needles still green, making an enclosure above her head, sat Rebecca. She had her arms wrapped around her knees, her head dropped forward, her cheek pressed against her kneecap.

Evan took off, trudging through another snowdrift like he was under water. He spotted her footprints now where she had walked around the same drift.

"She's here," he called out and pointed toward the fallen tree. He wasn't sure if Oscar heard him, but he kept going.

At the tree, he dropped to his knees before her. Her lips were purple, and her eyes were closed. There was evidence of frozen tears on her lashes and snow along the bottom half of her pants, but the rest of her looked dry. In her right hand, she clutched the photo album she had pulled out at dinner. It was open to the picture of her father.

"Rebecca."

Her eyes fluttered open. "C-c-cold."

"I know, honey." He slid off his coat and wrapped it around her as he picked her up.

"M-M-Mommy."

"I'm going to get you back to your mommy, okay? Hold on." He shifted her around so the coat was covering all of her. As he worked, she closed her eyes again and pressed her cold face against his neck. Her trust, her vulnerability, awoke a part of him he'd buried only a few minutes earlier. He wanted to be a father. He wanted someone to need him, someone he could love and teach and help grow into who they were meant to be. He couldn't pretend to ignore that part of himself. Not for long. Certainly not forever. He held Rebecca closer and said, "You'll see your mommy soon." Her skin was like ice against the warmth of his. They had to hurry.

Oscar arrived at his side. "Is she okay?"

"She's freezing."

Oscar removed his makeshift scarf and wrapped it around her head, neck, and most of her face. "You got her?"

"Yeah." Evan pulled her tighter against his chest.

"Let's go." Oscar helped Evan stand. "This way."

They started back, the three bodies moving in a huddle, Oscar blocking the wind from Evan and Rebecca.

Either they were walking a different route, or the footprints they'd made on their way to find her had already blown over. He hoped Oscar knew what he was doing. Or that he was using the compass.

Evan's foot caught on a tree root buried under the snow, and he tripped forward. He threw his weight to the side so he wouldn't crush Rebecca if he fell. His ankle twisted, and he didn't bother holding back the howl as pain shot through him. He landed on his right hip, Rebecca still in his arms.

Oscar had kept going but stopped with Evan's scream and rushed back to them. He dropped to his knees. "You okay?"

"Yeah. Just twisted my ankle." Evan held Rebecca out. "Here, take her."

She hadn't stirred with the fall, and once she was cradled in Oscar's large arms, she looked smaller than she had under the tree limb. Evan buried his gloved hands into the snow and pushed off the ground. His ankle throbbed as he put weight on it. His socks and pants were covered in more packed snow. At least the ankle was getting a cold compress. It would keep the swelling down.

He waved the other man on. "Go."

Oscar looked scared. Not an expression the big guy had shown yet.

"I'll be okay. Get her to the train. I'm right behind you."

"Okay." Oscar glanced around. "It's impossible to see out here. You should take this." He shifted Rebecca in his arms and held out the compass. "My phone's not getting a signal, but at least you'll know which way to go."

"No. You need it. Just in case." He had to scream to be heard over the wind. "You have to get her warm."

Oscar hesitated. He glanced at Rebecca.

"It's okay," Evan said. "Go."

Without another look his way, Oscar turned and ran off, moving faster than he had while leading Evan. In a matter of seconds, Evan lost sight of him. The wind died down for a moment, and he heard the river again. Thank God she hadn't ended up in the water.

A huge gust of wind slammed into him. He raised Kyle's scarf higher and started for where he'd last spotted Oscar.

He could barely see with the amount of snow whipping around him. So cold. How had Rebecca survived the short amount of time she'd been out in this?

Considering Oscar had taken Evan's coat with Rebecca, how was he going to if he didn't reach the train soon?

* * * *

"Evan's not back?" Kyle had to concentrate to keep from grabbing Penny and shaking an answer out of her.

She was coming down the steps to the first floor of the coach car where everyone had left the train on their search. She focused on the tray she carried with rows of filled coffee cups. "Not yet. So far just you, the prison guard, and his search partner." She pointed to the gray-haired ex-cop. He was wrapping a blanket around a seated, shivering man who worked with Diane in the lounge car.

"Prison guard?" Kyle asked. "Thought he was law enforcement."

"The term is Correctional Officer. And the name's Shepfield." The sound of the deep voice startled Kyle as the man approached. "Can you help me get everyone on board as they return? We need to keep a head count."

"Sure." Kyle planned on waiting by the door anyway.

Before they made it to the end of the car, two more people climbed aboard, one of them the conductor. He shook off the snow covering him everywhere, opened his coat, and asked, "Is she here?"

"No," Kyle said.

"How many are back?"

"Six," Shepfield offered. "Including you."

Penny tried to hand the conductor a cup of coffee. He shrugged it off and helped more people onto the train, getting a report from each, sending them into the dining area to get warm and have something hot to drink.

Kyle helped as much as he could, but as more and more people boarded with no sign of Evan, frustration overtook him. He went to the windows to search the way Evan had gone. No sign of him.

He wasn't waiting any longer. He headed for the door, and Penny shouted, "There she is."

Kyle returned to the window. Oscar was making his way toward the train carrying something—someone—wrapped in a coat. Evan's coat. But Evan wasn't with them. Kyle spun around and raced for the doors where Oscar was headed. By the time he got there, the conductor had taken Rebecca from Oscar and was carrying her up the steps. The girl's eyes were closed, and she wasn't moving. Sasha reached for her daughter.

The conductor said, "Let's let the doc have a look."

The doctor gestured for him to set Rebecca in the first row of seats. He leaned in close. "She's breathing." He stripped the coat off her shoulders and dropped it to the floor. "We need to get her into warmer clothes."

Kyle swiped Evan's coat off the floor and went to Oscar. He was stripping off his gloves, coat, and outer layers of clothing while Penny stood beside him with a cup of coffee. Kyle grabbed Oscar's arm and spun him around. "Where's Evan?"

"He twisted his ankle, but he said he'd be right behind me." Oscar looked out the window into the blowing snow.

Kyle fisted his hands in the fabric of Evan's coat. He didn't have to think about it. "I'm going to get him."

The conductor's voice rang out behind them. "I'm sorry, sir, you can't do that." Then, louder, he said, "No one else is leaving the train until the storm lets up. If we are still missing anyone, the rescue crew and search chopper will be on their way as soon as they can fly."

It didn't matter. Kyle was going.

The conductor gripped his arm. "I'm already going to be in more trouble than I care to think for letting passengers leave the train. I cannot lose anyone else. You stay on board." He returned to where the doctor was examining Rebecca. She had her eyes open and was holding her mom's hand.

Fuck staying on board. Kyle faced the end of the car, but the door was blocked by train personnel. He made his way up the stairs to the second floor. He'd get more clothes for Evan and head out another way. Oscar followed him to the vestibule doorway. "You're going after him anyway?"

"Yes." Kyle went through to the next car and continued on until he reached their room. Inside he grabbed his backpack and took out his laptop, then shoved a sweatshirt and pair of sweatpants inside. He took up Evan's coat again and paused with it in his hands. He was out there. Cold. Alone. Scared?

"You're in love with him." Oscar's voice floated in through the open doorway. "I saw how much he loves you, but I wasn't quite sure what you feel for him."

Kyle stared at the coat in his hands. If Oscar hadn't seen it, maybe Evan hadn't either. And Kyle hadn't bothered to say the words. He'd asked Evan to repeat them, but he had never...

You idiot.

He shoved the coat into his pack.

"You need someone to go with you," Oscar said. "Let me go back and get my gear."

"I'm not waiting. I'm going after him. Now." Kyle zipped shut his backpack and hefted it onto his back. He marched past Oscar into the hall.

"Here." Oscar caught up to him and handed him a compass from his pocket. "Take this. And..." He went to a small locker-type opening in the wall at the end of the car. He removed a flashlight and handed it to Kyle. "It'll be dark soon. There was a slope to my right, and I heard the river, but we stayed on the flatter area of land in a straight path southwest. We didn't make it the fifteen minutes before we found her. It only took a minute to reach her after I first spotted the slope. She was under a downed tree full of pine needles that made a sort of roof for her to hide under. You got your phone with you?"

Kyle pulled out his phone, and Oscar keyed in his number. "There. Call me if you find him or if you get into trouble. Hell, if you get a signal, call me in fifteen minutes either way. If you can't get him back to the train, find shelter, someplace where you can get him out of the weather and get him warm. The steeper areas might have alcoves or caverns."

"When I find him, I'm bringing him back here."

Oscar didn't argue. He said, "I'll open the door for you. Come on."

They headed to the other end of the sleeper car, farther from where they'd left the conductor.

"Be careful," Oscar said. "And come back for help if you don't find him in the next fifteen minutes."

Kyle gave a nod. Better than a verbal lie, wasn't it? He had no intention of coming back without Evan.

Chapter Twenty-Two

Evan had never been so cold. He loved the winters in Ohio every year when they visited for Christmas, but he was usually gone by the time the worst weather hit the Midwest. He'd been in Southern California too long. He wasn't used to this. And he wasn't wearing the right shoes. His toes and fingers stung. His ankle throbbed.

How long had it been since he'd last seen Oscar and Rebecca? He'd followed their path at first, but he lost sight of Oscar's footprints before long.

He should've reached the train by now. They hadn't walked this far to find Rebecca. He couldn't see the edge of the tree line or a clearing ahead where the tracks might be.

He was lost.

The storm had worsened. Maybe he was completely turned around, heading in the wrong direction. It's not like he knew a lot about hiking in a blizzard or hiking at all, for that matter. For all he knew he was walking in circles and would freeze before he ever found the train. He wished Kyle's grandfather were there. He had loved the outdoors and had spent a lot of time camping and hiking. He could've found the way without much effort.

The wind picked up, and a huge gust smacked into Evan. Then it died down without warning.

He heard the rushing water, stronger than before. The river. It was closer now. He was heading the wrong way. There was a clearing ahead. He'd go to the edge of the trees and get a look. Maybe he'd spot the train tracks curving through the mountainside and could follow them back to the train. He rounded the last tree, and the flat ground gave way to a slope, a drop-off that led to the river below. Startled, he slipped on the smooth surface of a rock hanging over the edge. He fell to his ass and tumbled down the embankment, snow kicking up into his face as he went. His right arm scraped the bark of a tree. He just barely missed another larger tree with his head. His injured ankle smacked against yet another. He cried out.

He kept falling, falling, finally landing. Not on hard ground as he expected. Water surged up around him. He flung his arms out to try to keep from going under. No use. Icy water rushed over his head, and he gulped in a mouthful. He couldn't get his feet under him. He thrashed his arms and legs until he found the ground below. He tried to stand, but his foot slipped on a smooth rock, and he landed on his back. More water surged over him. He coughed and choked and floated on the surface. He had to get out of the river, but his body wouldn't help him out.

For a moment, he thought he heard Kyle's voice call out to him.

Then it was gone.

* * * *

Kyle shouted again. "Evan!"

For several minutes, he'd been going straight southwest along the path Oscar had taken. He should've spotted Evan by now. Or at least the location where Evan and Oscar had found Rebecca. The wind had died down, and the snow wasn't kicking up as much as before, but the sun was setting. Soon he wouldn't be able to see much with only the flashlight.

Goddammit. He had to find him. Now.

He was going to kill the little fucker. As soon as he got him safe and warm.

Ahead was a downed tree with packed snow and footprints around it. He rushed forward. There was no sign of him. "Evan." He called again. And again.

Should he head back? Maybe they had crossed paths. The visibility had been shitty when he'd started out. Maybe Evan was already in their room, getting warm, drinking hot coffee.

No. Evan wouldn't be sitting around waiting for him. He was still out here. Kyle was sure of it. He went with his gut and got going again, heading farther away from the train.

He passed by three cabins, each thirty yards apart. He banged on the door and peered inside the windows of each in case Evan had taken shelter in one. All were empty. He pressed on, not allowing himself to think what would happen if he didn't find Evan.

He had to keep going.

But he couldn't be headed in the right direction. If Evan had come this far the wrong way, he would've stopped at one of the cabins. Unless he'd passed them when the wind and snow had reduced the visibility to nothing. He could've been twenty feet away and missed them. Kyle followed the swell of instinct and continued on.

He heard the rush of water. The river. Maybe Evan had used it as a guide and had gone the wrong way from where they'd found Rebecca. Kyle headed for the slope ahead. The roar of the water grew louder, but beneath that was another sound. A scream. Evan crying out.

Kyle charged forward, stumbling over jagged terrain and through a line of trees. He stopped short of falling over the edge of an embankment. The sky was growing darker, but he could still see the river fifty feet below. Amid the chunks of ice drifting in the water floated a red piece of cloth. A scarf, the other end still around Evan's neck. He was lying face up in the water.

"Ev!" Kyle rushed down the rocky hillside, adrenaline driving him on. He reached the edge of the river and didn't hesitate. He waded in.

Two steps and the water was up to his waist. He trudged through it and grabbed for Evan as soon as he was within arm's reach.

He pulled Evan against his chest. "Ev?" He was breathing. His eyes half open.

"Kyle?" His eyes fluttered and opened more.

"Are you okay?"

"Can't...can't feel anything."

"Hang on. I'm going to get you out of here. Just hang on." He dragged Evan backward toward where he'd entered the river, his own legs feeling the stab of icy water soaking through his jeans. Evan was like a deadweight. Kyle refused to let that thought linger. He reached the water's edge and lugged Evan from the river. They fell to the snow-covered ground. Rocks and branches jabbed Kyle in the side. That should've hurt, but he felt nothing. He was wet and cold. And more scared than he'd ever been in his life.

He had to get them moving. He yanked Evan's coat out of the backpack and tugged the wet scarf off Evan, followed by the hat and gloves. He traded them for his own, which were damp on the outside but not drenched like Evan's. Then he slipped the dry coat on him, rolling him to get it in place. That would have to do for now. "Can you stand?"

Evan didn't answer. His breathing was low and shallow, but he was still conscious.

Kyle got to his feet, slid the backpack on, and forced Evan up.

"I..." Evan leaned against him. "I can make it."

"I know you can." He held Evan tighter to him and took a step forward. Evan moved with him, Kyle half carrying him.

They'd never make it back up the hill and to the train like that. Evan was so cold, his teeth chattering and his body jerking with the intense shivers.

Kyle stopped and searched through the side pocket on his backpack for his phone. The bottom of the pack was wet from the river, but the phone was dry. He checked the display. No signal. It was getting dark.

Panic welled inside. He forced it down.

The cabins.

If they could make it to one, he could get Evan warm and dry and rested enough for them to head back to the train. He pulled out the flashlight and shone it around to get a better view. Farther down the embankment, there was a section of the slope that didn't look as steep with fewer rocks and more even ground. They might make that.

"Come on. This way." He got them going along the river, dragging Evan when his steps faltered, heading in the opposite direction of the train. It was their best hope.

When they reached the first of the small buildings, Evan was less alert, leaning more of his weight against Kyle. He hadn't said a word all the way from the river's edge, but he'd managed a few steps on his own. Kyle tried the door. Locked. It was unlikely anyone had come home since he'd pounded on it minutes earlier.

He propped Evan against the cabin wall beside the front door. "I'll be right back. Just stay awake until I come get you."

Evan didn't respond.

Kyle slapped him, then shook him by the shoulders. "Stay awake. Do you hear me?"

That did the trick. Evan jerked his head up and made eye contact with Kyle. He was still shivering. Wasn't that a good sign? Evan gave a slow nod, and Kyle resisted the urge to hold on to him. Instead, he headed for the nearest window, looking along the way for a rock to break the glass. He didn't need one. The window opened without trouble, but the screen was locked. One hard shove and it ripped and came loose, dropping inside the cabin.

He looked back to Evan. He had slumped to his ass on the ground, his head leaning back against the cabin wall.

Every instinct in Kyle told him to go back to Evan, but he had to get him inside. He propped one foot on a log of the exterior cabin wall, gripped the windowsill, and hoisted himself up and inside.

Thank God there was nothing directly underneath the window. He sailed through the opening without stopping and landed on his hands and chest, his shoes stuck on the ledge of the windowsill. He was in a living room. Hardwood floors, a couch, and a fireplace. A dining room at the other end of the house. All he cared about was the front door between the two rooms. He wrestled his feet free, then got himself moving for the door.

The lock gave his freezing, shaking hands trouble, but it didn't stop him for long. He flung the door open and found Evan still slumped on the ground. He was breathing, his mouth open, his eyes closed. Kyle slid his hands under Evan's armpits and hefted him against his body, then moved them inside and kicked the door shut behind them.

Less than ten feet to the couch and he tripped three times over his own numb feet as he dragged Evan across the room. He deposited him on the couch and knelt before him. "We have to get these wet clothes off you." Evan might not have heard him, but he kept talking anyway. "We have to raise your body temperature." Kyle fisted his shaking hands twice to get the blood flowing and then forced his fingers to work on getting Evan naked, stripping off the coat and the drenched clothes, socks, and underwear. He grabbed a quilt from the back of the couch and covered Evan in it, tucking it along his sides like Kyle's grandma used to do when he was a child and would stay at the farm with her whenever he was sick during the school year.

Evan hadn't stirred during the not-so-gentle removal of clothing.

"Ev." Kyle shook him. "You have to stay awake."

Evan groaned. It was the best sound in the world, and the brief glimpse of those blue eyes was the best thing Kyle had ever seen.

It wasn't enough.

He stood. He needed dry clothes and more blankets. He shed his own wet shoes and jeans and slid his backpack and coat off, then dug out the sweatpants and sweatshirt he'd brought with him. Crammed below the clothes was the journal. The sweats were dry, but had the journal gotten wet in the water? He wasn't about to check right then. He ditched the backpack on the floor, pulled back the quilt, and got Evan dressed, then went in search of more blankets. He found two rooms down a short hall. A bathroom and a bedroom. There were several more quilts on top of the made bed. He returned to Evan and covered him with the blankets. His breathing sounded less labored, but he was still too damn cold to the touch. "Stay awake, Ev."

Kyle forced himself to step away again. He closed the window and started a fire in the fireplace. It would take time for the fire to warm the room.

What else?

Body heat.

He stripped off the rest of his clothes and crawled under the blankets to lie behind Evan. He lifted Evan's shirt and brought him back against his own bare chest, letting his rising body heat warm Evan's. All he wanted was for them to be back in his apartment, eating takeout from Castillo's and talking about how hot Jake Gallagher's ass was. He kept moving his hands over Evan's skin, under the sweats, over his chest. He couldn't stop touching him.

Or stop taking in the details of the man in his arms. The disheveled blond hair plastered to the sides of Evan's head. A scrape over his left eye and smaller scratches on his right cheek. The full lips starting to turn a more normal shade of pink.

"Ev, you have to stay awake."

Evan groaned again. Or maybe it had been the word "okay."

Kyle held him tighter against his body. Still too cold. "Don't you dare leave me." He closed his eyes and listened to Evan breathe.

They stayed that way for what seemed like an eternity, but the shivers were gone, and Evan's body was warm to the touch again.

Finally, he spoke. "I feel better."

Kyle let out a long exhale. "Warm?"

"I don't remember warm."

"I'm going to see if there's coffee or something I can heat up for you to drink." He started to get up, but Evan gripped the arm he had across his chest.

"Don't go. Just...stay with me for a little longer."

They were silent, their bodies growing warm at every point they touched, and each man's breath fell in unison with the other's.

Kyle rolled Evan a bit so he could get a better look at him. "Ev..."

"Hmmm?"

He touched Evan's unscratched cheek, fingertips to flesh in a soft caress, emotions he'd promised he'd never feel for anyone surging through him. More than he'd let himself think when he'd realized Lorrie had been right about what he was feeling for Evan. More than he'd felt when they'd had sex on the train. Seeing Evan in that river, he would've given anything to save him.

The swell had returned, and it had taken Evan out to sea. Kyle had no choice but to follow.

He lowered his head until his forehead rested against Evan's temple. He whispered, "I'm scared," and hugged Evan to his chest until there was not an inch of space between them. "I...I love you." He buried his face in Evan's neck, breathing in the scent of pine and outdoors and underneath that, the musky scent of Evan—a very alive and breathing Evan. "I love you so fucking much."

The snore that followed wasn't exactly the reaction Kyle had expected.

Chapter Twenty-Three

Evan awoke sore and stiff. But warm. Hot, in fact.

Flickers of light danced across the walls and ceiling surrounding him. A fire burned nearby, offering an occasional crackle and pop in the otherwise silent cabin. The darkness of night was visible through the window across the room. Evan lay on a couch, Kyle half beside, half behind him, his face buried against the side of Evan's neck. Evan wished he could strip off the sweats he couldn't remember putting on and touch more of Kyle, feel more of his skin pressed against him. Kyle's hands were still moving all over Evan's body, like before he'd fallen asleep. Only these touches were different, more tender, more gentle.

"Uh, Kyle, I'm warm now."

"You sure?" Kyle asked, his voice muffled since he hadn't lifted his mouth from Evan's neck.

"Yeah. That fire is so dang hot, I'm about to sweat to death."

Kyle kept touching Evan, his chest, his stomach. He moved his hand lower, under the sweatpants, the strokes slow, purposeful, and unlike their urgent sexual touches on the train, like he wasn't trying to arouse Evan but experience him.

"I feel like I was out for ten hours. How long was I asleep?"

"Not that long," Kyle said. "How do you feel?"

"Good." With Kyle's focused attention, he was well on his way to feeling damn good.

"How about your hands and feet?"

"They're fine. See." He raised his hands out from under the blanket and bent his fingers several times to demonstrate.

Kyle turned each hand and examined it.

"I said they're okay. Where are we?"

"A cabin." Kyle slid his hand beneath the blanket again and swept a heated palm down Evan's chest to his abs and then lower, over his groin and along the inside of one thigh.

A cabin in the mountains. The two of them alone. Like Evan had been picturing at dinner on the train. "Is Rebecca okay?" His voice hitched. That hand was making it hard to concentrate. And to breathe.

"I think so. They had her back on the train, and the doc was checking her out when I left."

"And then you found me."

"I did. Are you sure you're warm?" Slowly Kyle ran his hand up Evan's thigh and cupped his balls, rolling them, then grazed his palm down the other thigh.

"Yeah. I'm warm."

Who was he kidding? He was on fire. And the burning logs in the fireplace were only part of why heat was blazing throughout his body. He couldn't hold still any longer. He moved under Kyle's touches, his hips shifting forward toward Kyle's hand, then back to meet his body.

Kyle drew his hand away. "Don't move. Lie still and rest."

"I'm fine. Please don't stop." Evan reached back for Kyle and was delighted to find only skin, no clothing to get in his way. He gripped his ass.

Kyle must have liked that. He cupped Evan's chin and kissed him, slowly at first. A kiss to his left eyebrow, his right cheek, his bottom lip. Only then did Kyle grip the back of his head and deepen the kiss, forcing Evan's lips apart with his tongue.

Evan faced Kyle, and without hesitation they were in each other's arms, the kiss turning passionate, their bodies aligning for just the right press of man against man.

Kyle pulled back and threw the blankets off and onto the floor. He helped Evan slide off the couch to the stack of blankets. Then he was on him again, the kisses building with intensity as Kyle flattened his naked body to Evan.

There was no way they could go back to how they were before they'd gotten on the train. Not because of the sex. Because of the way they'd touched, the words Kyle had said. *"I can do this."* He wanted to try, but what would he do when they finally made it to Ohio? Would he pull away?

No. Evan wasn't thinking anymore. He'd never felt so out of control. So on fire. So ready to explode. He thrust up, planting his foot on the blanket-covered floor for leverage. A bolt of pain shot through his ankle. He dropped back to the floor. "Fuck."

"What?" Kyle asked. "What is it?"

"Just my ankle." Evan tried to pull Kyle back down to him, but Kyle shook him off and crawled backward on his hands and knees over Evan's body, peeling the sweatpants off as he went. He slowly lifted them past Evan's ankle and off his foot. He examined the lower leg and, in a slow move, leaned forward and kissed the skin over and around the injured ankle. Kiss after kiss. Each one as gentle as the first.

It was all so different from any way Kyle had touched him yet.

Kyle sat up and stripped off Evan's sweatshirt, then returned to lie over him again. They touched, skin to skin, and somehow the slow move of Kyle against him felt like it was the first time they'd been naked together. Which was stupid. They'd touched and licked and sucked and fucked, but this...this was sensual. Passionate. Loving.

Kyle thrust forward, his dick fully erect and sliding along Evan's hip. Then he shifted, and the next thrust brought their cocks into contact, the sweet slide of their arousals working together to a new level of friction. This was definitely new.

Evan wanted more. He arched his back. "Oh God. Fuck me."

Kyle stopped and held himself above Evan so they were no longer touching. "We can't."

"Why?" He was expecting something about the twisted ankle, the fall into the river, the frigid walk to the cabin, and how he needed to take it easy.

He was already forming his arguments when Kyle said, "No rubbers."

Oh. Evan wrapped an arm around Kyle's waist and pulled him forward until they were back to the intimate touch of a moment before. He leaned in to kiss Kyle and said, "I trust you."

"Jesus." Kyle jerked back before their lips met. "Tell me you've never said that to some guy."

"What?"

"It's not about trust, Ev."

"It is if you're committed to someone."

"I guess, but it's not just about that in the beginning. I'm always careful, and I get tested every year, but I've been fucking other guys since my last test. I'm not going to put you in greater risk than I have to. Not even to slide my cock into you without anything in the way. No matter how much I want that."

"Oh." *Always careful*. Had Kyle ever gone bare with another guy? He'd never had a serious lover, never had a boyfriend, so maybe not. But he wanted that with Evan.

"Wait." Kyle sat up. "My backpack. I've got condoms and lube." He dug in his bag, and several strips of condoms landed on the floor beside Evan.

As Kyle searched the bag again, Evan stared at the massive pile of condoms. Apparently Kyle took the official Boy Scouts' motto to heart. *Be prepared.* Who knew when you'd have a shot at an orgy? "How many guys were you planning to hook up with during the week we were in Ohio?"

Kyle stilled, the lube in his hand, and his eyes widened. "Just you, you idiot."

"Oh. Come here." Evan tugged Kyle back to him. They kissed again, but then a thought stopped him. "Hey, you never told me what happened in that dream."

Kyle shook his head like he was finding the shift from talking to making out to more talking jarring. Which made sense. He'd probably never talked to the guys he was with. He barely knew any of them. "What dream?" he asked.

"With Jake Gallagher."

"Oh, man." He rolled onto his back and laughed, not looking like he was going to say anything more. It took a moment of Evan staring down at him before Kyle gave in. "I didn't like that he was kissing you. I grabbed him by his hair, yanked him away from you, and punched him in the nose. Then I told him to get the fuck out of Castillo's."

"No way."

"Yeah. As soon as he was gone…"

"What?"

"You kissed me, then turned me around, bent me over the table, and fucked the hell out of me."

"I fucked you?"

"Yeah," Kyle said. "Well, we never got to finish since I woke up when that guy broke into the apartment. Since then I've wanted to tell you…" Kyle glanced over his shoulder. "I should add more wood to the fire."

"What did you want to tell me?"

"It's not a big deal. I mean, I guess, I wouldn't mind if we…"

"If we what?"

Kyle intently stared at the ceiling and sighed. "I'd like you to fuck me sometime."

Evan was pretty sure he'd stopped breathing. He sucked in a gulp of air. "I didn't think you were into that."

"I'm not." Kyle gave up on the ceiling. "Not with just anyone."

"Oh. With me?"

"Yeah. I mean, if you want to."

"I want to!" How big of a dork did Evan sound like, practically screaming out the words? But he didn't need to worry. This was Kyle.

Who looked like his own brand of dork not being able to say what he wanted in bed.

Evan stroked himself. He was so damn hard just talking about it, thinking about how Kyle wanted his cock driving into him. "Grab a condom and put it on my dick."

"Now?" Kyle asked.

"Now."

"You feel okay enough to—"

"Kyle, I want your ass. Now."

"Okay." Kyle nodded and reached for a condom. "It's been a while."

A while. Evan liked the sound of that. He'd been on the receiving end enough times over the years to know how to make this good for Kyle. He'd take his time, draw out every sensation until Kyle was begging him to take him. He kissed him and said, "On your stomach." He sat up and took the condom from Kyle's hand, then waited while Kyle positioned himself on the blankets, his curved ass looking irresistible. Evan set the condom aside and stroked that ass, then spread the cheeks.

When his tongue made contact, Kyle rose off the blankets until he was on his knees. "Oh God. More."

He could do more. Evan buried his face in Kyle's ass. He licked and sucked, stabbing his tongue in and out, enjoying the heat of Kyle's body and the all-new begs and moans pouring out of him.

When the words of encouragement cut off and all that slipped out were loud, choppy breaths between the groans, Evan sat up and worked the condom on, then lube. Too much lube, but this time it was on purpose. He couldn't resist. He ran his lubed dick around Kyle's hole, along his crease, and then the skin leading to his balls.

Kyle groaned. "Fuck me, Ev. God, want you inside me."

"Lie on your side."

Kyle did as instructed without delay.

Evan settled behind him, raised Kyle's upper leg over his own, and positioned his cock right where he'd been dying to be for so long.

Before he could enter him, Kyle turned his head and said, "Kiss me."

The vulnerability of that request tugged at Evan's heart. He surged forward and met Kyle's mouth with his own, the kiss all moist lips, tongue, and deep breaths pouring into each other's mouths.

"Are you okay?" Evan asked.

"I'm more than okay."

With those words, the look of lust—and something more—in

Kyle's eyes, Evan pressed forward, and his cock stretched Kyle's body. He gave him a moment to adjust and breathe, then Evan shifted his hips in slow, measured movements until he was finally fully inside Kyle, the snug fit making him crazy. He ached to drive in and out and never stop. He kissed the back of Kyle's neck. "You okay?"

"Yes. You feel goddamn huge. I forgot that part."

Forgot? How long had it been? Evan licked Kyle's neck and sucked on his flesh.

"Oh God. Fuck me, Ev."

That was all he needed. Kyle wanted this. Evan drew back and thrust in. Again and again, focusing on the tight, sweet friction of Kyle's body on his dick.

"Yes, Ev. Yes!" Kyle arched and slammed his ass back.

Evan couldn't believe the pressure around his cock was Kyle. Not his hand, not his mouth, but Kyle's ass. He wanted to go slow, wanted to take his time and really feel every moment. But when they shifted so Kyle was on his knees, his forehead pressed into the blankets, Evan could barely keep from giving in and going at it like he'd never done before.

"Harder," Kyle cried out. "It's okay. Pound my ass. Been fucking dying for this."

Evan let go of any worry, any doubt, and fucked Kyle, grasping the flesh of his hips, burying his cock deep into him with every thrust.

Into Kyle.

His Kyle.

"EV," KYLE CRIED out again. He couldn't help himself. It was Evan. Fucking him. Finally.

"Touch yourself, Kyle."

He didn't think, just did what Evan told him to. He let go of the blanket where he'd been digging in with clenched fingers and reached for his cock. Like the night in his apartment when they'd jerked off at the same time, only this time Evan was taking his ass like he'd been dreaming for months.

That had his balls drawing up.

"Slow at first," Evan said. "I want you still hard when I come."

Kyle followed Evan's instruction. Gathering the lube still left on his balls, he rubbed it along his length in slow strokes while Evan thrust again and again. It was torture. Delicious, aching torture.

He wished it to go on forever, but he also wanted Evan to lose it inside him. He drove his ass backward, his body alive with sensations. The slide of Evan's cock in and out hitting that perfect spot over and over connected every thrust of pleasure in Kyle's ass to his dick. He jerked himself faster, his cock on fire in his fist. He squeezed his ass around Evan's dick, wanting to make this better than anything Evan had ever had. Another squeeze and thrust and Evan groaned loud and long, burying his cock deep inside Kyle's body as he came. They fell to their sides, exactly as they'd started.

"Oh fuck." Evan wrapped an arm around Kyle and plastered their damp bodies together. "That was…"

"Yeah." That was all Kyle managed when Evan didn't say more.

Evan slipped from his body and leaned away to work off the condom. A moment later, he pressed against Kyle's back again, wound an arm around him, and grasped his cock.

That was what Kyle had needed. He let his head fall back to Evan's shoulder. "No one touches me the way you do. No one has ever done to me what you do."

Evan whispered in his ear. "Come for me, Kyle."

He came, every muscle going tight, his body shaking. The release of tension and the flood of emotions—of all he felt for this man—overwhelmed him. A laugh surged out of his chest. He would've hated this moment a few days ago when he'd been living in denial. Before Lorrie had said those words that had scared him more than anything. That was until he'd seen Evan in the river.

The exhaustion from Kyle's two treks through the storm finally hit him. He grasped Evan's arm and wrapped it tighter around him, holding it to his chest. "Love you."

Chapter Twenty-Four

Evan rolled out from under the blanket, careful not to wake Kyle. The fire had died down, and the cabin had grown cooler through the night. He could put more pressure on his ankle as he crossed the room to the window with the screen lying broken on the floor below it. The storm was gone. No more wind, no new snow falling. It would be morning soon. They needed to head back. At first light. He just hoped no one from the train had been out in the dark looking for them.

He knelt before the fire and added the remaining logs from a basket in the corner of the room. They'd need to leave an apology note for breaking in to whoever's cabin this was.

The fire came to life again, and two words kept resurfacing in his mind. *"Love you."*

He'd been so relaxed and ready for sleep after the sex. He couldn't be sure he'd heard Kyle right. His heart had raced, and he'd jerked fully awake when the words registered, but by then Kyle was asleep.

Probably not a good idea to shake the hell out of someone when he was sleeping, looking blissed out on the high of sex. Not when he'd just saved your life. But Evan would've given almost anything to hear those words again. To know for sure.

He returned to their makeshift bed on the floor. He spotted the journal protruding from the top of Kyle's bag. There were yellow sticky notes poking out from several pages. He picked up the journal and lay beside Kyle again. He ran his fingers over the worn leather. Kyle must have known more about the sixty-year-old bank robbery by now. He'd been reading the journal before Rebecca had gone missing.

Evan tried to piece together what Kyle had mentioned about who Victor had lived with in Colorado. A group of Korean War veterans. Living alone in the wilderness and robbing banks. Maybe it was his fall down the mountainside the night before, but he couldn't focus. His mind wandered, and he was off plotting a new story about veterans working for the government to commit acts of domestic terrorism against its citizens in an effort to scare the public and increase federal funding.

He scrambled for Kyle's bag, and the journal slid off his lap. He needed a pen and something to write on. He found both and made notes for the fictional story he'd stumbled upon.

"What are you doing?" Kyle was rubbing the sleep from his eyes.

"I have an idea for a new screenplay."

"Screenplay?" With one quick roll, Kyle was on top of Evan, forcing him to his back, his arms above his head. Evan squirmed under the playful touches until Kyle spoke again. "All those boyfriends and you didn't learn it's impolite to work when you're in bed with your lover?"

Evan froze. Lover. Boyfriend.

Kyle smiled at him and caressed the skin where he'd been holding Evan down a moment before. "I'm glad you're still writing."

"I'm not letting one job and an asshole run me away from this."

"Good. Because I don't want to kick your ass. I much prefer eating it."

"I noticed that on the train."

"Never done that to any guy before."

All those men and he'd never... "You haven't?"

"I'm not a total slut." He laughed. Slowly, the laughter died off, and Kyle added, "It seemed too personal, too intimate."

"And having your dick inside some guy wasn't?" Although, Evan had always thought kissing was the most intimate act between two people.

"Guess I've been messed up about sex for a while now. I don't know." Kyle waved a hand through the air and asked, "You okay?"

"Yeah. All warm and my ankle hurts less."

"That's good, but not exactly what I meant."

Evan laid a hand on Kyle's chest, his gaze on the body above him. "Yeah. I'm okay." He was more than okay. He looked up at Kyle. "Are you?"

"Don't think I've ever felt this okay." They stared at each other for a moment more. Then Kyle looked to the window across the room. "It'll be getting light in another hour or so. We need to get back. They'll be looking for us, if they aren't already. I just hope we're not the ones holding up the train now."

"Yeah." Evan didn't want to go. Didn't want to lose this moment. "Okay."

"But let's eat and take advantage of a real shower first."

"We shouldn't take their food."

"We already had sex on their blankets. Nothing else could be that rude. We'll leave them some money. You're not walking back without food in you. I'll go see what they have." Kyle leaned forward and planted a quick kiss on Evan's lips, then stood and left the room. Evan settled into the blankets and watched the fire burn.

A moment later, Kyle's warm lips were on his again. "Time to eat."

"Oh man, I fell asleep?"

"Not for long. All I found were some frozen pizzas and fries. Nothing in the way of breakfast food." Kyle set a plate in front of Evan and turned to lie facing him with his own plate of food on the floor beside him. "I tried to call Oscar again, but I'm still not getting a signal, and this place doesn't have a phone."

Evan couldn't stop watching Kyle. Now that they weren't on the train, everything seemed more real, less like he'd been in a dream world. He focused on the conversation and said, "Maybe they never get a signal out here. Storm or no storm."

"Maybe." Kyle grabbed a slice of pizza and took a bite. When Evan didn't follow suit, he said, "Eat."

"I am." Evan bit off the end of a fry and threw the rest back to his plate.

"You fucking eat some pizza, or I really am coming over there to kick your ass."

"You're so bossy." Evan picked up a slice and took a bite.

"I'm only bossy when I'm right."

"Yeah." Evan swallowed and added, "I'm only bossy in bed."

"So I've noticed." Kyle's face flushed. He dipped his head and dragged a fry through the mound of ketchup on his plate, swirling it around with a great deal of concentration. Instead of eating the fry, he asked, "Have you always been like that?"

Evan went for another bite of pizza before answering. "I've never been like that before."

"I liked it."

His cheeks full of food, Evan stared at Kyle. Finally, he gulped down a swallow. "Yeah?" He shoved in another bite before he said something embarrassing.

"It was the best sex of my life."

It suddenly became impossible to swallow. If Kyle didn't stop saying stuff like that, Evan was never going to finish a meal again. He'd choke on everything he tried to eat.

* * * *

Kyle ran his tongue along the skin of Evan's neck, loving the shudder that worked its way through Evan's body.

It reminded Kyle of that night in the hallway at his apartment. Evan up against the wall, their bodies moving together, his lips on Evan's skin, and Evan's hand on his ass. Only this time, they were naked and wet, the warm water of the shower raining down on them, filling the small bathroom with the sound of a light rainfall. Not the best water pressure but better than a freezing dunk in the river.

Kyle bit and sucked at Evan's skin. He liked the idea of a mark on Evan's body coming from him instead of the fall into the river.

Evan gasped and bucked against him.

Damn, he had to quit doing that. Kyle pulled back. "Careful of your ankle."

"It barely hurts."

"Maybe you shouldn't stand. You could get on your knees." He liked that idea. He threw Evan a smirk. "And while you're down there…"

"Nope." Evan pressed on Kyle's shoulders, encouraging him to his knees. "You're going to suck me off." His voice wasn't harsh. It was matter of fact. A statement of what he wanted.

Kyle nodded. He couldn't get enough of Evan's cock. He buried his face against the wet blond hair above Evan's dick and breathed deep, taking in the scent of the soap they'd borrowed, and under that, the scent of Evan's need. He gripped the hard cock in his hand and gave a slow stroke, teasing the sensitive skin under the head. Leaning forward, he licked the tip, savoring the salty flavor.

He'd never get enough of this.

He drew Evan into his mouth, wetting the length with his saliva, focusing on taking in as much as he could, then concentrating on the suction as he drew back.

"God, that feels good." Evan leaned back against the shower wall. "Touch your dick. Jerk off. Make yourself come while my cum fills your mouth."

Holy shit. Evan was going to kill him talking like that. Kyle took hold of his own cock with his free hand and sucked harder on Evan's. Then he did something with his hand and tongue as he pulled up that Evan must have liked.

"Oh God. Do that again."

Kyle did. He didn't think he could get any more creative or give a better blowjob than he was. He looked up and found Evan staring down at him, panting, his mouth open, his tongue wetting his lips. He was close. That inspired Kyle. He bobbed his head faster, his hand on his own cock working at the same speed as his mouth, the two touches in sync. Evan's hand landed on the back of his head. Not holding him there, more like moving with him, becoming a part of the blowjob. Evan's fingers dug into his hair, and a moment later, he groaned and came.

The warm cum hitting Kyle's tongue and the back of his throat felt like an awakening, opening the door to a place where sex wasn't about power or control or taking what he wanted. He sat back and continued jerking off, speeding toward his release.

Evan grabbed Kyle's hand still wrapped around the base of his cock. He sucked two fingers into his mouth. When he released them, he spit on the ends and said, "Stick your fingers up your ass. I want to watch you fuck yourself."

Damn. Where had this Evan been hiding? Kyle reached back and groaned as his fingers made their way exactly where Evan had instructed. He gave several more quick pumps to his dick. "Fuck. Ev!" He fell forward and pressed his forehead to Evan's hip as he shot. And shot. And shot more, coating Evan's calf with his cum. He threw his head back and focused in on Evan's eyes.

EVAN COULDN'T GET over the way Kyle looked right then. On his knees, staring up at him, his wet hair plastered to his forehead in a way he'd never wear it in public, one hand still on his dick, his fingers up his ass. Evan had never seen anything look better. He brushed the tips of his fingers along Kyle's cheek, over the dark stubble.

When Kyle spoke, he slowly removed his hands from his own body and ran them up Evan's thighs, the touch surging excitement throughout Evan again. So did Kyle's words. "I love the way you tell me what to do. I can't believe you've never been like this before. It seems so…"

"Natural." It did. Like a part of him was waking up, finally finding the road home after being stuck in a blinding storm so far from where he needed to be. "I wasn't like this with—"

Kyle stood and put a finger to Evan's lips. "I don't want to know. All I care is how you are now. With me." He leaned in and kissed him. A long, drawn-out kiss that was all about that one touch. Not sex. Not getting off. Kyle spoke again with his lips lingering over Evan's. "I can do this."

"You keep saying that, but you don't really say what you mean."

"Us…me…you…you and me…"

Evan smiled as Kyle fumbled with the words.

"Dating," Kyle said. "A relationship."

"You think you're ready? I mean, you're awfully young to be doing something like this."

"I think I might be. I mean, I—hey, you're teasing me."

It took a minute or two for Kyle to join Evan in his laughter. Evan couldn't remember when he'd ever laughed so much before or after sex. Reluctantly, he shut off the cooling water.

A loud scraping sound came from outside the bathroom, like someone had run into one of the wooden chairs in the dining room.

Chapter Twenty-Five

"Shit!" Kyle pulled aside the shower curtain and grabbed the two towels they'd found in a hall closet. He threw one to Evan. "The cabin owners must be home."

Perfect timing.

For Evan, maybe.

Kyle had been about to do some teasing of his own that involved wrestling Evan to the blankets in front of the fire, holding him down, and riding his cock for an hour or two, pausing anytime Evan got close to coming.

Evan rushed to dry off. "Guess we really have to go now." His voice sounded more disappointed than Kyle liked hearing. There wasn't anything he could do to stop the inevitable. They had to get back on the train and head home.

Kyle hurried to dress. He didn't want to explain what they were doing in someone else's cabin while naked. Evan joined him. When they were fully clothed, they headed into the living room.

"Hello?" Kyle called out. "We were trapped in the storm and needed a place to stop."

Silence. No one was there.

But someone had been. The blankets were in a pile like they'd been kicked around, and his backpack was open, its contents strewn across the floor.

"Fuck." Kyle crossed the room. He grabbed his pack and searched through the items on the floor.

Evan stood in the hall doorway. "The apartment. The train. Now this. It all has to be about the journal."

Kyle sifted through the bottom of his bag. "Dammit. It's gone."

"The journal? It's right here." Evan pointed to the floor on the far side of the couch where the journal was half hidden under a side table. "Maybe whoever was here didn't see it before we interrupted him." He picked up the journal and handed it to Kyle.

It was dry and looked like it had stayed that way during their stroll through the river. "What was it doing under there?"

"I saw it sticking out of your bag earlier. I was going to take a look, see if there was more about the bank robbery, but I decided it wouldn't be right for me to read it."

"I'd like you to. I don't think Grandpa would mind so long as it was you. You already know what's in it. Maybe when we get back to the train." Kyle ran a hand through his hair, fighting his need to pace around the room, curse at someone, punch their lights out. He said, "They must have followed us here."

"It's got to be the same person who searched our room on the train."

"But that wasn't just us."

Evan picked up a blanket from the floor. "Maybe they were covering their tracks. Or they weren't sure which room was ours."

"Yeah." Kyle set the journal on the couch and dropped to sit beside it. "I guess I don't want to believe Grandpa did it."

Evan sat beside him. "Did what?"

"Those guys wanted him and Joe to hide the money for them."

"How much money was it?"

"It doesn't say."

"Did he do it?"

"I think so. I was just getting to that part when you came back into the room yesterday. Since then I've been a little...distracted." Not that he'd go back and do anything differently. Except for Evan's ass ending up in that river.

The assured smile on Evan's face looked good. "It'll be light enough to head out soon. Maybe you should read more before we go."

"Yeah." Kyle picked up the journal and leafed through it until he reached the part where he'd left off. He read aloud.

> *"I knew I had to leave, to go home. So when Joe spoke up today and told them we'd hide the money, I didn't protest. I knew it was the wrong move, but I couldn't do anything except hide the truth.*
>
> *"They didn't want to know where we'd take the money. If they didn't end up in prison, or perhaps even if they did, they'd find one of us later to show them where the money was. Until then, Joe and I would be the only two people to know where we would hide it.*

"The threesome left to retrieve the money where
they'd temporarily stashed it as they'd fled Denver.
The rain that had been threatening us all day finally
came, turning into a downpour before long. Joe and
I waited in our tent. He didn't speak as he slowly
undressed me, as he kissed and caressed my body, as
we made love. After, he held me and said, 'In Ohio.
We'll go together. That way it'll always be close to
one of us.' Without having to say anything to him, he
knew where I wanted to spend the rest of my life.

"An hour later, we loaded the trunk of our car with
the bags that held the stamp of the Denver Bank and
Trust, and we left Colorado."

Kyle stopped reading and closed the journal. "I guess he did it."

"What are you doing?" Evan asked. "You aren't going to read anymore?"

"Not now. We have to get back to the train. They've got to be ready to leave by now. They'll probably send search-and-rescue out after us soon, if they haven't already."

Evan nodded, then said, "You need to read the rest as soon as you can, though."

"Yeah." A part of him didn't want to know the rest. Another part knew he owed it to his grandpa and what he'd written in the letter to Kyle about learning from his mistakes. "I have to read it."

"Maybe it says where they hid the money. Maybe no one ever came for it, and it's still there."

"I can't imagine Grandpa would put that in writing." Why? He'd talked about his male lover in the journal. After Kyle got back to the train, after he made sure Evan was safe, he'd read the rest. And he'd deal with whoever was after the journal. He started picking up the remaining blankets. "Let's go. I want to see who was here."

Evan stopped him. "What do you mean?"

"I'm going to find out who broke in here. He's probably headed back to the train. Maybe we can catch up. I've got to try and make a deal with him."

"He works for the network. He's probably been paid a shitload of money."

"Then I'll talk to Hastings myself. They might as well give up. They are not getting this journal. And I'm not letting anyone else find out about it. Grandpa didn't know what else to do. He was afraid. It was a different time. If he didn't want his kids or his grandkids to know about his relationship with Joe, or about what he did to help those bank robbers, then I have to respect that."

"I don't want to betray him either."

That had never crossed Kyle's mind. Not once. Not even with Evan's career on the line. "I know that." He faced the window; the sun was rising.

"What are you thinking?" Evan asked.

"They've gone to all this trouble. Whoever this guy is, he's going to take another shot on the train. I'll just have to convince him there's nothing in the journal about where the money is."

"Sure." Evan rolled up a blanket and threw it at the couch. "Because I bet he'll stop to talk to you and believe whatever you say."

"I have to try. I have to find out who hired him."

"What do you mean?"

"Maybe it's not your boss."

"He's not my boss. Then who?"

"Maybe someone who thinks this money belongs to him. There were four men involved in that bank robbery."

"They'd all be in their eighties. Or older. If they're still alive."

"Not their kids. Not their grandkids."

"And what makes you think you can talk them out of wanting to take a look at the journal?"

"I don't know." He had to try.

"They could be dangerous. This isn't one of your mysteries."

"Well, it's certainly inspiring one."

"I noticed that." Evan watched him for a moment, then added, "I'm glad you're writing again."

"Thanks to you. And Grandpa." Kyle walked to the dining room table and wrote a note explaining why they'd stayed in the cabin, and leaving it with his name, number, and some cash.

The sun had risen, and light poured into the cabin, making it look like a different place than where they'd spent the night together. Would they ever have another night like the one they'd just shared?

"What are you thinking now?" There Evan went again, making him put his thoughts to words. With two best-selling novels, Kyle would've figured he'd be better at it than he was.

"I'm going to miss this place." He'd never said that about somewhere he'd spent less than twelve hours. "I liked it here. I liked you here."

"Me too."

Unrestrained, more words poured out of Kyle. Maybe that was

what it meant to be in love with someone. You showed them everything. Even what you didn't want anyone to see. "What if I can't write when we get to Ohio? What if everything is different when this trip is over?"

Evan didn't answer right away. He pinched his bottom lip between his teeth. Slowly, he released it, and said, "You'll write. Because sometimes different is better." They were silent, their gazes locked for a long while, and then Evan added, "You haven't told me yet."

"What?"

"About Mac. Who does he choose?"

Kyle tried to find a gut response, blurt it out, and then he'd know what he should do. It never came. "I don't know yet."

* * * *

"What part of no one else leaves the train did you not understand?" The conductor glared at Kyle from the open door of their room. Kyle and Evan had been back for several minutes, and after checking on Rebecca and receiving major hugs of thanks from Sasha, they were getting warm and eating the food Oscar had brought for them when the conductor appeared at the door, pushing Oscar aside.

Kyle held nothing back as he responded. "Evan twisted his ankle, fell down an embankment covered in rocks and ice, and landed in a freezing river during a blizzard trying to find a little girl you lost on your fucking train, but he's okay, in case you were wondering."

The conductor's face was devoid of expression. Then he nodded. "Good. Okay. I've got to go check with the engineer. This train should be moving any minute now." He added a mumbled, "Glad you're okay," and took off down the hall.

Oscar remained at the door, smirking for a moment longer, then said, "I'm sorry for all the inconvenience, and I hope you enjoy the rest of your travels with us." He winked and turned to follow the conductor.

Kyle stood. "I'll be right back."

"Okay." Evan slurped more of his soup. He'd already had two bowls and three pieces of bread since they'd been back. Nice to see him eating like a normal person again.

Kyle jogged after Oscar. "Wait up." He stopped at the end of the hall, and Kyle asked, "We're leaving soon?"

"Yep. The train that's behind us came in during the night. They've got the tracks clear now. A chopper's been out looking for you since daybreak."

"I'm sorry if I've gotten you into trouble, but I'm not sorry I went after him."

Oscar waved the apology off. "You did the right thing. What anyone in your shoes would've done. If it had been my wife out there and anyone had tried to stop me, I'd have punched their lights out."

"I would have too, if it came to that. Do you know if there was someone else out in the storm last night? They would've gotten back on board before us this morning."

"Yeah. A man. Guess after we found Rebecca, he'd heard that you boys were missing and wanted to see if he could help. He knew the conductor wouldn't let anyone off the train, so he went out on his own. Got turned around in the storm and had to wait it out in a cabin until morning. I was hoping that's what you two were doing."

"We did. What does this guy look like?"

"I didn't see him. Just heard someone had come aboard this morning, but from what my buddy was telling me, it sounds like it was that big guy, Shepfield. I get the impression he thinks the conductor's an idiot."

The prison guard. He should've thought of that connection, and maybe he would have if he hadn't been hiking through a blizzard and having a record number of orgasms. Had Shepfield known someone at a prison where he'd once worked? Someone who knew about a bank heist in the fifties? Or maybe he'd known the bank robbers themselves. At least one of them had been caught. He must've been convicted and served time for it. With someone shot and killed at the bank, he would have also done time for more than the theft.

Oscar cocked his head to the side. He looked odd without the Santa hat on. "Why are you asking?"

"I just need to know. Can you find out for sure if it was Shepfield who got off the train?"

"I'll check."

"Thanks. For everything."

Oscar turned to leave, then stopped, a smile on his face reminiscent of the first time Kyle had seen him, sans the red hat with the swinging ball. "I'm really glad Evan's okay."

Kyle gave a nod. He was too.

He couldn't fathom the alternative.

Chapter Twenty-Six

The train horn blared as they barreled through another intersection. Kyle read the last sentence and slowly closed the journal. He couldn't shake off his sadness at the final words. Sadness for his grandpa, for a man named Joe he'd never met, for himself and Evan and the ten years of their lives he'd wasted.

He stared at the back of Evan's head and listened to the slight wheeze that wasn't quite a snore, just the way Evan had sounded when Kyle had sat watching him sleep in the Motel 6 on their first trip to California.

The relief washed over him. Evan was alive and safe. Yet Kyle almost couldn't breathe at the thought that both those things might have come to an abrupt end, that the day before could've ended differently in many ways.

He forced himself to focus on what he needed to do next. When the laptop booted up, he sat at the table, pulled out his phone, and connected it to his computer. He hoped they were far enough out of the mountains now he'd get a data signal. He did.

A quick search for the Denver Bank and Trust robbery brought up thousands of results. A scan of the first page revealed articles, blog posts, newspaper clippings, and photos related to the theft. He clicked on a link titled THE KOREAN WAR BANDITS and read the page.

> The gang of Korean War veterans robbed a total of nine banks in Colorado, Kansas, and Nebraska in the early 1950s until all four men were apprehended less than two weeks after their final robbery at the Denver Bank and Trust on July 28, 1953, where a security guard was shot and killed. To this day, the location of the stolen money from their last heist is unknown. Due to the timing of the robbery, just minutes after an armored truck made a regional

drop, it was the largest cash bank heist in the United States until 1997.

Some believe the gang hastily buried the money near their campsite outside Denver, Colorado before they split up and ran from the police. Hundreds of treasure hunters have scoured the area in search of the money but have uncovered nothing. Others believe it's an urban legend that the money is still hidden somewhere, and that the funds were actually divided among the families of the bank robbers before the arrests were made and are now long gone.

The first man arrested, Charles Sybert, was stopped and taken into custody as he fled the robbery at the Denver Bank and Trust. The other three men were apprehended one week later, all three in different locations and all three arrested within forty-eight hours of each other. Each served their time in the same federal penitentiary just north of Denver. Charles Sybert and George Johnston subsequently died in prison. Sybert from a knife wound and Johnston from a fatal reaction to penicillin. Vern Paskowski and Henry Thompson died after their releases from prison. Paskowski was killed in an automobile accident, and Thompson was ironically shot and killed while he was a bystander during a robbery at a livestock auction. The premature deaths of all four men have led to more mystery surrounding the missing money, making this one of the most popular bank robberies for historians and treasure hunters alike.

Kyle clicked more of the related links. All confirmed the same basic information as the first article. He shut his laptop lid.

All four men served their time in the same prison, and he'd bet he had already met someone who worked at that prison during at least part of their time there. Tomorrow, he was getting some answers.

He crawled into bed beside Evan, then hesitated. What the hell? It was getting easier to go with his instincts where Evan was concerned. He leaned down, kissed him on the temple next to the scratches above his left eye, and tucked the blanket higher around his shoulders.

* * * *

Evan awoke a little sore and with that drowsy feeling of too much sleep, despite how much he'd needed it. The chug and sway of the train wasn't helping him shake off the foggy feeling. But the press of a warm body along his back, an arm wrapped around his waist, and a hand rubbing his bare stomach did.

"You awake?" Kyle asked.

"Yeah. What time is it?"

"Late. You slept twelve hours, even with the nap when we got back yesterday."

"Oh man. Guess I was tired. Did you get any rest?"

"Some. Been writing."

"Yeah?" He rolled to face Kyle. The dark stubble he'd been sporting the day before was gone. Evan ran a hand along the smooth line of his jaw. "You'll have the book done in no time."

Kyle turned his head and kissed Evan's palm. "They said we'll be in Chicago early tomorrow. I guess they're hauling ass. Oscar said they're making arrangements for everyone's connections. We should be able to catch another commuter train home to Ohio like we'd planned and be there in time for Christmas Eve dinner at your mom's."

"Good." Evan's mom went all out every year, hosting both families for a huge feast, with drinks and games and gifts and Christmas carols. It would suck to miss it.

"Yeah. Thank God," Kyle said, "because if we missed the party, your mom might've killed me."

"Why you?"

"Because this is the first year it's just us coming home, and nothing like this ever happened with—"

Evan pressed a quick kiss on Kyle's lips. "Don't." He didn't want to think about Dennis or anything else right then. Kyle was still being the affectionate man he'd been in the cabin. Evan didn't want to let the rest of the world in. Not yet.

"It's just…" Kyle rolled onto his back and folded his arms behind his head. "Your mom adored him."

"She adores you too. You're like a son to her."

Kyle looked shocked by that. Then the expression was gone. He sat up with a start. "I got us something to eat." He leaned over the edge of the bed and lifted a tray.

Despite his words to Kyle, Evan couldn't believe he hadn't considered what his mom would think of him and Kyle together. What would everyone think? Their families had no idea anything was going on, or had ever gone on between them. Was this going to be the worst Christmas surprise ever? Or would they be happy for them?

Kyle shifted around to the other end of the bed so they were facing each other and placed the tray between them. A small bowl of fruit, two cinnamon rolls slathered in creamy frosting, and a single bottle of juice. "They don't have much left in the way of breakfast. I thought we could share."

Evan reached for a fork, but Kyle was faster. He scooped up a piece of pineapple and held it to Evan's lips. Evan hesitated a moment, letting the reality of Kyle's action sink in. He opened his mouth and sucked the fruit and juice from Kyle's fingers, the sweetness bursting over his tongue.

Kyle spoke as he picked up a grape. "I finished reading the journal." He popped the grape into his mouth and got another he fed to Evan.

Who knew it would be so hard to concentrate while being hand-fed fruit in bed. "You finished it? Did it say where they hid the money?"

"No. Grandpa wrote mostly about his last week with Joe. He brought him to the farm with him. Introduced him as a friend from the war. Joe stayed there for a week."

"Maybe the money's at the farm."

"Maybe. I don't know where it would be that no one would've found it. Maybe buried someplace, but I can't imagine Grandpa would have taken the risk to hide it where his family might've seen what he was doing."

"You're right. Especially after all he went through to hide the truth."

"There's a letter to me at the end," Kyle said. "Written in the pages of the journal. Dated the same day as the first letter."

"What did it say?"

"I don't know." He shrugged and ate another grape. "I haven't read it yet. I just...couldn't." His dark eyes held the same sadness as the day of the funeral when they'd watched those old movies. "It's all that's left."

"I'm sorry."

Kyle stared at Evan, his dark eyes going from that sad, serious expression to something lighter, happier. "Thanks." Kyle rolled his finger through the icing of a cinnamon roll, tore off a piece, and held the roll up to Evan's mouth.

That did it. Evan was convinced he hadn't woken up yet. Might as well go with it. He licked the frosting off the length of Kyle's finger before eating the bite of roll.

Kyle leaned in, his gaze focused on Evan's mouth. He ran his thumb over Evan's lips, then followed it up with a swipe of his tongue across the bottom lip. He topped that off with a long kiss that brought their tongues together. Like a slow dance that was becoming more sensual with each lingering touch of their mouths. Kyle pulled back and smiled. "Frosting. On your lip."

No way that was a dream. Nothing in dreams felt that real. Evan closed his eyes and let out a soft moan. Who knew fruit and pastries turned him on? He opened his eyes, afraid the embarrassment he hadn't felt at his reaction would come barreling to the surface with one look at Kyle. He should've known better.

Kyle threw him a smirk, that cocky look of confidence he'd seen him flash dozens of guys. Evan had never been on the receiving end. And he'd never seen it mixed with such intimacy. And maybe more.

Kyle said, "I talked to Shepfield."

"What?" It was hard to be pissed while turned on and being hand-fed in bed, but Evan was managing it. "By yourself?"

"He's not the one who followed us. At least, I don't think so. I searched online about the bank robbery. All four men were convicted, and each served time at the same prison in Colorado. Figured I'd see if I could confirm whether our helpful ex-prison guard worked there. Found out this morning he's never worked at any prison outside California, and now he works private security in LA."

"How did you find that out?"

"I asked him."

"You're some detective. Didn't you think he'd wonder why you're asking about his past?"

"I told him I was researching prisons for one of my books. Asked him all kinds of questions I didn't need to know the answers to."

"And you think he was telling you the truth?"

"I do." Kyle ate a piece of pineapple, then brought another to Evan's lips.

"Uh, Kyle, I didn't hurt my hands. I can feed myself."

"I know." He looked at the tray between them. "Can't seem to stop myself, though. I love watching your mouth."

Yeah, this was better than the dreams. "If you squeeze the next piece over your dick and balls, you can watch my mouth suck it off you."

Kyle's eyes widened. He scrambled for the front of his jeans and threw them open. "You have the best ideas."

"I do." Because no matter what they'd been through on the train, this trip was the best idea he'd ever had.

He just hoped when they got to Ohio, he'd still feel that way.

He wanted to believe Kyle's actions and words meant something—wanted to believe what Kyle had said in the cabin about a relationship.

Because if it wasn't true, losing this was going to be worse than six months ago. Worse than losing the job. Worse than anything.

Chapter Twenty-Seven

"Maybe we should leave the room for a while." Kyle was finding it hard to concentrate on revising the chapters he'd already written, and time was ticking by in that annoying way it had a tendency to do. He couldn't send the pages to Sue Ann yet. There was an element missing from his writing. The ideas were good, but the spark that was undeniably his style wasn't there, and he couldn't get it back. His mind was on something else.

Since he'd talked to Shepfield, a nagging doubt had lingered. Shepfield had been telling the truth, he was sure of that, but the guy had also left something out.

Across the small room, Evan lifted his gaze from the notebook he'd been scribbling in for an hour. He was wearing his glasses, a snug white T-shirt, low-rise jeans, and nothing else, looking so damn sexy. That was the other thing that was making it hard to concentrate.

"Why should we leave?" Evan asked.

"So someone will come after the journal again, and we can get a look at who it is."

"Did you miss the part where they might be dangerous?"

"We can't very well find out what's going on if we just sit here."

Evan pushed his glasses up and glared at Kyle, a determined I'm-going-to-kick-your-ass look.

Fine. Kyle faced his laptop and opened his manuscript again.

Five minutes later, he'd read the same sentence three times. He closed his computer and grabbed the journal from his bag. He had marked several sections as he'd read the final pages, and there was one entry he kept coming back to. His grandpa and Joe's drive from Colorado to Ohio.

I know now that sleeping with the closest friend I've ever had was one of my worst mistakes. It would have been easier if I'd never traveled down this road with him. Because now walking away seems impossible. But I have to. No matter what we feel, no matter how good our time together has been.

We are too different. We want different things. We want different lives. I'll always care for him, but he can no longer be my future. I have to let him go, let him meet someone else, let him have a life, let him be happy without me.

Focusing on what was best for Joe made every decision, every action easier.

Kyle stopped reading.

Mac.

Part of Kyle had been determined to make it work between Mac and his best friend, but his grandpa's words confirmed what he hadn't wanted to face.

He had been too close to the storyline without realizing it. Without understanding what he'd been feeling for Evan, he'd been inserting his own life into his novel. He'd been hoping for the past six months, whether he wanted to accept it or even acknowledge it, for something to happen between him and Evan, for it to be more than friendship, more than sex, and he couldn't write his novel with an ending other than the one he'd wanted for himself.

He got out a pen and the pad of sticky notes, wrote a quick note, and stuck it to the journal's page. He closed the book and watched Evan again. He was tapping the pen to his cheek, his eyes scanning the notebook on his lap, that serious concentrated frown that meant he was on to something. Not frustrated. About to explode with excitement.

In a flash, Evan leaned over the notebook and put the pen to paper.

Kyle smirked. Without a single doubt, he knew what he wanted. Nothing else mattered but that truth. It was stronger than any fear, any reasons why he'd stayed away from relationships. From love.

A confidence he never thought he'd have when he'd first admitted to Lorrie she might be right about what he was feeling for Evan surged through him. He picked up his laptop again. He had to give Mac the future he'd known all along the man needed. Even if that was the opposite of what he wanted for himself and Evan.

It had been a mistake for Mac to become lovers with his friend. His future was with the cop.

And that didn't have to mean anything for Kyle's own life. For his future with Evan.

When he had that pivotal scene done, he returned to the beginning of the book and finished revising the chapters he needed to send to Sue Ann, then outlined the major points for the rest of the book, typing furiously to get it all down. He didn't stop writing when Evan whispered that he was going to go call his mom and left the room. Or when Evan returned and wrote more in his notebook. They were quiet as they worked, and a few hours later, Kyle felt a hand thread through the back of his hair. Then the hand moved lower and another joined it to massage his shoulders.

He closed his eyes and let the warmth and relaxation of Evan's fingertips work through him.

Evan leaned against his back and whispered, "Take a break." Then his lips were on Kyle's neck. Kyle tilted his head to the side and let Evan explore. Everywhere. Anywhere he wanted. "Sounds good. What—" He sucked in a sharp breath. It was hard to talk with Evan's mouth working his blood to the surface.

Evan stopped and walked around him. He sank to his knees. "Yes, what were you going to say?" He popped the top button on Kyle's pants, the palm of his hand rubbing his cock through the jeans.

"What did you have in mind?"

Evan smiled, his attention on undoing the pants. "I thought maybe you'd want to do a little reading."

Kyle shifted in the chair, pushing his dick closer to Evan's face. "Reading, huh?"

"Yeah." With his free hand, Evan reached backward for something on the bed. "You read this nice article about Jake Gallagher while I blow you."

Kyle took the magazine from Evan. "Read the article? I don't think so."

"Okay." Evan pushed the magazine toward Kyle while his other hand continued to work on getting his pants open. "Look at the pictures, then. There's more inside with his shirt off."

"No way." Kyle tossed the magazine over his shoulder. "I'd rather watch something else." He squirmed again until he had his ass to the edge of the chair. Something better—much better.

Evan had the jeans open. He worked them down Kyle's hips, and Kyle lifted his ass to help get them lower. His hard cock was straining against his briefs. Would the crazy, hard-in-an-instant erections ever stop around Evan? That sent doubt trickling along his thoughts. Passion never lasted long. What would they be like in five years?

Ten? Would Evan still drive him crazy? Would he still surprise Kyle? Take the lead in that confident way that drove Kyle nuts? Would they still touch each other with an intensity that heightened every moment of arousal? Would they fuck each other against the hall wall because they couldn't wait to get to a bed?

Guess he'd find out. He had every intention of seeing what it was like to be with someone that long.

Evan peeled back Kyle's underwear and gripped his cock. He tilted it toward his mouth, his warm breath blowing across Kyle's slit. Kyle breathed deep and waited. To see those full lips open wider, to feel that moist tongue stroke him and the wet heat of Evan's mouth drag over his dick. Then Evan surprised him yet again. He kissed the tip of his cock, closed his eyes, and rubbed his cheek along Kyle's length, like a cat lazily marking his territory with his scent. The frames on Evan's glasses bumped the head of his cock.

A hiss escaped Kyle's throat. Uncontrollably, he surged off the seat. "Ev..."

Evan dropped his hand to Kyle's thigh and forced him to remain still.

On the upstroke of cheek to dick, Evan tongued under the head of Kyle's red, swollen cock. Another hiss, louder, longer, and Evan clutched his thighs in both hands. He was killing him. Slowly. Kyle wanted to grab that blond hair and sink into his mouth, fuck him like mad. One slow touch to his dick and he was out of control.

Evan sat back and pulled his glasses off. He leaned forward again.

"No," Kyle said.

Evan stilled and threw him a questioning look.

"Leave them on. You look fucking hot like that."

The hint of a blush appeared on Evan's cheeks before he slipped the glasses on and finally sank his mouth onto Kyle's cock, giving him the longest, most intense blowjob he'd ever had.

And not once did he stop watching Evan's blue eyes through the lenses. Or worry about whether sex with Evan would always be like this.

They had a long time to find out.

* * * *

Evan made one last note in his notebook. He was vibrating with excitement. He couldn't wait to get back to LA and really get going on the new script. He'd had a ton of plot lines and character details rolling around in his head during the past twenty-four hours.

He set the notebook on his bag. Kyle was asleep on his side, his face pressed against Evan's hip, his left arm draped over Evan's body like he'd done all night long. They hadn't turned the bed back into a bench since their first night in the room. Didn't look like they would need to today either.

At this rate Kyle would miss the entire morning, their last on the train, but he'd spent so much of the past two days writing, he probably needed the extra sleep.

Evan, on the other hand, had gotten too much. He felt like he'd slept through so much of his life lately. He was finally awake, finally alive again.

They'd be in Chicago by early afternoon. He couldn't imagine leaving the room they'd shared for such a short time. So much had happened there, so much had changed between them.

He wanted to believe it would continue when they stepped off the train, that the Kyle who'd emerged in the last five days was ready for exactly what he'd said he wanted.

Evan spotted the blinking battery light on Kyle's laptop. The cord was dangling off the table. He carefully slid his leg out from under Kyle's, got up, and plugged in the computer. The journal sat open on the table beside it.

Kyle had said he wanted him to read it. He took a seat in the chair and read a few lines. A lot of what Kyle had already told him. He flipped the page. More about Victor's travels with Joe, and their adventures. Evan flipped through more pages and stopped on one with a sticky note. The journal read…

> *I know now that sleeping with the closest friend I've ever had was one of my worst mistakes.*

That struck a nerve. Had him gripping the journal in clenched hands. He eased up. Victor's words were not Kyle's.

Or at least he thought not. Then he read Kyle's note on the side of the page.

> *Thanks, Grandpa. I could not have said it better.*

No. That was not the Kyle he'd slept beside all night. The one who'd held him and gently kissed every scratch on his cheek and the scrape above his eye before they'd fallen asleep.

Evan read the rest of the journal entry.

*We want different lives. I'll always care for him, but
he can no longer be my future. I have to let him go,
let him meet someone else, let him have a life, let him
be happy without me.*

Then he read Kyle's note again.

When had he written that? He hadn't acted like it had been a mistake. Or had Evan missed something because he was so damn happy? Maybe once they'd gotten on the train again, Kyle had wished he could take back what he'd said in the cabin.

But it didn't seem like that was true the previous night.

Before the soft kisses, before the tender way Kyle had wrapped his arm around him, the sex had been off-the-charts explosive. Evan had gone down on Kyle while he'd been sitting in the chair, and then Kyle had taken him to bed, and they'd made out like sex-crazed teenagers. When Kyle had gotten it up again, he'd fucked Evan, touching him everywhere with his hands, his lips, his dick. It was like Kyle had wanted it all, hard and intense, and he'd planned to have it all night long.

Maybe he'd known that was going to be their last time. Maybe that was why he'd been so out of control.

Seeing Evan floating in the river had freaked Kyle out. That was obvious by the way he'd clung to him on the couch in the cabin. Maybe that was why he'd said he wanted to try to make a relationship work. Maybe he'd meant it. For now.

What about in six months? A year? Two? Would Kyle run when he couldn't live with his mistake any longer?

No. Kyle had been telling the truth. Evan had felt it in his touch, in his kiss. The note in the journal didn't mean anything.

He took in the details of Kyle on the bed. His dark hair sticking out all over on the pillow they'd shared a moment ago. His long, lean legs protruding out the bottom of the white sheet. And that sheet accentuating the perfect curve of his ass.

Kyle was his now.

Evan believed that with everything he was.

His phone beeped, and he checked the display. Another message from Dennis. He sent a reply. When they got back to LA, he had to talk to him. He had to explain in person.

Kyle would understand. After everything they'd shared, he'd understand Evan had to do this.

Chapter Twenty-Eight

Kyle awoke to the sound of a phone beeping. He stretched and opened his eyes, not wanting to face the fact that their days on the train were almost over. In Ohio, he stayed with his parents and Evan with his mom. What would they do this year? He couldn't ask Evan. How much of an asshole did that make him? But it wasn't like he'd ever experienced bringing a guy home with him.

Beside him on the bed was a handwritten note from Evan.

Went to get lunch.

An alert on Evan's phone beeped again. Maybe it was his mom checking on their status. Kyle hesitated, then picked it up and read the text.

From Dickhead. At the airport. I'll see you soon.

Soon? Kyle scrolled through the previous messages to read the entire exchange.

The first from Dickhead: I want to see you. Want to be with you. Don't want this to be our first Christmas apart in ten years. Want us to get back together. Miss you.

No response from Evan.

Another message from Dickhead: Booked a flight to Ohio for Christmas Eve. Tell me you'll see me, that we can talk, and I'll come.

Another: Evan, I love you. Want us to make this work. One word from you, I'm on the plane.

Evan responded an hour ago: We need to talk. I'll call you in a few minutes.

Then a half hour later, the last text from Dickhead: At the airport. I'll see you soon.

Kyle tossed the phone into Evan's bag and got off the bed. What the fuck?

Evan probably figured what they had going on would never last, that Kyle would never stick around, and was considering taking Dickhead back before he lost him a second time.

Kyle paced the room. What a fucking idiot. Thinking Evan would ever trust him. Would ever trust he could make this work.

He wanted an explanation.

Although hadn't he already gotten one? He'd broken Evan's heart once, and he'd waited too long to make up for that.

He dressed, packed his bag, and sat in the chair, glaring at the glass door to their room.

He didn't have to wait long.

Evan slid the door open, carrying a tray with wrapped deli sandwiches, bags of chips, and sodas from the lounge car. He gave a reluctant smile, then set the tray on the table. It wasn't like Evan not to say anything. Probably didn't want to admit he'd been rethinking his future. He'd never had trouble being honest with Kyle. Guess they'd ended up fucking up their friendship after all.

Well, Kyle had no intention of helping Evan say the words to end this.

Evan sat and passed him a sandwich.

They ate in silence, and ten minutes later, downtown Chicago rolled into view.

"Guess it's time to go," Evan said. He tucked his half-eaten sandwich in the plastic wrap and set it on the tray.

"Guess it is." Kyle wadded his empty wrapper and tossed it across the room. It landed in Evan's open bag on the floor.

"Hey." Evan glared at him, then stood, picked up his bag, and fished out the wrapper. "What's the matter with you?"

"Just want to get off this train. I'm sick of being cooped up in here."

"Cooped up?"

"Yeah. Aren't you sick of this small fucking space? Of looking at my face day in and day out?" God, he was being an asshole. Jealousy did not sound good on him. Too bad he couldn't stop it, couldn't stop the anger and disappointment and loss thundering through him. Was this how Evan had felt ten years ago when Kyle had walked out into that back alley?

No wonder he doesn't trust you. No wonder he wants someone else.

"I knew it." The bag in Evan's hands fell to the floor. "I knew you'd freak out. I just didn't imagine it'd be this soon. I thought there was some other reason for that note."

Kyle lifted his head. The scared expression in those blue eyes gave him pause. No matter what, Evan didn't deserve the way he was speaking to him. Didn't deserve...

Wait. "What note?"

Evan rushed forward and dropped to his knees before Kyle. He gripped Kyle's thighs in his hands. "Please don't do this. You're just scared. It'll be okay if we take this slow. You'll see. It's not going to be how you think it will. It doesn't have to change you."

"What are you talking about? What note?"

"In your grandpa's journal. You said it was a mistake to sleep with me." Tears flooded Evan's eyes. "Please, Kyle, don't do this. Don't leave me."

Kyle's chest tightened at the look on Evan's face, but then the words registered. A surge of laughter poured out of him.

Evan jerked his hands away and sat back on his heels. "What's so funny?"

"That note was about my book. About Mac."

"Oh."

Kyle pulled Evan's hands back to his thighs and covered them with his own. "So what? You thought I was lying to you in the cabin when I said I wanted us to be together?"

"No. I thought you might be scared."

"Thanks for the faith, Ev." He'd meant it as a joke, but anger was pushing aside the humor and relief. Seriously, he asked, "Do you trust me?"

"I thought so, but…"

That shouldn't have been a surprise. But it still hurt like hell. "Are you thinking about going back to him?"

Evan's jaw dropped. "What?"

"Dickhead wants you back. You never said what you were going to do, but I'm guessing you're still considering it. I'm guessing you think he'll give you the future I can't."

Evan sat there with his mouth hanging open, his eyes wide, saying nothing.

"Shocked I'm able to read you so well? Seeing the text messages on your phone didn't hurt." Well, it had hurt, like hell, but he was trying to make a point.

Evan's shocked expression morphed into a half smile. "You're jealous."

Kyle surged out of the chair and stormed past Evan to the other side of the room. "Damn straight, I am. He had you for ten years, Ev."

"He didn't have me. We were partners."

"And you want that back."

Evan's hands were on his arms, forcing him to turn around. "No. I want that with you. But I do need to talk to him. I wanted to wait until we got back to California, but he wouldn't take no for an answer. I tried to tell him over the phone, but he kept cutting me off. He'd already booked a flight. Once I told him I had to talk to him, he was coming no matter what else I said."

"What do you need to talk to him about?" Kyle spoke again before Evan could answer. "Why not go back to him? I mean, if you don't think I can handle this, then you better take him back before you lose him too."

"What does that mean?" Evan dropped his arms to his sides. "You think I need a guy to be happy? You think I'm weak, don't you? That's why you came looking for me out there in the storm. You thought I'd get lost and need you to save me. Like always."

"What are you talking about?"

"I know what you did to that guy back in high school. I know you went after him. You thought I needed you to protect me. Well, maybe I did then, but I don't now."

"Fine. Next time your ass is floating in a goddamn river in the middle of a blizzard, I'll leave you there."

"Fine."

They were both breathing heavily, staring at each other. Kyle couldn't find the words to show Evan he could be trusted. Maybe that was because there was no reason for Evan to do it.

A knock sounded on the door. Neither moved at first. Another knock. Kyle gave in and opened the door. Oscar stood in the hall, the Santa hat back on his head, crooked this time and looking less jolly than before.

He said, "We're pulling into the station, and I wanted to talk to you before you had to take off."

"Were you able to find out more about the guy who got off the train?"

"Not really. Apparently, no one got a good look at him but the conductor, and when I asked, he refused to tell me who it was. All I know is the man who went out after you was a big guy. Older than me. He was wearing a hat, scarf, and long coat, so no one else saw much of him to describe." What Oscar did know fit Shepfield. Even if he'd never worked in a prison in Colorado, it didn't mean he didn't know someone who did. Or maybe he was working for someone now, supplementing his retirement. Hadn't he said he had a job? Working private security in LA. The kind of person a television network with a lot of cash to burn might hire to steal the journal.

Oscar held out his hand. "Sorry I couldn't find out more."

"That's okay. I appreciate your help." They shook, and Kyle

added, "Thanks again for everything."

"Sure. You boys take care now. It was a pleasure having you in my car." His smile was less full, his posture no longer as official-looking as he gave a nod and walked away.

Perhaps Oscar was done working the rails after the train ride from hell. Kyle wanted to mention he felt bad about that to Evan, but he couldn't say anything, couldn't force the words from his mouth.

Would it always be like this now? Anger and unease between them?

Not if he could help it.

Evan picked up his bags and headed for the door. Kyle stood in his way. They shifted sideways at the same time, and the move forced Evan to look up.

Kyle wanted to make Evan talk to him, make him say what he was going to do, why he needed to talk with Dickhead, but his eyes held a sadness Kyle hadn't ever seen from Evan. And when he spoke, his voice sounded like the shy, quiet kid Kyle had met in their high school English class.

"I can't believe you think I'd go back to him after everything we've done. Everything I've said to you. I can't believe you don't trust *me*."

"When I saw he was coming, I lost it."

"I tried to tell him not to come. That I would see him when we got back."

"Why were you going to see him?"

"I don't love him anymore, and he deserves to hear that from me."

A high better than any drug he'd tried in his youth swelled through Kyle. "Because you love me?"

Evan dropped his head forward and laughed. "You are the most frustrating man."

"I'm going to show you, Ev. I won't hurt you again." Was he making promises he couldn't keep? His gut clenched at that.

"How do you know?" There was that uneasy voice again. "This is completely new for you. How do you know you won't get scared? Or make a mistake? I can't be with you and then see you with someone else. That…" Evan shook his head. "If you think you need time before you're ready, I want to know now."

"I'm ready."

Blue eyes scanned Kyle's. "I want to believe that."

The train came to a stop at the station. The end of the line. Kyle opened his mouth to speak, then clamped it shut. If Evan didn't trust what they'd done together, how Kyle had touched him, what he'd said, what more could he do to convince him?

He threw a tip for Oscar onto the table, hesitated, and tossed out a few more bills. He owed the guy more than he could repay with cash.

Evan stared at the pile of bills for a moment, then turned and walked out. Kyle grabbed his bags and gave the room one last look.

For the first time in his life, he'd let himself feel something. Would it have been better if he hadn't? Even if he had to watch Evan walk away?

Chapter Twenty-Nine

Kyle tossed his bags onto the bed in his old bedroom at his parents' house and changed into the new blazing red, scratchy sweater his mom had knitted for him. He hated how he looked in red, but he wore whatever she made for him every year. The tradition was as old as he could remember.

He was home.

He fished out his laptop and booted it up. It had been great seeing his mom and dad, Lorrie, and the kids, but he only had an hour until they needed to get to the Christmas Eve party. He had something to take care of before then.

He sat at the wood desk he'd used in his high school days, trying not to think about the angered, hurt words he and Evan had exchanged, where things were headed, or what Evan would do.

Once his laptop was online, he searched for what he'd been contemplating throughout the cab ride from the train station. Only so many people knew his grandfather had befriended the four bank robbers. He wanted to rule everyone out, make sure it was the network coming after the journal. That meant ruling out any family members of those four men who'd stolen the money. He keyed in the names of each man.

Numerous sites came up. All discussing the Denver Bank and Trust's theft and the four men responsible for it. Some reporters and treasure hunters had gone to the prison during the 1950s and '60s and had interviewed the men, though none of the robbers would reveal if they knew where the money was located. Kyle finally found a site that explained the more personal details he was after.

Of the four men, only Vern Paskowski was married.
He fathered two children, a son and a daughter.
Both currently reside in California where their father
had spent his final days.

If the man who'd broken into the cabin hadn't been Shepfield or someone else working for the network, could it have been Paskowski's son? Or maybe the daughter had sent someone. Maybe the two were working together.

Kyle searched for more information on Paskowski's children, finally locating a name and a California telephone number for each. He dug out his phone and made two calls. Neither answered, and he left a message asking them to call back no matter what day or time, even on Christmas. He needed to ask them an important question about their father.

He tossed his phone aside and clicked a link for the son's Facebook page. The profile picture was too young for the description Oscar had given of the man who'd gone after him and Evan in the storm. Maybe it was an old photo.

Was he on the right track? Maybe it hadn't been a relative of the bank robbers. It was definitely not a relative of his grandpa's. Only Kyle knew about the journal, let alone what had happened during that year of his grandpa's life.

Who did that leave? A random treasure hunter?

His gut said no. It had to be someone closer to the original men. Someone who knew about the journal's existence, since that was what everyone believed held clues to the treasure. Who knew his grandpa had kept that journal?

The women who visited their campsite? Maybe.

Who else?

Joe.

Was he still alive? Did he have any family? The journal mentioned a brother and a new baby.

Kyle searched for "Joe Morrison." The web search indicated *98,200 results*. He searched again, this time adding in "Korean War Veteran." *26 results*. Bingo. He started with the first and found he didn't need the other twenty-five. The link provided a list of obituaries for veterans from the war. There were two Joe Morrisons. The first died in the war. The second died in 1958. That had to be him. He had lived for only five years after the journal ended. Kyle read the text on the scanned newspaper clipping of the obituary from the *San Francisco Chronicle*.

The obit was brief. It mentioned Joe's brave service in the war and listed the names of those he was survived by, including his parents, his brother, and…his young son, Victor Morrison, who, according to the paper, resided in San Francisco with his mother at the time of his father's death.

Victor Morrison.

He had a son. A child he'd named after Kyle's grandpa.

It had been love. For both men.

Kyle ran another search and found the phone numbers for four Victor Morrisons in California but none in San Francisco. He expanded the search and found more scattered throughout the US. Best to start with the one closest to where the obituary indicated they had lived. He dialed the number and left the same message he had for the children of Paskowski, only this time, the words felt oddly more personal for him.

The door to his room swung in and slammed against the wall with a bang that had him flinching. Lorrie was standing there, her arms folded across her chest. She looked pissed off and disappointed at the same time. "What the hell happened?"

Kyle set aside his phone and closed his laptop lid. He did not want her to see what he'd been looking at. "What do you mean what happened?"

"I saw the two of you. Something is messed up."

He and Evan had barely talked on the train ride from Chicago to Toledo or in the cab to Liberty Falls. Evan had stared out the window next to him, his closed notebook on his lap, while Kyle had reread various parts of the journal.

The final pages were emotional. Entries about how it had felt for his grandpa to be home after two years, to see his parents and the farm, to have validation about the future he wanted. There were mentions about life and love and how hard it was to know something was right but to know it wasn't right at the same time. Kyle had felt the desperation in his grandfather's words, the despair in having to make a choice. If his grandpa had been with Joe in today's world— and not during a time when just being in a known gay bar could get you arrested, or worse—maybe he would've asked Joe to live with him, run the farm together, maybe they would've had a future. But then Kyle wouldn't have been born. Neither would Lorrie or her kids. It was the kind of thing better left unexamined.

As he and Evan had driven past the welcome sign for Liberty Falls, he'd closed the journal, the sadness of his grandpa's past and the uncertainty of his own future smothering him in the backseat of the cab. Evan had looked at him but hadn't said anything. He'd turned away again, and Kyle had closed his eyes and listened to the tires rolling over the wet surface of the road, the spray of salt kicking up and smacking into the sides of the cab as they made their way through the remnants of the snowstorm.

When the cab had dropped them off, they'd stood at the curb of Kyle's old home with his family and Evan's mom, all talking excitedly, asking about the weather and the stranded train, passing out hugs until the cold forced them indoors. Evan had crossed the street with his mom without a look back, and Kyle had gone inside with his parents, Lorrie, and her kids.

"I fucked up, all right?"

"I figured," she said.

"Gee, thanks."

She took a seat on the edge of his bed. "What did you do?"

"Nothing."

"I'm guessing that's the problem."

"Hardly. We did exactly what you thought we'd do. We fucked all the way here."

Her eyes widened, and then she laughed. The sound of it pissed him off. "That's not the only thing I thought you'd do."

He stood and grabbed the backpack with the journal inside. He wasn't taking his eyes off it. He headed for the door. She beat him to it and stepped in his way.

"I'm not talking about this," he said. "We have to head over. They're going to wonder where we are."

She gave him a long stare.

He went for a distraction. "Where's your husband?"

"He's helping a friend."

"On Christmas Eve." With his kids so damn excited about the holiday and presents and candy and Santa Claus. "Nice."

Lorrie took a step back and gave him a more pissed-off look. "For your information, Brett's friend who was laid off the same day he was just got a job. He has to drive his own rig, but it wasn't running, so Brett offered to help. They have until the day after Christmas to get it fixed, or his friend is going to lose the job. Maybe out in Hollywood, everyone has a good paying job, but it's not like that here. Not this year." Her voice had risen, and she'd stepped closer into his space as she talked. She never spoke to him like that.

"I'm sorry," he said. "I didn't realize."

"You don't live here, Kyle, so try not to judge what you aren't around to see."

He didn't bother to tell her she'd been doing the same thing to him. Only she was usually right about his life. He pulled her to him and kissed her on the forehead. "I won't. I'm sorry."

"And don't think I don't know what you're doing, trying to get the conversation off you and Evan. You're not as slick as you think you are."

He laughed, her words easing some of the tension in his chest. "Fine, but we need to get to the party."

After a long stare, Lorrie finally let him pass. He knew the truth, though. The discussion wasn't over. She just wasn't mean enough to deny Christmas Eve to her waiting kids.

The doorbell rang downstairs.

"He made it!" Lorrie did a little hop and took off for the staircase.

Kyle followed her but paused halfway down the stairs as Lorrie went to open the door in the entranceway below.

Brett stepped inside, a huge smile plastered on his face as he held out his arms for Lorrie. With a matching grin, looking so happy to see him, she fell into her husband's arms, and he held her tightly in his.

"Did you get it fixed?" she asked.

"Yeah. He's all set."

"Oh good." She hugged him again. "I'm glad you made it for the party."

"Me too, Daddy." Their daughter ran into the room, followed by her brother and Kyle's parents, everyone dressed in the green and red knitted Christmas sweaters, smiles all around.

It was nice to see his parents happy. Not their usual troubled expressions whenever he did a video chat with either of them during the year. They liked it best when everyone was home together for the holidays, not when he was two thousand miles away.

Maybe it wasn't only for himself he needed to consider moving home.

Was that still what he wanted?

No, Evan needed to be in LA.

Kyle would just have to learn to write there or find another career. Unless Evan decided he really didn't trust him and that his heart was safer without the risk.

They needed to talk again. Which was funny, since Kyle had been trying to avoid this exact thing his entire life. In the past six days, he'd thought and talked more about his feelings, about relationships and love than he imagined possible for a lifetime. And here he was, needing to say more. He just wished he knew what the hell he was supposed to say.

He joined his family downstairs, and the group headed out. They crossed the street, but Kyle stopped at the edge of his parents' driveway.

Evan's childhood home. It looked the same as it always did.

Decked out in red and green exterior Christmas lights, plastic reindeer on the lawn, and a giant Santa riding in his equally plastic sleigh. Gloria Walker loved the holiday as much as her son. Every year, she made plates of cookies to trade with Kyle's father for help putting up the decorations.

That first year after Kyle's family had moved to town, she and Evan had invited them for Christmas Eve dinner. Since then, it had become a tradition.

Gloria had once dreamed of a big family, but when her husband had run off while she was still pregnant with Evan, life had thrown her a curveball. A single mother who'd never had a job, who didn't want to lose her home and wanted to give her son every opportunity, she had given up her dreams of a house full of kids and focused on work and her only child. Kyle saw how much Christmas with Evan and Kyle's family, especially Lorrie's kids, meant to her.

If Evan didn't have kids, she'd never be a grandmother. Kyle had never given that a thought until now. He imagined she longed for the day Evan would bring his own family home for Christmas.

And Evan wanted the same thing.

Shit. Could he do this? Kyle had been saying it for days now, but as he stood there face-to-face with the reality of what a future with Evan would be like, he had to ask the question, had to make sure. Evan deserved that.

It didn't take him long to settle on the truth. With Evan, it was all or nothing.

Kyle wanted it all.

He crossed the street and went inside. Gloria had a hold of him before he had a chance to shut the door behind him. She was always so excited to see him, and this year her hug lasted longer than usual. She pulled back and took his face in her hands. She had the same blonde hair and blue eyes as Evan. Although her eyes were more the color of the sky before a storm, not clear and bright like Evan's.

"What's wrong with my boy?" she asked. "I thought you said he was doing better."

"He is. He was."

Her eyes widened, and he hated that panicked look.

"He's going to be fine. I'll make sure of it."

She stepped back and studied Kyle with a long stare. She must have liked what she saw. A slow smile emerged. "I think maybe he will be. Finally."

"Yeah." Had everyone been waiting for them to get together?

She slipped her arm in his and walked with him to the living room, where his family was already admiring the eight-foot decorated tree, frosted snowman sugar cookies, and hot cocoa in candy-cane-colored mugs.

Evan was sitting in a chair by the fire, sipping from a red and white mug, watching the kids look over the wrapped gifts. He had a smile on his face, but it wasn't the dimple-flashing one Kyle had grown addicted to. The scrape above his eye had a bandage covering it. No doubt Gloria had smothered it in antibacterial cream. Always the overprotective mother. She didn't need to worry. Evan could take care of himself. No matter what Evan had said on the train, Kyle never doubted that.

Evan leaned back in the chair. He had his leg propped up on another chair.

Kyle went to him. "I thought your ankle was feeling better." Okay, maybe Gloria wasn't the only one with the instinct to overprotect. And in the process, he'd made Evan feel weak. Wasn't that what he was trying to tell him on the train?

"It's fine."

"Does it hurt?"

Evan lifted his head and met Kyle's stare. "Yeah, it hurts."

Now, that wasn't about the ankle.

Kyle sat on the stone ledge in front of the fireplace, picked up the metal poker, and stoked the fire, watching the flames come to life. Things had to be okay between them. He needed to have Evan in his life. No matter what. "I'm sorry for how I acted when I saw the messages on your phone."

"If I'm supposed to trust *you*, then—"

"Oh, I see. Is it always going to be like this?"

"Like what?" Evan asked.

"You worrying I'm leaving every time I walk out the door? I don't know what else I can do. What else I can say." Yeah, he did. He could tell Evan the truth. Repeat those words he'd whispered in the cabin before he'd realized Evan had fallen asleep. "Ev—"

The doorbell rang.

"That's Dennis," Evan said.

Perfect timing, Dickhead.

Chapter Thirty

Dennis stepped through the living room archway, looking larger and more threatening than ever. Although, the threatening part had nothing to do with his size.

Kyle wasn't sure why he was mentally referring to Dickhead as Dennis again, but it probably had to do with subconsciously accepting Dennis might be back in their lives for good. No matter what happened between them, Evan was just the kind of guy who'd stay friends with his ex.

Gloria drew Dennis down for a hug, and Kyle's parents stepped forward to greet him the same way. All sported smiles to see the one person they thought wouldn't be there that year, or ever again. Although, there was also disappointment mixed in with the smiles. Maybe everyone had been waiting for Kyle to get a clue, and they thought this year was finally when they'd get the news they'd been waiting ten years to hear.

Dennis passed out hugs and set down an overnight bag.

Dickhead.

Okay, maybe Kyle wasn't done with the nickname yet. Because that was a very dickhead thing to do, acting like nothing had changed. Like he and Evan hadn't come to Ohio at different times and via different modes of transportation. Evan stood and crossed the room. Dennis met him halfway and gave him a hug. A simple platonic hug, the same as he'd given everyone, and Kyle wanted to rip Dennis's arms off.

This jealousy shit had to go.

Or maybe not. Maybe it was justified.

Dennis was watching Kyle over Evan's shoulder, and the pointed stare said a lot.

He knows.

Or he suspected something. Or maybe Kyle was seeing things. Maybe Dennis wanted Kyle's help getting Evan back.

Fuck that.

Kyle clutched the fireplace poker in his fist. When he realized what he was doing, he set it on the stone ledge. He was pretty sure shoving an iron poker up someone's ass was not the best way to say "Merry Christmas."

Two hours later, after they'd stuffed themselves on turkey and all the fixings of Gloria's traditional Christmas dinner until no one could move from the table, Dennis leaned over to Evan and whispered something. Evan laughed, and his eyes lit up. That look was so like the ones on Evan's face in the cabin, in the shower, in their shared bed on the train.

Kyle stood. He couldn't take another second of Evan pretending nothing had happened between them. Although what was he expecting? For Evan to stand up and announce to everyone he'd licked, sucked, and fucked Kyle all the way from California to Ohio? No, but he could've at least told his mom they were together. What? Like Kyle had told his? He piled dirty plates on his until he had a stack that would make his hasty exit look less like he was the biggest asshole around. He carried the plates to the kitchen and heard footsteps behind him.

"What happened?"

"Lorrie…" He set the plates on the counter and turned on the water to fill the sink. He was as familiar with Gloria's kitchen as his own mom's. "I told you, nothing happened."

"I thought—"

"Just forget it." He went to fetch more plates.

She grabbed his arm before he reached the doorway. "What is the matter with you? Why is Dennis here?"

"Because he knows he has a shot at getting Evan back."

She stared at Kyle, saying nothing.

"Evan doesn't trust me. I don't think he ever will."

She still didn't move or speak. Then a noise came from outside the kitchen door, and she pulled him into the pantry closet. She tugged the string above their heads for the overhead light and searched his eyes, her mouth hanging open like she couldn't believe what he'd said. "Are you an idiot?"

"What?"

"Seriously." She held her hand up in front of her in a let-me-explain gesture. "Okay, not an idiot. Maybe you're some sort of genius. You know, like people who are really good with numbers and dates but they suck at personal, human interaction. Only you're really good at casual sex but forget real relationships."

"I did everything I could to show him he can trust me." He played with the edge of a label coming loose on a can of mushroom soup. "I would do anything to be with him."

"You really do love him."

He gave up on the label before he left Gloria with a can and no idea what to find inside. "I do."

She squealed and clapped her hands together, the sound shrill in the small closet. She threw her arms around his neck and squeezed so tight he couldn't breathe. In a quick move, she stepped back and smacked his arm. "Then what are you doing washing the dishes? Go out there and fight for him."

"I'm not sure... I'm not sure that's the right move."

"For you?"

"For him." He stepped out of the pantry before Lorrie asked more questions. He came face-to-face with Dennis, holding two empty glasses. They stared each other down for a moment, and then Dennis crossed the kitchen to where a bottle of whiskey sat on the counter. "Your dad wants another drink."

"Lorrie," Kyle said, "give us a minute alone."

She slipped around him and whispered, "You aren't going to hit him, are you?"

He gave Lorrie a pointed look, and she walked out of the room. The door swinging shut behind her left a repetitious squeak in the silence of her exit.

Dennis faced him. They glared at each other again. Neither said a word until Dennis set the glasses down, leaned back against the counter, and folded his arms over his chest. "You're an idiot."

"Seems to be a common conclusion. You're not my favorite person right now either."

"I left him because of you."

"What are you talking about?"

"I knew he loved you. I knew that part of him would never let you go. That he'd never love me the way he does you. I learned to be okay with that in the beginning because I wanted him. But I saw you the night he won the National Screenwriters Competition. You were so damn proud of him. One look at you and I knew you felt the same for him as he does for you."

This was not what Kyle had expected. Far from it.

Dennis reached for the whiskey and poured a shot into each glass, running the flow of whiskey from one glass to the other and spilling another shot in the process. He slammed the bottle down, grabbed a glass, and knocked it back in one try. The glass hit the counter again, his fist clutching it and holding on. "I tried to give him everything he wanted. And he wanted you. The hardest thing I've ever done was walk away from him." He faced Kyle. "Last week, I made up my mind. Six months and you hadn't made a move."

"He was hurting. Some asshole broke his heart."

"And now?"

What could Kyle say to that? He'd been a coward once, but he'd taken a chance on the train, in the cabin. He wasn't about to run now.

Dennis focused on the cabinets behind Kyle. "I missed him something fierce. I kept picturing him—how much he loves Christmas. I wanted to be a part of that. If you weren't going to be with him, then I couldn't stay away any longer. Hell, now that I'm here, I don't think I can leave again even if I thought it was best. Which I don't."

That was more in line with what Kyle had been expecting. "We slept together." *Well, shit.* He hadn't meant to blurt it out like that.

Dennis fetched a dish towel and swiped at the spilled whiskey on the counter, scrubbing so hard he'd likely sand away some of the countertop with the whiskey. He stopped cleaning as quickly as he'd started, the towel clutched in his large hand. "You're good at the jealous-boyfriend thing, I'll give you that."

Kyle ran a hand through his hair. Well, if he was going to be good at only one aspect of being a boyfriend, it made sense he'd pick the one that made him look like an ass. Evan deserved better from him.

Dennis threw the towel into the empty side of the sink. "I came here because I thought maybe I'd read you wrong. That maybe you didn't want or couldn't handle a relationship with him." He turned back to Kyle again. "But..." He shook his head.

Kyle didn't want to be even more of an ass, but it was now or never. "I want everything with him."

"Sure you do," Dennis said. "For now. I don't know why I thought walking away was a good idea. I know guys like you." He gripped the full glass of whiskey in his hand and headed for the kitchen door. He paused beside Kyle. "I'm not walking away again, and if you think I can't convince him you're not worth the risk, you are sadly mistaken."

"I'm not letting him go." The words came out easier than any Kyle had said over the past six days.

"It won't matter. Someday you're going to break his heart. I plan to be there for him when you do."

Dickhead.

* * * *

Evan leaned back in the chair and let the warmth from the fire wash over him. The chatter filling the room and the laughter from the kids sounded nice. Like family. He sipped more of the eggnog Kyle's mom had given him. It was as spiked as the stuff she made every year. At this rate, he'd be asleep soon.

He rested his head on the back of the chair, closed his eyes, and listened to Dennis's deep voice as he offered to get another drink for Kyle's dad. If Evan didn't think too hard, this reminded him of any other Christmas over the past ten years.

But it wasn't. No matter how much eggnog he sipped, he couldn't force away the memories of the last six days. He didn't want to.

The crackle of the fire sounded louder as he sank into the memories of the cabin. The wind blowing outside, Kyle so warm against him, making love to him on the floor. The shower with Kyle on his knees before him. The intense way it had felt to let go with him.

In the cabin, Evan had known he could trust Kyle, and that this time he wouldn't get hurt. How had he let that feeling slip away?

Because he'd felt the fear even before he'd seen the note in the journal. Before their heated exchange of anger. Before the long ride to their parents' houses in silence.

Like every other year, they had passed by Liberty Falls High School, and it hurt to see the building, looking so similar to when they'd first met. Back then, he would've given anything to spend one night in Kyle's bed. Which was laughable. After all they'd done over the last several days, he still hadn't been in Kyle's bed. Considering the train's bench where they'd slept, they hadn't really been in a bed at all.

And maybe he hadn't really had Kyle.

He wasn't sure he could handle the heartbreak of having been so close to what he'd always wanted and never really having it.

Although that wasn't right. He'd had it.

He needed to talk to Kyle, but first he had something to say to Dennis.

The doorbell rang. A moment later, Evan heard a muffled voice in the hall near the front door. "I'm sorry to interrupt your holiday, but I'm looking for someone. He has something I need, and it can't wait."

"Who are you looking for?" Gloria asked.

"Kyle Bennett."

Evan sat up with a jolt. He jumped out of the chair and headed into the hall. A man wearing a long wool coat stood in the foyer by the front door.

No, not him.

It couldn't be him.

Chapter Thirty-One

Evan rushed down the hall in the other direction and shoved the kitchen door in. He ran into Dennis. Literally. His chest collided with the glass of whiskey Dennis held out in front of him.

The liquor splashed onto Dennis's dress shirt. "Dammit." As soon as his gaze connected with Evan, he stepped back and his expression softened.

"I'm sorry." Evan couldn't come up with any other words.

"You didn't mean it," Dennis said. "Are you okay?"

There was no time to answer. Evan faced Kyle and was momentarily distracted. He'd never seen Kyle looking so…frightened. A panicked longing filled those dark eyes.

Is it me he wants? Or me he's afraid of?

Evan couldn't examine that right then. "There's someone here you need to see."

"Who?"

"I think the person who's been after that book you'd like no one else to get a look at."

"Here?" Kyle rounded the kitchen counter and headed into the hall. Evan followed. He heard Dennis step in line behind them.

Standing beside Gloria at the end of the hall was Nate, his gaze scanning the room until finally spotting Kyle. He glared at him, his white eyebrows creating lines above the anger in his eyes, looking so different than the man they'd met on the train. This was the first time Evan had seen him without Penny. Maybe she had a calming effect. Or maybe Nate was an actor. He hadn't given them a clue he'd wanted the journal before now.

Gloria gave a nod to Nate. "It was nice to meet a friend of Kyle's from California. I'll leave you alone to talk." She disappeared around the corner, returning to where the rest of the family was waiting in the living room. Every year they sang carols and opened gifts after dinner.

Kyle's niece peeked her head around the corner. "Look, Uncle

Kyle. It's Santa Claus." She giggled and pointed at Nate.

Lorrie called out for her from the other room. "Leave Uncle Kyle and his guest alone."

Without taking his eyes off where the little girl had been, Nate said, "You have a nice family." He slid a hand inside his coat and then out again. At his side, he held a handheld hook, the kind used to carry bales of hay. He had the wooden handle gripped in his fist and the end with the metal hook made for stabbing the hay pointed at the floor.

"You don't need that," Kyle said. "You're not going to hurt anyone."

Nate still hadn't looked away from the living room doorway. "When I couldn't find the journal, I thought I'd try looking for the money myself, but I have been all over that damn farm, and I cannot figure out where it could be. Then I found this hook in with the horse supplies and figured it wouldn't hurt to have some incentive when I came to talk to the one man who has what I need." He slowly turned his head toward Kyle. "I need to read that journal."

"So it was you all along," Evan said. "In our room on the train. In the cabin. You followed us here from California."

"You have no idea how far I'll go."

"Did you pay that guy to break into Kyle's apartment? Or did the network hire him? Are you working for them?"

Nate focused on Evan. "No one hired me."

Kyle approached Nate, speaking in a surprisingly calm voice. "Let's go outside, away from my family, and I'll talk to you about it."

"No." Evan advanced toward them. "You're not going anywhere with him." Dennis clasped Evan's forearm, stopping him. Evan tugged free. He was not going to let Kyle walk outside alone with the person who'd been following them, who looked crazed with anger, holding a weapon.

Kyle spoke to Nate again. "I want to help you if I can, but I don't want you around my family with that thing." He gestured to the hook in Nate's right hand. "And I don't want them to know about the journal." He took another step closer to Nate, and so did Evan. They were flanking Nate now. If Evan did this right, he could force the hook away before Kyle got too close.

The music for "Winter Wonderland" started up on the piano, and the families in the next room began singing. They sounded nicer than previous years. Perhaps the family sing-a-long fared better without him and Kyle there. Guess they weren't going to be trying out for the Gay Men's Chorus of Los Angeles as one of their first activities together as a couple.

The idea they had "boyfriend" outings in their future spurred Evan on. He inched closer to Nate.

"Get me the journal," Nate said, "and I'll leave you alone. If you don't..." He raised the hook and gripped it tighter, holding it close to his chest.

Kyle spoke in the gentlest tone he'd used yet. "Nate, you're not going to hurt anyone."

"You have no idea what I'll do to get this done." Nate moved fast. He nabbed Evan by the arm and yanked him forward, the hook raised in the air, heading for Evan's throat.

"No!" Kyle charged toward them.

Chapter Thirty-Two

The cheerful, happy singing of "Winter Wonderland" continued in the next room. Kyle didn't hesitate. He grabbed Evan by the waist and tugged him backward. He wasn't going to watch someone hurt Evan. Not again. He didn't believe Nate would go that far, but he wasn't taking a chance.

Nate still had a grip on Evan's arm, though. Until Dennis had Nate's throat clenched in his large fist. Nate dropped the hook and let go of Evan in exchange for clawing at Dennis's forearm.

Finally, Dickhead had great timing and was using his size for something good.

Kyle took another step away, bringing Evan's back against his chest. He pressed his lips to Evan's ear. "Are you okay?"

Evan nodded.

The singing in the other room continued as if they hadn't heard the commotion.

Dennis had Nate against the wood door, one hand pinning Nate's right wrist to the door, the other hand wrapped around his throat. It didn't look like he was going to let up.

"Let go of him." Kyle had to get Nate out of the house before his family finished their song and came to get them for the next one. Otherwise, he'd have to explain why Dennis had a death grip on their visitor.

"I'm not letting him go," Dennis said over his shoulder. "He's staying right here until the police arrive."

"I need to talk to him alone."

Evan gripped Kyle's free hand. "Don't." Kyle still held Evan in his other arm, their bodies pressed together. He couldn't let go.

Dennis turned his head sideways and glared at Kyle. His gaze dropped to where Kyle had his arm wrapped around Evan, then where their hands were clasped together. He glared at Kyle again. "Are you in some kind of trouble? Did you bring it here and put everyone in danger?"

Evan finally moved forward, separating them. "This isn't Kyle's fault."

"Then what is going on?" Dennis asked.

He must have loosened his grip. Nate shoved Dennis and charged forward toward Evan and Kyle. "I need to know where it is."

Dennis seized Nate again and yanked him back to where he'd had him pinned before, slamming Nate against the door, banging his head in the process.

"Stop," Kyle said. "Let him go. He's not dangerous."

"How do you know?" Dennis gave another shove to Nate. "He came here with a weapon."

Nate shook his head. "I want the journal, and then I'll go."

That wasn't going to happen. Kyle tried to keep his voice calm, show Nate he could trust him. Knowing his track record with getting people to believe that fact, he didn't hold out much hope. "I can't give you the journal, but if you come with me and leave here without any more trouble, I'll help you find what you're really looking for."

"You can't let him go," Dennis said.

"I can handle this."

Evan faced Kyle. "Like you handle everything?"

What the hell did that mean?

A chorus of "Let it Snow" broke the silence left by Evan's harsh tone.

"Okay," Nate said. "If you can help me find where it's hidden, I'll go with you."

Kyle grabbed for his coat and backpack. "Tell my dad I borrowed his truck, and I'll be back as soon as I can."

"You're leaving here alone with this crazy person?" Dennis asked.

"He's not going alone." Evan reached for his coat and stood before Kyle.

The truth slammed into Kyle. He'd never been alone. He'd always had Evan, supporting him in everything he'd ever done, through the ups and downs of his writing career, through the loss of his grandpa.

He had to stop being jealous and overprotective. Evan deserved more respect than that.

He had to let Evan make his own choices. About his future. About Dennis. About the two of them. He had to trust him.

* * * *

"How do you know where the money is?" Evan whispered from beside Kyle in the truck.

Kyle glanced back at Nate, who sat in the backseat of the cab, staring off into the darkness of the fields surrounding them. The hook Nate had retrieved from Gloria's foyer floor lay on the seat next to him.

"I don't know exactly." Kyle tilted his head to indicate Nate behind them, hoping Evan would get that he didn't want their visitor to know there was nothing in the journal about where the money was hidden. "I didn't get a chance to read all of the journal, so there may be something in there." Of course he had read the entire thing, and Evan knew that.

Evan got it. He gave a nod.

"I think he's right, though," Kyle said. "I'm betting it's at the farm. Can you get the journal out of my bag?"

As he pulled out the journal, Evan said, "There's something I don't get. Why would they come to Ohio? After all Victor had said about not wanting anyone to know they were..." He trailed off, and Kyle didn't need him to finish.

"They knew the money needed to be close to one of them, somewhere it could be accessed quickly, and somewhere no one else would find it. Joe wouldn't let Grandpa hide it on his own, so the first time Grandpa came home, he brought Joe with him." And no one had suspected they were anything but friends. Although, if his grandpa's family were as perceptive as everyone around Kyle and Evan—or perhaps if his grandpa and Joe were as shitty at hiding what they felt for each other as he and Evan were—then everyone knew.

Evan turned to Nate. "So the network didn't hire you?"

Kyle watched Nate in the rearview mirror. The moon was high, and the rays were reflecting off the snow, casting a white glow through the truck's window, illuminating Nate's face and beard. He did look like Santa Claus.

"No," Nate said. His tone was harsh, but the man had tears in his eyes. Maybe Dennis had been right. Maybe this guy was certifiable. Nate opened his wallet and pulled out a picture. He held it up so only he could see it, then gently tucked it back into his wallet again. "A man named Hastings came to see me, though. That's how I remembered about the money. About the story I'd heard when I was a boy. I figured the network had to know more than I did. I followed Hastings to your grandfather's attorneys, and from there I found out who the journal was going to be sent to."

"Why did Hastings come to see you?" Kyle asked.

"I don't believe explaining myself was part of our deal. You keep your journal, and I get the money. That's it." He went back to staring out the window, squeezing the wallet between his hands.

"Ev," Kyle said, "why don't you read the journal and see if you can find anything? The last note I added is where they arrived in Ohio." When Evan gave him a questioning stare, he said, "Maybe you can find a clue I missed. Check the glove box for a flashlight."

Evan stared at him for a moment more, then found the flashlight and opened the journal. He shone the light on the page.

"Don't read it out loud."

Evan looked at him again and nodded.

Nate laughed. "I already know what you're trying to hide."

Kyle glared at Nate in the review mirror. "And what's that?"

The man smiled, the look more like the ones he'd given his wife on the train than any look he'd had since showing up in Ohio. "Besides the fact your grandpa hid stolen money, which makes him an accessory to the crime? I know everything."

"You're Paskowski's kid." It made sense, even if the names didn't match up. He was acting like the money belonged to him.

Nate met Kyle's gaze in the mirror and laughed again. "You're smarter than your books imply."

Evan spun around in his seat. "Shut up." He faced the front of the truck and continued reading in silence, flipping pages every few minutes.

Kyle shifted his focus back and forth between the road ahead and Nate's image in the rearview mirror. "You think because your father stole it, you get to keep it?"

He didn't respond.

A mile from the farm, Evan closed the journal and said, "I know where it is."

"What?" Kyle had read that book from cover to cover. Nowhere did it say where the money was hidden. "How do you know?"

"He didn't write exactly where it is, but he wrote about something else."

"What?"

Evan ran his index finger along the journal's spine. "The place he and—" He gave a quick glance Nate's way. "Where he was last with his lover. I think it's near there."

"Oh, yeah. That." Okay, so Kyle hadn't exactly read it cover to cover. "I sort of skimmed that entry when I saw what it was about. It, uh, it looked…descriptive."

"It was." Evan paused, then added, "I imagine he didn't want to forget it. He was in love."

"Yeah." Kyle turned his head. Thanks to the light of the flashlight, he stared into those clear blue eyes. "He was."

They held the stare between them. He couldn't read Evan's expression.

A minute later, he made the turn onto the lane leading to the farm, snow crunching under the truck's tires as he drove toward the farmhouse. The two-story house with a wraparound porch sat in the middle of the three-hundred-acre farm. To the right of the house was the barn where Kyle had spent so much of his childhood. It was there he'd first kissed another boy during the summer his grandpa had hired Kyle and his friend to muck out the horse stalls, wash the tractors, and do other odd jobs. It had taken Kyle the entire summer, until their last week, to work up the nerve to kiss his friend. That was when he'd first learned he could convince another guy to do almost anything using only his mouth and nothing close to words.

That memory sent his thoughts in a direction he didn't care for. Had he pushed Evan too hard? To a place they shouldn't have gone, right as Dennis was heading back to Evan?

He couldn't think about that right then. He had to get rid of Nate before anyone else learned about the journal. But what if they actually found the money? What then?

The lights were off in the house, and the only illumination came from two sources outside: a high-voltage security light attached to the front of the barn and the Christmas lights strung along the roof of the house. Kyle's cousin had moved to the farm after their grandfather had passed away. He and his family went to his in-laws' in Toledo every Christmas Eve.

An arc of snow on the ground turned from white to green to red to white again as the Christmas lights cycled through their rotation. There was also one of those blow-up lawn snow globes with fake snow pelting the reindeer and the Santa trapped inside. The entire blow-up lawn ornament swayed in the breeze and made a squeaky sound as it rocked. What would his grandpa make of seeing something like that on his farm?

For Kyle, it was a reminder his cousin had young children living there. No matter what happened, if the money was at the farm, it couldn't stay there. It was too dangerous.

"When will they be home?" Nate asked.

"We have a couple of hours."

Kyle parked in front of the barn's sliding double doors that spanned almost the full height of the building. He exchanged a look with Evan, and they got out of the truck, Evan carrying Kyle's backpack with the journal inside. A gust of icy air smacked into Kyle, kicking up loose snow and blowing it in his face as if the farm were sending him a warning to get back in the truck and leave.

Even if Nate changed his mind, Kyle couldn't. He had to know the truth.

Nate got out of the truck, hay hook in his hand.

"You don't need that anymore," Kyle said. "You and I both know you aren't going to use it." It was a bit of a gamble, but Kyle was confident that the Nate they'd met on the train wasn't the kind of guy who would slash at someone with a hay hook. No matter what the reason was that he was so adamant about finding the money.

Nate sighed and tossed the hook into the back of the truck. It slid several inches, causing a fingers-on-the-chalkboard scratching sound along the truck's bed until it collided with the tailgate. Nate winced. "Sorry."

Kyle rolled his eyes and faced Evan. "Lead the way."

Chapter Thirty-Three

Evan headed toward the walk-in door at the end of the barn closest to the house, trudging through the loose snow that had fallen in the past few hours. He hoped he was right about this. It wasn't like the journal specifically said where they'd hidden the money.

Nate and Kyle kept up at his side, unease and determination radiating off both men as they strode through the snow. There was something they were missing about Nate, some detail on what was driving him and why he wanted this money.

They reached the barn door, and Kyle opened it. He flipped on the overhead light and took a step inside. The horses whinnied. "Sorry girls," he said. "Not time to eat yet."

Evan followed him in. The creak and bang of the large sliding doors as they shifted in the wind, the shuffling of the horses' hooves, the smell of hay and manure... It all brought back those days during the summer when he and Kyle had helped out on the farm. When he'd watched the shirtless Kyle shovel out the horse stalls, his tanned back rippling with the heft of each load, his ass on display as he bent to thrust the shovel in again. Evan hadn't done much to help with the chores, he'd been too busy staring and trying to keep his hard cock from jumping out of his pants.

He smiled. He couldn't help it. After all the years since that summer day in the horse stall, he'd finally gotten everything—and more than—he'd been picturing that day.

Kyle cleared his throat and gestured for Evan to go on ahead.

"Sorry. Memories."

Kyle gave him a knowing smirk.

They walked past the horse stalls toward the back of the barn. Kyle's cousin only had the two horses he kept as pets for his daughters. The rest of the hay he sold as needed throughout the winter to local horse and livestock owners. The hayloft should still have a good supply left. Evan just hoped it was laid out in the same configuration as it always was. That way they could get to the exact location from the journal. He stopped at the ladder that led to the loft above. He signaled for Nate to climb first, then Kyle.

There was a hesitation before Kyle put his hand on the ladder like he was going to make Evan go up before him. "That ankle is still bothering you."

"A little." Which meant there was no way Kyle was letting him climb last. He'd want to be there to catch him if he fell. Kyle had always been protective of him, but it had taken on a new intensity in the past six days. It was going to get old fast. They'd have to have a talk at some point.

They stood still for a moment more. Just the two of them in the dim light of the barn, an intimacy passing between them that had nothing to do with sex.

Kyle nodded and whispered, "Be careful." Then he climbed the ladder first.

The hayloft was warmer than the first floor. Neat stacks of hay bales nearly filled the entire upper half of the barn except for a narrow walkway around the inner edge of the center opening where the hay was raised and lowered into the loft. There were new planks of wood at various locations across the walkway's floor, most likely to replace the ones that had rotted throughout the years. If the money was in the hayloft, how had it survived all this time? How had no one found it in sixty years?

"Where to?" Kyle asked.

"They were in that corner." Evan pointed to the right back corner with the flashlight. "They had just hidden the bags. It doesn't say where, but it sounded like it was close by. It would have to be somewhere private." He looked to Kyle. "As private as somewhere they'd have to hide in order to have sex."

"It actually mentioned the bags?"

"Yeah."

"Jeez." Kyle grabbed the flashlight, and Evan tried not to laugh. He understood why Kyle had skimmed certain parts of the journal. It wasn't like Evan had even felt all that comfortable reading about Kyle's grandpa having sex.

They moved along the walkway until they faced the far corner of the loft. The bales were in tightly packed stacks that spanned from the walkway to the back wall, each stack climbing high above their heads, stopping short of a narrow wooden ledge that ran the perimeter of the barn where the angled roof met the outer barn walls. "We need to get into the corner."

Kyle surveyed the hay around them. "It'll take us forever to make a path."

"Well, well," Nate said. "Guess I should've brought the hay hook after all."

Kyle glanced his way, and Nate shrugged, then flashed a smile.

Maybe Dennis had been right. Maybe Nate was crazy. Evan held back a laugh. "It's okay," he said. He took the flashlight from Kyle. "We don't need to move the hay. They were up there." He pointed the light toward the top corner.

"All right." Kyle looked around again. "There should be a ladder up here somewhere." He and Nate turned to search along the walkway.

They didn't have time for that. They couldn't spend all Christmas Eve in the barn. Their families would be worried. It would take finesse to keep the bales from toppling over, but they could climb the sides and crawl along the tops of the stacks. Evan slipped the flashlight into the backpack, then put a foot on the edge of a bale and gripped the one above his head. In no time, he'd made it halfway.

"Ev," Kyle shouted from below. "What the hell are you doing? Get the fuck down here."

He stopped and looked back at Kyle. "Trust me."

"I do, but...we can find a ladder."

"It's okay. I'm almost there."

"Okay. I'm coming up."

"No. One at a time or we might knock it all down."

"All right."

Evan reached the top of the hay bales and knelt on the flat surface. He could see across the layer of hay to the back wall. The stacks were twenty rows deep, each stack reaching to the same height as the one he knelt on. Except for five locations along the back wall where angled reinforcement beams ran from the wall to another beam above him near the center of the barn's roof. The angled beams prevented the bales closest to the back wall from being stacked as high as the rest.

He crawled toward the largest opening in the far corner and shone the flashlight over the edge. The taller stacks around the opening created an eight-by-eight-foot alcove made of two barn walls and two walls of hay with an angled beam along one side of the hay.

"I was right," he called out. "This is where they were."

"EVAN," KYLE YELLED again toward the top of the hay bales. He spotted Nate watching him. "What?"

"Penny and I knew the two of you were fucking each other. She said it was love. I told her maybe it was for him, but I wasn't sure about you. Guess she was right. She's always been smarter than me. She came up with the idea to take the train."

Kyle ignored him and focused again on where Evan had disappeared. "Evan!"

Nate continued. "I can see why your grandfather left the journal to you. Considering how much he loved his friend too."

"Shut up." Kyle couldn't hide the amusement in his voice. Nate was growing on him, crazy and all.

Evan peered over the edge of the bales. "Come up here."

Kyle put his foot on the first bale, but Nate stopped him. "I'm going first."

"That might not be a good idea."

"Why? Because I'm older than your father? I can make it."

Kyle looked up at Evan and then back at Nate.

"I'm not dead. Get out of my way." Nate shooed Kyle aside. The climb took twice as long as it had for Evan, but Nate managed, and Kyle quickly followed.

They crawled their way to join Evan in the corner, where he sat with his feet dangling over the edge of the bales. He pointed downward with the flashlight, and they all looked to the alcove below. Evan smiled and dropped down first. Nate went next. He staggered a bit on the landing, and Evan reached out to steady him. Nate recovered, and Kyle followed.

He landed on both feet, and Evan put a hand on his arm when the bale below him shifted. Kyle resisted the urge to reach out to Evan in return. Not yet. The next time he touched him, he was saying a lot more than he wanted Nate to witness.

Evan shone the flashlight around, lighting up the small space. They were surrounded by two walls of the barn and two walls made of hay. Standing on the tightly packed hay bales in the corner, they were hidden from view from anywhere else in the hayloft.

"How did you know this was where they were?" he asked Evan.

"Your grandpa mentioned the loft was filled with straw back then. They'd found a place to be alone in the corner, a private alcove by an angled beam. Just them, a blanket, and the bottle of wine they'd taken from the cellar."

"A cellar?" Nate asked. "Maybe that's where it's at."

"No," Evan said. "I thought the same thing, but then he said this…" Evan pulled the journal from the backpack. He stopped short of opening it and lifted his head. "I forgot. Sorry."

"Go ahead." Kyle flipped a hand through the air in Nate's direction. "He already knows."

"Okay. I'll just read the first part." Evan read aloud.

> *"Joe's gone now, and I can't let go of today, of the last time we'll ever be in each other's arms. We spent the afternoon in the alcove made of straw in the upper right corner of the barn. Where I had spent hours as a child, hiding from my brothers, running my toy tractor along the angled beam until I couldn't reach any higher. No one would look for us there. It was the perfect place to say good-bye to my youth.*

> *"We lay on the blanket for a while sipping the wine we'd found in the cellar, trading the bottle back and forth, neither of us speaking, Joe was still a touch out of breath from the climb to heft the bags into place. We were so close to each other. Even in the low light, I saw the scar above his eye that reminded me of all we'd lived through in Korea. Even over the straw surrounding us, I smelled his familiar scent. He was all I could see, all I could feel, even without touching him. A part of me knew I'd carry those sensations with me for the rest of my life. But this was the last time they'd be real. I knew as I reached for him, it was the last time we'd make love."*

Kyle sucked in a deep breath, the ache of his grandpa's pain so real to him. What must it have been like to be gay back then? To feel like you had no options? Like no matter what choice you made, you'd lose?

Evan slowly closed the book. He wouldn't look at Kyle. He said, "This has to be where they were. But where would they hide it?"

Kyle examined the walls. They were thin. Too thin to have a secret compartment filled with bags of money. "He said Joe had to climb?"

"Yeah." Evan shone the flashlight above their heads.

A long ledge ran above them along the side of the barn from corner to corner. Without looking, Kyle knew both the opposite side and back wall of the barn had the same construction. The wooden planks had probably been added at some point to protect the hayloft's contents from any leaks where the roof met the barn's outer walls or to create another level of storage. He could not recall his grandfather or cousin ever utilizing the small space. He pointed overhead. "There. That ledge has been there as long as I can remember."

Evan nodded. "That wood looks old. Do you think it'll hold us?"

"Maybe."

"We could climb back up to the top of the hay and stack more bales until we can reach it."

They set to work, scaling the sides of the hay, then stacking bales into a crisscross pattern to create a makeshift ladder. Nate remained in the small enclosure below, standing still as Kyle and Evan moved the bales around. The man looked exhausted.

"Move back," Kyle called down to him, and then he rolled a hay bale into the enclosure. "Have a seat."

Nate nodded and sat on the bale. He watched as they finished creating the ladder above.

After a few minutes of work, Kyle and Evan were eye level with the ledge. At this angle, they could see it was actually made up of a long beam. The beam created the outer edge of the ledge and ran the length of the barn. It had flat planks of wood attached above and below, and each plank spanned from the beam to the barn wall. The money could be hidden on the other side of the beam in the space between the flat boards.

Kyle and Evan stood on the top hay bale, staring into the dark space above the ledge. The barn was even darker at this height, the boards of the ledge shielding most of the light from below. They'd need to use the flashlight to get a good look. Kyle paused. What if they found it?

"Want me to look?" Evan asked.

"No. I have to do this. I already know he helped them hide the money. Actually seeing it won't make a difference."

"Here." Evan handed over the flashlight.

"Thanks. Wait here for me while I check it out?" Their fingers touched as Kyle took hold of the flashlight.

"I'm not going anywhere." Evan held the touch for a moment more before letting go.

Kyle wanted to believe those words meant something more than what they were actually discussing. Now wasn't the time to ask. He gave Evan a nod, then hoisted himself onto the ledge. The space wasn't tall enough to stand, especially with the angle of the roof overhead, so he had to remain on his hands and knees. He bounced a little to test the sturdiness of the aging wood. The best approach would be to move along the floor over the beam, rather than put his weight over the empty space alongside it. He moved forward along the beam's path.

He started in the corner, shining the light around, searching the walls and floors for any sign of a hiding spot or loose floorboards. He made his way toward the front of the barn, the boards below him creaking as he went. He searched that corner, then returned to where he'd started. Nothing.

The exterior barn walls were one-board thick. The rafters of the roof overhead were smaller than the beam below him. There was no place to stash anything as large as a bag of money except under the floorboards. The boards were old, but the few he'd examined were still firmly secured. He couldn't pry them loose with just his hands.

Besides, they couldn't pry up every board in the place. They'd be there all night. He wanted Evan's opinion, but he couldn't see him from this angle. He crawled forward. The floorboard under his right knee gave a little. The rotting wood had it sagging in the middle, creating a sliver of space between it and the next plank. He slid his fingertips into the crevice and tried to pull up the end of the plank. It wouldn't budge.

Something told him not to give up. Not yet.

He set the flashlight down so it shone over the area where he worked. He tried the next plank that was just as sunk in as the first. It was even more secure. He moved forward and tried another. He was about to give up and tell Evan they'd need a crowbar when the last plank he tried loosened on the first pull. He yanked on it more, and the board jerked free, sending him flying backward on his ass, almost smacking himself in the forehead with the piece of wood still clutched in both of his hands.

"Kyle!" Evan called out. "Are you okay?"

"Yeah. I might have found something. Hang on." Kyle tossed the plank aside and grabbed the flashlight. He shone the light into the space below. There were cobwebs and stray stalks of hay. He could see all the way down to the other boards secured to the bottom of the beam. There was nothing inside the opening. No bags. No money. He got on his belly, stuck his arm inside the hole, and pointed the beam of light one way and then the other. He almost missed them. They were smaller than he expected and tucked far into the space, with years of dust and cobwebs covering them.

He'd definitely found something.

He reached inside until he had his arm stretched out all the way and his head plastered to the floorboard beside the hole. He grabbed hold of the first bag and yanked it forward an inch. A plume of dust flew into the air and out of the hole. He coughed and waited until the air cleared, then dragged the bag toward him and out through the opening. Despite the faded material and the dust covering half the letters, he could make out the words *The Denver Bank and Trust* stamped on the side of the bag. He held it in his hands for a moment, feeling the weight of its contents and of the truths he'd learned over the past six days.

When he could move again, he crawled to the edge of the makeshift loft. "Climb down, Ev. Stay off to the side by Nate." Nate was still seated on the hay bale in the alcove below, staring at his shoes.

Evan made his way down. Once he was next to Nate, Kyle said, "Watch out." Then he dropped the bag to the hay bale beside Nate and Evan. Dust and hay particles blew into the air on impact.

"Oh my God," Evan said as he stared down at the bag.

"Stay back." Kyle gestured to Evan. "I'm coming down." When he reached the alcove, he added, "There are at least five more bags that I can see."

No one moved a muscle, all staring at the small bag lying on the hay before them.

Finally Evan said, "Want me to..."

"Yeah." Kyle pointed the flashlight at the bag. "Go for it."

Evan sank to his knees, opened the bag, and slid out a metal tackle box. He lifted the lid. Inside were bundles of cash. Evan picked one up. "They're practically like new."

Transferring the money into the box had been a wise choice. The bag had several holes that probably hadn't been there on the day it had left the Denver Bank and Trust. Whatever had chewed through the bag would've destroyed the money inside had it not been protected. "Old bills, though."

"Yeah," Evan said. "They don't even make thousand dollar bills anymore. This is what?" He held up the bundle and examined the edge of the stack. "A hundred bills per bundle."

One hundred thousand dollars in Evan's right hand.

Evan set it in his lap and pulled out more bundles from the box, dropping each to his lap until he'd counted twenty packets of money.

Two million dollars. Lying across Evan's lap.

"Holy shit," Evan said. "How much was stolen?"

Nate finally lifted his head and spoke. "Ten million dollars."

For sixty years, ten million dollars had been stuffed under a floorboard in his grandpa's barn. Kyle had to let the shock of that settle before he spoke. "The bank was a regional drop, and the robbery was timed just right, or they never would've gotten away with that much." Although, the robbers hadn't really gotten away with it. His grandpa had.

Nate laughed—a high-pitched sound that confirmed the crazy theory. Kyle shone the light on the man's face. Nate stared at the money while he spoke. "I used to hate that money. My mom talked about it like it was evil. That it was more important to my father than she was. She said he left us to go find it. Which I guess wasn't true. He knew where it was all along. When she learned he'd gotten sick, she said he didn't fight to live. I thought he had been miserable, had left us, because he'd let that money slip away from him. That he wanted it more than he wanted us." Nate looked up at Kyle. "But it wasn't the money he wanted. It was your grandfather."

Shit. "You're Victor Morrison."

Chapter Thirty-Four

"Victor Morrison?" Evan asked. Where had Kyle heard that name?

Kyle glanced his way. "I did more searching today and found Joe's obituary listing his only son."

"Named after your grandpa?"

"I guess."

Nate nodded. "But since I never knew my father, I didn't want to use the name he'd given me. I go by Nate, short for the middle name my mother picked out, Nathaniel."

Evan felt the weight of the money on his lap. Kyle looked like he felt the weight of the world.

Nate continued. "My father left when I was a baby. Right before he died, he sent me a letter, told me about traveling with his friend from the war, about the bank robbers they'd met, and the money he'd hidden for them. I was just a little boy then, but he said if I ever needed anything, I should come to Ohio and talk to Victor Bennett. He said he wished he could've been a dad to me. Wished he could've loved my mother, married her, and had a life with us. Twenty years ago, before my mom died, she finally told me the truth. That my father was gay and was in love with Victor. It's why he said he couldn't stay with her. He tried to live a different life when he first came to San Francisco and met her, but he couldn't do it. She said if I ever wanted to go find the money, there was a journal detailing my father's affair with your grandfather and that maybe it had something in it about where the money was hidden. She wasn't sure."

Nate looked again at the stack of bills on Evan's lap. "When Hastings came to see me, he said my father had camped for months in the early '50s outside Denver with a man named Victor Bennett. He wanted me to tell him what I knew about their time at that campsite and the men they stayed there with. When I said I didn't know anything, he mentioned the journal your grandfather kept. Guess some of the women who used to visit the campsite saw your grandfather writing in it. I figured it wouldn't be long before the network found the money. I spent a lot of years hating my father. Hating your grandpa. I thought they were selfish, weak men."

Kyle strode across the length of the small enclosure to the side with the angled beam, the hay crunching under his heavy steps. He stopped and stood with his back to them.

That was better than the punch Evan expected Kyle would hand out to anyone who talked shit about his grandpa.

Nate's hysterical laugh from earlier was back. "I never thought I'd do something like this. I never wanted anything from that man."

"Then why now?" Evan asked.

Nate reached into his back pocket for his wallet and removed the photo again. "My granddaughter. She's dying."

Evan leaned forward and let the money slide from his lap to the floor made of hay. He got up and sat beside Nate. "I'm sorry."

"It's a rare brain cancer. She's four years old, and this thing inside her I can't see is killing her." He sounded so distraught and helpless it tore at Evan's heart. "There's a hospital in Boston with an experimental treatment, but my daughter doesn't have insurance or the money to pay for it. I've already sold our RV, our home, cashed out my retirement to cover the costs of her treatments till now. When Hastings came to talk to me, I pulled out my father's old letter, and I knew I had to find the money." He lifted his head and spoke louder to Kyle's back. "Once I knew you were getting the journal, we came to California to find you, and we followed you to the train station. Penny said we should get on the train and use the opportunity to talk to you. We had to max out our credit cards for the tickets. She said we should tell you about everything and see if we could come to an agreement about the money. I couldn't take that chance." He looked at Evan, desperation visible on his face. He was asking for understanding. "But I didn't hire anyone to break into his apartment or the cabin you mentioned." Kyle had probably been right. Shepfield might be working private security and doing dirty jobs on the side for the network. Maybe one of those jobs had been to hire a junkie to break into Kyle's apartment.

"But I did..." Nate hesitated. "I did break into your room on the train. I wanted it to look like a robbery, so I searched all the rooms in your car. I didn't take anyone's money, though. I hid it somewhere else in their bags, figuring they'd find it later." He looked at the picture in his hand.

The smiling little girl had red curly hair. It was short and wispy. Not like it had been cut. Like it had been lost to chemo and was just starting to grow back. "She's very cute," Evan said.

"She's a sweetheart. Never complains about being sick."

Kyle hadn't said a word. Hadn't moved. Even in the dim light of the flashlight, the tension in his body was unmistakable. No matter what Victor had done, Kyle would always love his grandpa.

"I can't believe the money's real," Nate said, almost in a whisper. "It's really here."

Kyle finally faced them. "You should take it. All of it."

"What?"

"I'm not going to stuff it under that floor again when you have someone who needs it. Take the money. Go spend the holiday with your family."

That shouldn't have surprised Evan, but it did. Like someone had sucked all the air from the hayloft, the breath caught in his chest. He loved this man so damn much.

"But what do I do with it?" Nate asked. "Even if I only spend a fraction of it, how will I explain where I got the money?"

When Kyle didn't speak, Evan asked, "You didn't have a plan?"

"No." Nate laughed. "Stupid, huh? I was focused on getting this far. She needed me to do this, so I did it." Despair worked its way over his face like someone had drawn a blanket over him, smothering his hopes. Evan could relate. Being so close to something you wanted so badly—something you needed with everything you were—and not knowing if you should go for it was torture.

Nate shook his head. "Now that I'm here I don't know if I can do this. That money doesn't belong to me. A man was killed for it."

"You can do this," Kyle said. "For your granddaughter."

The howl of the wind outside sounded louder in the silence after Kyle's words. The large double doors thumped against the barn, and Nate jumped with the sound. "Where do I say I got the money?" he finally asked.

"The truth," Kyle said. "We call the police and tell them about the journal, that you've found the money. There's no one to claim it. The bank's insurance covered the stolen funds. No individuals lost their money. The insurance company took a hit, so did the bank in the long run, but both companies folded in the early '70s. They can't even charge anyone for a sixty-year-old bank robbery, even if there was someone to charge. Whoever finds the money will get to keep it." He looked at Evan. "Isn't that how it works?"

And that was exactly what the network had been counting on.

Could it be that simple?

Although, this was nothing close to simple.

Telling Nate to call the cops, to let everyone know about the journal, had to be killing Kyle. Evan stood. "All that will take forever. Besides you've come this far to keep your grandpa's secrets."

"Ev..." Kyle gave him a look Evan knew well. He wanted Evan to know the truth without having to say the words. It was the same look he'd given him on the train when they'd reached Chicago. And at his mom's house right before Dennis walked in. "Grandpa would never want a little girl to die in order to keep those secrets."

"I can say it was my father who hid the money," Nate offered. "That your grandpa knew nothing about it."

Kyle shook his head. "That wouldn't be fair."

"I don't owe him anything. He's gone, but you have a family to think about. A promise to keep."

"It doesn't matter now." Kyle looked defeated.

"It does matter," Evan said. There had to be something. Had to be a way to make this work for Nate and his granddaughter. For Victor. For Kyle. The wind outside surged again, and desperation swept over Evan, as if time was running out, like when he'd been lost in the storm. Then the howl of the wind died down, and he landed on the perfect solution. One that would help Nate and put an end to any more hired junkies or ex-prison guards coming after them for the journal. He grinned at Kyle. "I know how we can get Nate money right away and still keep your grandpa's secret." He turned to Nate. "And not touch a dime of this stolen money. We just have to talk to one man."

Kyle stared at him for a minute, his expression serious, and then he returned the grin with a slow, drawn out acceptance. "Hastings."

"They were willing to pay you just to get a look at the journal in case it had any information. A little negotiation and I bet they'll be willing to pay whatever Nate thinks he'll need to know exactly where the money is."

Kyle stepped closer. "I love the way you think. They'll pay." He moved to stand in front of the hay bale where Nate sat. "That's if you don't mind being on TV."

"*American Treasures*?" Nate asked. "How would that work?"

"First we put the money back under the floorboards. Then you call Hastings and tell him you know what he's really after and that you know where the money is hidden—that you've seen it for yourself. Then you make a deal with him and get the payment before you tell him the rest."

Nate sat taller, more animated than he'd looked yet, even on the train. "What rest?"

"Let me think for a sec..." Kyle paced the small hay enclosure. He wore a concentrated frown like when he was stuck on a scene and had to make a decision on how to press ahead. Then the frown dissolved. He faced Nate. "The story your mom told you. About how your father got the scar over his right eye."

"He got that in the war."

"Yeah, but I think your granddaughter's life is worth one lie." He asked Evan, "You okay with this?"

"So far. How do you get from a scar to this barn?"

"Joe got the scar when he was visiting his war buddy's home. He decided he'd found the perfect hiding place, so he'd crept out of the house in the middle of the night, alone, to hide something, then he'd fallen and cut his head on a nail." Kyle looked back to Nate. "Your mom wouldn't tell you what he was hiding or why, but she did tell you where he hid it. After Hastings came to see you, you were curious, so you went to find out exactly what your father was hiding. When you saw the money, you were too freaked to touch it, so you left it right where your father had hidden it sixty years ago."

"Hastings will pay me before I tell him all that? Before I tell him where the money is?"

"If you tell him you've seen the money? Yeah, I think he will. It'll be the biggest treasure they've aired yet."

"This," Evan said, "might actually work."

"Yeah, it will."

"Okay." Nate had his gaze locked on the picture in his hand. "I'll tell them whatever I have to if it means there's a chance for her."

It took them an hour to return the money to the bag, put it back, secure the floorboard, and rearrange the hay bales. They drove to the motel in Liberty Falls where Nate had left Penny earlier that evening. It was snowing again, and all three men rode in the cab of the truck in silence. Maybe Nate and Kyle were on the same shocked page as Evan. After all, they were driving away from ten million dollars in cash.

At the motel, Nate got out of the truck, and Kyle rolled down the driver's side window. "Have a good Christmas."

Nate gave a nod and said, "You've given me the best gift this year. Hope. Thank you." He turned and went inside.

Kyle stared at the closed door of the motel room for a moment more. "We better get back."

"Yeah," Evan said. Time to go to his mom's house. Alone. He wanted to crawl into Kyle's bed with him and sleep for three days, even if they would miss Christmas. But they also needed to talk. Maybe Kyle thought so too. He hadn't driven away yet.

"How are you doing with all this?" Evan asked.

"I'm fine." Kyle laughed and dropped his head to the headrest behind him. "It's been one hell of a week."

"Yeah." Evan turned in Kyle's direction and rested his temple on his own headrest. "You didn't once think of keeping that money for yourself." It wasn't a question. He knew the truth.

"I guess I didn't." Kyle faced him. New snow was falling, and the windshield was covered again, transforming the truck's cab into a cocoon made for two. Like they were lying in bed, the covers over their heads as they talked. The motel's neon vacancy sign cast a muted blue glow through the layer of snow. "How'd you know that?" Kyle asked, his brown eyes dark and serious even with the eerie shade of blue surrounding him.

"I know you."

"Yeah. We make a good team."

"We do." A surge of need rushed through Evan. Nothing sexual about it this time. It was a longing for words and promises that had gone unsaid. Or had they?

Kyle studied him for a moment. "You look exhausted. How's the ankle?"

"A little sore." He wished he could lean forward and fall into Kyle's arms, but he couldn't give in. Kyle switched on the windshield wipers, the privacy of their sanctuary broken by the squeak of rubber against glass and the bright blue neon in full illumination. Snowflakes fell before the truck's headlights. The snow didn't comfort Evan the way it had on their previous trips to Liberty Falls. Getting the smallest glimpse of each flake as it moved through the beam of the light and not being able to see it fall to its final destination didn't seem fair. He closed his eyes. He just wanted to catch a flight with Kyle and head back to California. He sighed and faced him again. "Take me home?"

Kyle reached out and stroked his cheek with an open hand. "You got it." He faced front and put the truck in drive.

Too bad he hadn't meant that the way Evan wanted him to. When they passed by the sign that read WELCOME TO LIBERTY FALLS, OHIO, HOME OF THE PERFECT CHRISTMAS TREE, Evan forced the words out. "I have to talk to Dennis."

"I know." Kyle didn't say anything more until they were turning down their parents' street. "It's okay, Ev. No matter what you want to do."

"I know exactly what I want." Evan waited for Kyle to ask what it was or to make a joke, something. But he said nothing. He gave a nod, parked the truck, and got out, trudging through the snow for his parents' house. He had his shoulders hunched, his head hung low.

He was hurting. He really didn't believe they were going to make this work.

Six days before, if someone had told Evan he'd spend the last hours of Christmas Eve with two million dollars lying across his lap and a brokenhearted Kyle walking away from him, he'd have laughed his ass off.

The two million dollars had seemed more likely.

Chapter Thirty-Five

Kyle stood in the dark at the window of his old bedroom, watching the house across the way. Only one low light remained on in Evan's old home. In the kitchen. It was killing Kyle waiting and letting Evan do this on his own.

But he had to.

He turned away from the window. That didn't mean he was about to wait until Christmas morning to find out what happened. He needed to talk to Evan. Tonight.

He lay on the bed, his clothes and shoes still on, and he waited.

A moment later, Lorrie stood at the bedroom door. "Mom and dad are putting the kids to bed. They wanted me to come get you. Time for our traditional Christmas Eve nightcap." Kyle didn't want a drink, didn't want to celebrate. He wanted to be alone. He lifted his head, and her smile faded. "I'll tell them you're already asleep." She went to leave.

"Lorrie." He rolled to his side. "Are you happy?"

"Right now?"

"In general, are you happy with your life? Are you happy with Brett?"

She crossed the room and leaned down to hold his face in her hands. "It's a good thing you're a writer. Such an imagination but clueless about so many things in your own life. Yes, I'm happy." She let go and stood up. "I may not have the most glamorous life like everyone out there in Hollywood, but I wouldn't trade it or my family for anything. I love my kids. I love Brett. I love our life together."

How had he not seen that? Maybe he hadn't wanted to know love made life better, grander, made the tough times bearable. Until now.

Lorrie added, "It's the kind of love I think you have a shot at, baby brother. If you let yourself." She kissed his cheek and left.

He fell back to the bed again. She was right. What a coward he'd been running from it for so long, thinking he was too good for commitment, thinking that fucking every guy he possibly could was the only way to really feel alive.

He had to talk to Evan.

He rolled off the bed and went to the window. Where were they? In the kitchen with that lone light? Or in the darkness of Evan's old bedroom? Were they talking? Touching?

He crossed the room and sat at the desk. He opened his grandfather's journal and turned to the handwritten letter on the pages that followed the final entry.

> *Dear Kyle,*
>
> *I'm not sure if you've read this journal, but I hope you can. I'd like for one person to know the truth—to know what I've done. Perhaps a confession from your old grandfather is too much to put on your shoulders, but the shame and guilt is more than I can bear some days. I lied. I helped men cover up a crime that included the death of an innocent person. I took what wasn't mine and kept it from those who it did belong to. All to hide the fact that I loved another man.*
>
> *I was a coward.*
>
> *I am ashamed of that, of all I did, and can't bring myself to leave this journal for your father and aunts to find.*
>
> *I had thought leaving Joe and going home was the right decision for me—the right decision for everyone. Only, my heart was with a man who lived two thousand miles away. He was my home, and I left him alone to face a future I didn't have the courage to live. He died of cancer five years later. When I called to talk to his family, his mother said he'd given up. He'd stopped fighting. I had done that to him.*
>
> *I loved your grandmother. I loved our life together, our kids, our home, but a part of me was never there*

with her. A part of me died in a hospital in San Francisco.

Regret is a horrible thing to live with. The family I had helps me see life often takes surprising, wonderful turns, but I'll never forget the life and the young man I walked away from. I'll never forget the love I learned to give another person through him. I'll never regret a single day I spent with him. I only regret not being there for him in the end when he needed me the most.

My hope for you is you'll live your life so you'll never have to regret the choices you've made, the experiences you've avoided, or what you've let slip away.

I know you love him. He's the right future for you. He always was.

Kyle turned the page. It was blank. He flipped through more pages until he stared at the last blank page of the journal.

He grabbed his phone and sent a text to Evan. I need to see you.

* * * *

Evan reached into the soapy water and washed a plate, then another, letting his hands linger in the warmth of the water between each dish. He heard Dennis step into the kitchen. There was no mistaking that slow, measured walk. Dennis located a towel and dried the dishes from the dish rack, putting each away in its proper place. He was comfortable in that room, knew where everything went. They'd done this before. Too many times to count.

Dennis had been his family, but that had ended six months ago. Maybe they could get that back. Maybe not. It no longer mattered. Evan had to take a chance on the future—the family—he'd always wanted.

"I love you," Dennis said, his voice so low Evan barely heard it over the slosh of the water as he washed a wineglass. "But I had to let you go. I wasn't who you wanted. I'm still not, am I?"

Evan stared out the kitchen window above the sink. Somewhere in that house across the street, in the dark, was Kyle. He rinsed the glass and set it in the dish rack. He picked up another. "I did love you."

"I know." Dennis gripped Evan's upper arms and turned him until they faced each other. "But you belong to him."

Evan nodded. The water from his hands dripped onto the floor. "I didn't mean to hurt you. I didn't know how he felt when I e-mailed you. Or maybe I did and didn't want to see it... I don't know. After contacting you again, seeing that you wanted me back and that I got your hopes up, I thought I owed you an explanation."

Dennis dropped his hands to his sides. "You don't have to explain. When I first met you, I thought all I'd ever have was one night. You were so young, and it wasn't exactly the right thing for me to do— sleeping with a student. When you kept coming back, kept wanting to see me, I let myself hope we'd have a future together. A life."

"We had a life."

"But it was a temporary stopover for you. You had to wait for him."

"You were never that to me."

Dennis held his gaze on the wet glass in the rack. He gave a quick nod. "Thank you for saying that, but it's time for you to go to him, isn't it?"

God, Evan wanted to believe that, but what if Kyle still wasn't ready?

Dennis spoke again. "I told him I was going to fight for you, wait around until he screwed you over so I could get you back, but seeing you with him earlier, being here with you alone like this." He shook his head. "I realize now that's not what's best for me. I can't say this doesn't hurt, but I want to be with a guy who wants me. Not someone else."

"You deserve that."

"I do. So do you." Dennis met his gaze again. "He's a gamble. You know that, right?"

"No." Evan faced the sink, focusing on the house across the street again. "He isn't. He just needs time to get used to this."

"If he hurts you, I'm going to kick his ass."

They laughed. It wasn't a joyful sound, but it was nice to know Dennis wanted to try for something other than anger or pain.

"I might let you do that."

Dennis sighed and said, "I'm going to go get my bag. I'll stay at the motel tonight."

"But it's Christmas Eve."

"I have to go. For me."

Evan got that. "I'm sorry you came all this way for nothing. I tried to tell you on the phone."

"I know. I didn't want to hear you. And it wasn't for nothing. I needed to see you two together. Otherwise, I would've kept holding on." He stood taller, his gaze focused on the kitchen door. "If I leave early tomorrow morning, I can make it to my sister's in Chicago for Christmas dinner."

"Okay. I'll finish up here and be out in a minute." To say good-bye. For the last time.

Dennis nodded and walked out of the kitchen.

Evan wiped his wet hands on a towel. He had a call to make. He couldn't put it off any longer. He dug out his phone and dialed.

"Merry Christmas, Evan." Miguel's voice sounded cheerful over the lively music in the background. Their usual family Christmas party at Castillo's. "How's it going there in Ohio?"

Evan couldn't find the words to answer. Too much had happened to go with a standard "Fine. How are you?"

"What's the matter?" Miguel asked, his voice serious in an instant.

"If I stay in California, can I come back to work?"

"Of course. What happened?"

"I didn't take the job. They asked me to do something I couldn't do."

"I'm sorry, kid."

"It's okay. I'm not giving up."

"No, you're not. Did I ever tell you how I got from college ball to running a restaurant?"

"No."

"I met my wife during our junior year. I was totally smitten from day one, but she was dating someone else. At the homecoming game, I was determined to impress her. My dreams of playing pro ball died that day when I blew out my knee. In my anger and resentment, I dropped out of college and ran from everything. From everyone. Family. Friends. My wife, although we were just friends back then. After five years of doing nothing and getting nowhere, I finally accepted my dad's offer to work in the kitchen of the family business. Washing dishes every night at Castillo's, I had a chance to get to know the family I hadn't bothered to spend time with before then. My dad, grandparents, brothers, and cousins. I also had a chance to win over the love of my life when my wife starting coming in on Wednesday nights after her late shift at the hospital. I found out years later it was my grandmother who had invited her to dinner that first night she'd come into Castillo's. That football injury was the best thing that ever happened to me. Sometimes what we need the most comes to us in ways we can't imagine will work out to be anything but pain and heartbreak." He paused. "Kyle hasn't come around yet, has he?"

"You knew?"

"Kid, everyone knew."

"Yeah, I guess so. He says he's ready. I'm not sure if he is. But he will be. Someday."

As the words left Evan's mouth, his phone chimed the alert for a new text message.

* * * *

Kyle's phone beeped with a new message.

From Evan: I need to talk to you too.

Kyle responded with: Meet me in an hour. Where we first met.

How?

It'll be open. Just come. Please.

Kyle stuffed the phone into his pocket and went to the bookshelf beside his desk. He searched for his old high school yearbook and finally found it on the bottom shelf, the spine covered in dust. He flipped it open and searched through the pages. The name of the man he needed to talk to had to be in there. He just hoped the guy would help him out on Christmas Eve.

It was the most romantic plan he could come up with.

Chapter Thirty-Six

Evan pulled into the Liberty Falls High School driveway and parked next to the only other vehicle in the dark lot, the truck Kyle had driven to the farm earlier.

This was crazy. They were going to get arrested for breaking into their former school on Christmas Eve. *The New York Times* best seller and the wannabe screenwriter were about to make the local news. Evan got out and went to the nearest set of doors. He found the last one beside the gymnasium unlocked and knew where to go from there.

Like instinct, like heading home.

Up the stairs, second door to the right. And straight on till morning? He took a deep breath and let the hope wash over him.

The halls of the school looked similar to when he'd last been there, with a few notable differences. The walls were painted a bright shade of blue instead of the drab off-white they'd been, the banners and posters were more artistic, and there were far more signs for campus teen groups and activities. A flyer caught his eye, and he stopped before the bulletin board.

> *Liberty Falls High School LGBTQ & Straight*
> *Alliance. Come one and all to join the fun at our*
> *New Year's Bash.*

Yeah, some things were different, all right.

For the better.

A low flicker of light filtered into the hallway through the frosted glass window on the door to their old English classroom. Where he'd first laid eyes on the dark-eyed transfer student. Evan reached for the doorknob and told himself it was the cold he'd walked through outside causing his hand to shake.

He didn't make it one foot into the room before he froze at the sight before him. The overhead lights were off, and every student desk in the room was covered in lit candles. In the middle of them all was a red blanket spread out on the floor with two fluted glasses and a bottle of champagne at one corner, as well as a two-foot-tall fake Christmas tree with round ornaments too large for the tiny tree and a string of twinkling lights that must have been battery powered for all the illumination they gave off. The room smelled of peppermint. And Kyle's cologne.

Which made sense. Because waiting there next to the tree was Kyle.

He didn't look like the casual, take-it-or-leave-it guy Evan had first seen in that room. He had his hands awkwardly at his sides, his body held perfectly still like he wasn't breathing, and his eyes... Those serious brown eyes were watching Evan with a new expression. Hope? Or something more.

Evan stood in the doorway, unable to speak.

"Hey," Kyle finally said. He smiled, and his entire body relaxed.

Evan couldn't move. He looked again at the candles, the blanket, the tree, then at Kyle.

He wasn't sure what he'd expected, but it wasn't this. Never this. Kyle took a step forward, and Evan shook his head. He didn't want him to say anything he'd regret later—anything he wasn't ready to say.

"I have a confession to make." Kyle took another step forward. "I never had any plans to go to college in LA like I told you I did. I was going to go to Ohio State or someplace closer to home." Another step. "I went because of you."

Oh God. Evan shook his head again. "Don't."

Kyle stopped moving forward. "What?"

This could hurt worse than anything Evan had been through yet. No matter how over-the-top romantic Kyle made the moment. "Don't do this if you aren't ready."

"Ev, I may not have been ready ten years ago in that motel room, but I am now." Kyle moved again, bringing them closer. So close. "I want us to be together. Really together."

Evan tried not to think too much about those words. He nodded and kept staring at the candles, the blankets, the glasses, and the bottle of champagne. "I know you do."

"No. You don't." Kyle shifted forward, their bodies almost touching now. "I want to live with you. Make a life together."

The words sounded like a dream. Like something Evan had read once. Or maybe something he'd written.

"Unless…" Kyle paused. "If you want him back—"

"No!"

A second passed, maybe two. Then Kyle reached out and yanked Evan to him. The force of his body slamming against Kyle's pushed the air from Evan's lungs. Kyle clung to him, holding the back of Evan's head so he was flattened against his shoulder.

"Uh, Kyle, I can't breathe."

Kyle pulled back and gripped Evan by the biceps like he couldn't let go.

Every touch on the train, in the cabin, every whispered word, every moment of finally feeling like he was awake and alive came rushing back to Evan, and he knew…this was it. "This is what you want?" He had to ask. Had to hear Kyle say it again.

"For the past six months, I thought what I was feeling was lust, about having you in a way I never was able to before. Well, I guess it's that too, but it's more. Bigger. Something. You know?"

"For a writer, you suck with words."

A laugh surged out of Kyle, and he dropped his arms to his sides. "Yeah."

It didn't matter. "It's just…" Evan looked to the little tree by the blanket. The lights were fading like the batteries were running out. He met Kyle's stare. "We do this, and that's it. No one else but me."

"I've been thinking about that." Kyle stared at the floor before him like he was considering something. The likelihood he could keep his dick in his pants? Probably not a good sign it was taking him so long to do the calculations. He met Evan's gaze. "It's been no one but you for a while now. I can do this, Ev." He stepped close again. "I can do this."

Evan wasn't sure who moved first, but the space between them shrank in an instant, and they were in each other's arms again, their lips and tongues and bodies coming together as easily as if they'd been sharing that touch for years. Kyle wandered his hand up and down Evan's back, the contact soft and so like the way he'd touched him in the cabin.

Evan sank into the sensations of Kyle's hands on his body, his mouth pressed to his, the slow, gentle sweeps of hand and tongue that had nothing to do with getting off, that had everything to do with—

In a flash Kyle broke the kiss and slid his lips along Evan's skin to his earlobe.

"I love you, Ev." He leaned back and held Evan's face in his hands. "I love you."

No matter how long he'd waited to be in this moment with Kyle,

Evan's own reaction surprised him. He bounded forward and wrapped his arms around Kyle's neck. The action of a boy with a crush. Exactly what he would have done at the age of eighteen.

He didn't care because Kyle held on just as tightly and said, "I'm sorry I made us wait."

"It doesn't matter anymore."

"I can do this now. I can."

Evan pulled back but didn't let go. "Stop talking. Just…stop." He brought Kyle down to him, kissed his forehead, then his nose, caressing Kyle's cheeks with his thumbs. "I trust you." He kissed him deep and long, pouring all the passion he felt into it. He tugged on Kyle until they were lying on the blanket, then straddled him, lifting the scratchy red sweater and kissing everywhere he could reach, not wanting this moment to end.

Kyle sat up on his elbows. "I want you inside me again."

"Here?" Evan looked around the room. Sex on the floor surrounded by dozens of burning candles had to break some sort of fire code.

"Fuck me," Kyle said. "Right here. Right now."

They'd just have to be careful because they were doing this. "I take it back."

Kyle cocked his head to the side, looking younger and more innocent than he had at eighteen. "Take what back?"

"You are perfect with words." Evan pressed forward until their lips met, until Kyle was on his back, their limbs tangled together.

It wasn't the lust-filled moments of their initial gropes in that motel room in Iowa. It wasn't the heated rush of their first touches ten years later. It wasn't the intense desire of the train or the deliberate, passionate way they'd made love on the cabin floor. This was all of it, everything at once, and when Kyle raised his legs and Evan worked his way into him, it felt like coming home after years of traveling alone.

* * * *

When Kyle finally caught his breath, he said, "Damn. That was…something else." Guess acting like a jealous asshole wasn't the only part of being a boyfriend he was good at. Apparently he could do romance with the best of them.

"Yeah, it was." Evan dropped onto the blanket beside him. "I can't believe we just had sex in our high school." He laughed, and the sound filled the room, bouncing off the block-concrete walls.

An alarm sounded from inside Kyle's bag. He reached over and got out his phone. "It's midnight." He rolled on top of Evan and tugged the little Christmas tree closer. "Merry Christmas."

The tree teetered from the weight of the four oversized ornaments, and Evan laughed again. "Charlie Brown's tree has nothing on this one."

"Hey, I had less than an hour to find something in my mom's stuff that would fit in my bag. I can put it away if it's offending your delicate holiday sensibilities."

"No." Evan rolled them over. He kissed Kyle on the mouth, his jaw, his cheek. "It's perfect." He lowered his hand, grazing his fingertips down Kyle's body, then gripped his cock, stroking it with a squeeze at the top. "Best present ever."

No matter how great that touch felt, there was no way Kyle was getting it up again. Not yet. Not after the intensity of that orgasm. He squirmed and poked Evan in the side. "You're a dork."

Evan rolled around, releasing Kyle's cock as the touches turned playful. "Never said I wasn't." He pinned Kyle to the floor with his entire body. "I was president of the dork club in high school."

Kyle had never heard Evan laugh so much. Never seen him this happy. Hell, he'd never been this damn happy. He flipped them again, straddled Evan's legs, and clasped his wrists, pressing them to the floor above Evan's head. "Why wasn't I invited to this club?"

Evan wriggled, trying to get free. "Popular jocks weren't allowed to join."

"Who said I was popular?"

Evan stopped his struggling and stared up at him, then rolled his eyes. "They voted you captain of the football team your first week here. It took me twelve years to get the treasurer slot in drama club."

Kyle released Evan's wrists and lay beside him, his palm on Evan's chest. "I never asked you to be anything but who you are."

"I know." Evan rolled to his side and propped his head on his hand. "What now?" His naked body was on display before Kyle, the candlelight accentuating the taut muscles and smooth lines.

"I'm thinking we rest up, and then I bend you over the teacher's desk."

Evan's mouth dropped. "We can't do that. Can we?" He looked to the desk in the front of the room. "I think I had a dream about that once."

How long had Evan been waiting for this? From day one? "You want to know what we do now?" Kyle waited until Evan turned his way. "For starters, when we get home you stop sleeping in the spare room."

"We could stay here."

Kyle glanced around the room. "Might not work out so great when the kids show up for class. Besides, I only gave the janitor fifty bucks, and he didn't seem too excited to come out on Christmas Eve to begin with. He might not cover for us staying here."

"Now who's the dork?" Evan smacked his arm. "I meant move back to Ohio. Get our own place here."

"Not an option. You have a career in LA."

"Yeah, waiting tables. Some career." In a more earnest tone, he said, "It's okay. You want to live in Liberty Falls, and I think maybe I do too."

Kyle shook his head. This was not up for discussion. "No, we're heading back home. You have a pitch session next week."

"I'm fine with moving, really. You've been thinking about it for a while and—wait." Evan shot up to a sitting position. "I have a what?"

This was fun. "It's for a cable network that does some wicked cool shit."

"What are you talking about?"

"I spoke with Sue Ann, and she contacted the studio that bought the film rights for my first book. They called in a favor for me. You have an appointment next week."

"But…"

"But what?"

"I wanted to do this on my own."

"You're going to. I got you a foot in the door. That's all. You and your ideas have to do the rest." He tugged Evan back to the blanket and leaned over him. "You're going to pitch one of your original ideas and land a deal. Then you'll have a show to produce, and I've got a book to finish. We'll take the train back on New Year's Day like we planned."

Slowly, a smile turned up the corners of Evan's mouth. "Okay."

Now or never. In for a penny…

"Then…" Kyle took a deep breath. "We should wait awhile, a few years probably. Hell, maybe longer. Let me get this whole…partner thing down, but then I want to adopt a girl first." He shrugged. "I liked having a big sister. That's assuming you want to adopt over the surrogate thing."

Evan studied him, all the seriousness in the world pouring out of those blue eyes.

Kyle tried not to laugh at that look. This was even more fun. He lay back, tucked his arms behind his head, and waited.

Evan lifted up and stared down at him. "But…"

"But what? I like kids, Ev."

"Yeah, I can tell. But…you want to be a father?"

"It's not that weird. A lot of men do."

"Yeah. I just thought—"

"I don't want to wake up one day and realize I avoided everything that could've meant something in my life."

Evan gripped the back of Kyle's neck and jerked him forward, crushing their lips together in a kiss that proved how right it had been to mention this now. Kyle didn't want to leave anything unsaid, leave anything for Evan to worry about when it came to the two of them and their future together.

Then, just as abruptly, Evan pulled back. "Wait."

"What?"

"I have an idea."

Better than the bending-him-over-the-desk thing? "What's your idea?"

"For my new screenplay. I've got to write it down." He scrambled over Kyle, landing half on him, and reached for the backpack. "Do you have paper in here?"

Kyle got out a pad of paper and a pen and handed them over. Evan wrote like mad for five minutes while Kyle lay on his back, staring at the classroom's ceiling. No perfect white swirls here. There was a water stain above them and flaking paint in the corners. Real life wasn't perfect, but it didn't mean he had to avoid living. "It's going to suck being married to a writer, isn't it?"

Evan stopped writing and carefully set aside the pen and notebook. With one swift movement, he lunged for Kyle. "Yeah, it is, but it'll be better than ending up with Candace Grey." Evan kissed Kyle's bare chest, one kiss after another as he worked his way lower to his abs, then lower still.

Candace Grey? Kyle lay back, enjoying the slow way Evan was wetting his balls with tongue and lips. He nearly forgot what they were talking about. Then the name came back to him. "Who is Candace Grey?"

Evan lifted his head. "Captain of the cheerleading squad."

"From high school? I don't remember her."

"She was at every pep rally and game."

"I have no memory of any cheerleaders. I do remember this good-looking blond guy who was into watching old movies and came to all my games. One look at him and I spent the entire season jerking off in the last stall of the locker room."

"You did? Thinking about me?"

"Yeah."

"Oh man. We were so stupid." Evan laughed. The sound surged through the empty room.

Kyle thought about his grandpa's life and roads not traveled. He stared at Evan's ridiculously wide grin. He'd almost lost this. Almost let it get away for the second time.

"What?" Evan asked.

"I like visiting with our families"—he stroked his thumb over one of Evan's dimples—"but I'm looking forward to heading home."

Evan leaned into the touch. "Me too. I say next year for Christmas, we take the train again."

"I say after a visit with the folks, we rent a cabin in the Sierras for a week."

Evan laid his head on Kyle's chest. "That sounds perfect."

Like instinct, holding nothing back, Kyle stroked the blond hair. "We'll need a truckload of lube."

Evan's body shook with the laughter. "And frosting. Lots and lots of frosting."

Yeah, Kyle could do this.

So long as he was with Evan, he was home.

ABOUT THE AUTHOR

Sloan Parker writes passionate, dramatic stories about two men (or more) falling in love. She enjoys writing in the fictional world because in fiction you can be anything, do anything…even fall in love for the first time over and over again. Sloan lives in Ohio with her partner and their neurotic cats. Her greatest moments in life are spent with her family, her friends, and her characters.

To contact Sloan, find out about her other books that are available for purchase, and read free stories, visit: www.sloanparker.com.